D1480433

Once Upon a Time,
There Was You

Once
Upon a Time,
There Was You

A NOVEL

Elizabeth Berg

RANDOM HOUSE
LARGE PRINT

Copyright © 2011 by Elizabeth Berg

Published in the United States of America by Random House Large Print in association with Random House, New York.
Distributed by Random House, Inc., New York.

Cover design: Shasti O'Leary Soudant
Cover illustrations: Lincoln Seligman/The Bridgeman Art Library (seascape), Jonathan Barkat (boats)

The Library of Congress has established a cataloging-in-publication record for this title.

ISBN: 978-0-7393-7813-7

www.randomhouse.com/largeprint

FIRST LARGE PRINT EDITION

Printed in the United States of America

10 9 8 7 6 5 4 3 2 1

This Large Print Edition published in accord with the standards of the N.A.V.H.

To Kate Medina

Marriage is a funny thing. Even when it's over. Maybe especially then.

—ROBIN BLACK,
from **If I Loved You, I Would Tell You This**

There are two dilemmas that rattle the human skull: How do you hold on to someone who won't stay? And how do you get rid of someone who won't leave?

—from **The War of the Roses**

There are rocks deep enough in this earth that no matter what the rupture is, they will never see the surface. There is, I think, a fear of love. There is a fear of love.

—COLUM McCANN,
from **Let the Great World Spin**

Prologue

When John Marsh was a young boy, he used to watch his mother getting ready to go out for the evening. He stood beside her dressing table and listened to the **mbuh** sounds she made tamping down her lipstick, and he took note of the three-quarter angle with which she then regarded herself in the mirror, as though she were flirting with herself. He watched how rouge made her cheeks blossom into unnatural color, and how the little comb she used to apply mascara made her blond lashes go black and spiky. She always finished by taking her hair down from pin curls and brushing it into a controlled mass of waves, which she then perfumed with a spicy scent that reminded him of carnations and oranges, both. Finally, "How do I look?" she would ask him, and he never knew what to say. What he felt was: **Gone.** For though he had stood beside her, watching her every move as she transformed herself, he was never sure that the made-up woman before him was still his mother, and this made for a mixed feeling of fear and confusion. Nonetheless, he always smiled and said softly, "Pretty."

Before he turned six, she was off living in another state with a man who did not care for children. The rare times John saw her, she came and stayed in a nearby Howard Johnson, and she would buy him dinner there. While he ate, she would sit smoking, sneaking looks at her watch.

Many years later, on the eve of his wedding day, thirty-six-year-old John sat in a bar talking to his best friend, Stuart White (Stuart himself happily married for twelve years), about how he was suddenly consumed by doubt. He sat morosely on the stool, chatting now and then with the women there, many of them beautiful, and understood that it wasn't that; it wasn't that he wanted anyone else. When the blonde sitting next to him offered a cigarette, John took it.

"What are you doing?" Stuart asked. "You don't smoke. And Irene **hates** cigarette smoke."

"Yeah, I know," John said. "I think she has an allergy or something." He put a match to the end of the cigarette.

"Whoa," Stuart said. "Are your **hands** shaking?"

"My hands aren't shaking!"

"They are, too, man. Look at them."

John looked at his hands, and his friend was right: there was a fine tremor.

He ground out the cigarette, shoved his face into his hands, and moaned.

Stuart said, "Okay, okay, buddy, you just need to calm down. Try this. Think about when you asked Irene to marry you. Why did you ask her?"

John looked over at him. "She didn't wear makeup?"

When Irene Marsh was a young girl, she used to have a play space in the basement where she lined up her many baby dolls. One by one, she fed them, burped them, and rocked them to sleep. It brought her a rare peace, to care for her babies. It took her away from what went on between her parents, the yelling and the hateful silences, which were worse than the yelling. She sang lullabies into plastic ears and rocked inert little bodies; she prayed each night on her knees to get old enough to live with someone else, in love.

Which was why it was a little surprising that, on her wedding day, she sat weeping in the bride's room. The place was ornately decorated: a multi-tiered chandelier, embossed ivory wallpaper, two elegant club chairs upholstered in tangerine silk, the table between them holding a bouquet of white freesia and a crystal bowl full of Jordan almonds—for good luck, Irene knew. In the adjoining powder room was a vase of creamy white orchids, pristine linen hand towels, and a gold basket of might-needs decorated by a length of wide satin ribbon. When Irene had shown the bathroom to her best friend and only bridesmaid, Valerie Cox (Valerie herself happily married for nine years), Valerie had said, "Oh, everything is so **pretty**!" Irene had stood there, imagining herself as the speck on the ground, Valerie as the plane rising higher in the air. What Irene had felt about the décor was only a sense of outrage, at the excess.

Fifteen minutes before the ceremony was to begin, Irene sat on the bench before the white vanity with her back to the mirror. She had just put on her wedding gown, a dress that was purposefully plain and might in fact work for everyday, were it not floor length and made from ivory Qiana. Her hair was loose about her shoulders, not as yet styled into the upsweep she'd planned; her satin heels lay in a little jumble on the floor beside her, her veil across her lap. The bridal bouquet sat unpacked in its box in a corner of the room.

"But I thought you were **sure**," Valerie said. She was standing before Irene, holding her friend's trembling hands in her own. "You said you were absolutely sure!"

"I know, but I want to go home. Will you take me?"

"Well . . ." Valerie didn't know what to do. She spoke in a near whisper, saying, "Irene. You're thirty-six years old. If you want children—"

"I know how old I am! But you shouldn't get

married just to have children. I can't get **married** just to have children!" She drew in a ragged breath, snatched a tissue off the dressing table, and blew her nose.

Valerie spoke slowly, carefully, saying, "I don't know; getting married to have children isn't such a bad idea. And besides, you **love** John. Don't you?"

Irene stared into her lap, picked at one thumbnail with the other.

"**Irene?**"

She looked up. "I can't go through with this. Please, Vee. It's wrong. Go and get the car, okay? We have to hurry. If you don't want to, I understand. I'll take the bus. There's a bus that goes by here."

Valerie cracked open the door to see if anyone was out in the hall: no one. Then she knelt on the floor before Irene and looked directly into her eyes. "Listen to me. If you do this, you can't take it back. Do you understand that? It's not just a little tiff and then you apologize and get married next week instead. If you do this, it's the end of you and John. Do you understand that?"

Irene nodded. "I do. So to speak." She tried to smile.

Valerie stood, crossed her arms, and sighed. "What about all those people out there? There must be two hundred people! Do you want me to make an announcement or something?"

"Oh. Yes. Yes." Irene rose and carefully draped

the veil over one of the club chairs. "Apologize for me, okay? Say I'm sorry. I **am** sorry. And be sure to say that I'll send all the gifts back, right away. Tomorrow. I know this is hard. I'll make it up to you, I promise."

But then Irene's father poked his head in the door and said gruffly, "Let's go," and Irene put her veil on, stepped into her shoes, and linked her arm through his.

"Irene?" Valerie said, and Irene said, "No."

Once Upon a Time, There Was You

1

When eighteen-year-old Sadie Marsh comes from California to visit her father in Minnesota, she sleeps in a bedroom decorated for her much younger self: a ruffled canopy bed, a white dresser with fairies painted on it, wallpaper with pink and white stripes, a bedside lamp with a wishing well base. Neither John nor his daughter has ever made a move to change one thing about that room; Sadie still sleeps under a pile of stuffed animals, the ones she left behind.

It's a warm Sunday in late August, and John is sitting on the front porch, feeding peanuts to the squirrel that has ventured up the steps and over to him. He's waiting for his daughter to come out the door to announce that this is really it; she has everything now, she's ready to go to the airport. She's been here for the usual length of time—one week. She's not even gone, but already he is feeling a wide band around his middle start to tighten. When he drops her at the airport, neither of them will express any regret at her leave-taking: it is an unspoken agreement that they keep every parting casual, that they do not make a bad situation worse with what they both would describe as fussing and carrying on, a phrase that John's Atlanta-born mother was fond of using, and one that she in fact employed every time **they** parted. "No fussin' and cahn' on, now," she would say, her white-gloved hand beneath his chin, her eyes crinkled at the sides the way they did when she smiled. "I'm gon' see you real soon, just you wait; you won't hardly know I've been gone."

He did wait. And wait.

Sadie has Irene's looks: auburn hair, hazel eyes that lean toward green, a fair complexion that burns at the mention of sun. She's tall, with a delicate bone structure, wrists so tiny she can almost never find a watch to fit her. But her nature is more like her father's: she's an outdoor type, confident in athletics, a person who is more irritated than inspired by poetry, an even-keeled young woman who rarely takes things personally. She has a loud laugh, an infectious one; even when Sadie was a toddler, Irene would say, "You can't hear her laugh and not join right in, even if you're mad at her. **Especially** if you're mad at her."

John hears Sadie coming down the stairs and tosses the rest of the peanuts into a corner of the porch. The squirrel stands there on its hind legs, its tail flicking, then opts for running off the porch rather than heading for the feast. "Hey!" John says. He moves to the top step to watch the squirrel run to the elm tree on the boulevard, then rapidly ascend. From the highest limb, it stares down at John. "Get your **peanuts**," John says, pointing, but the squirrel only stares.

"All set, Dad," Sadie says. She has her over-stuffed backpack in one hand, her suitcase in the other, and he can tell from the tone of her voice that she, too, is having a hard time keeping upbeat. Never mind a deep and abiding love; he and his daughter really **like** each other. One week four times a year is not enough for either of them, but it is the best solution for now. In winter and summer, Sadie comes to St. Paul; in spring and fall, John goes out to San Francisco, where he stays in a hotel and visits with both Irene and Sadie, but that never quite works out—if he sees Sadie alone, she seems to feel bad for her mother; if they all get together, it's excruciating. The truth is, John doesn't like Irene much anymore, and he doesn't think she cares for him, either. They've grown apart in large ways and small. Irene identifies herself as a conservative liberal now, which John can't fathom. She's overly concerned about order and cleanliness in her flat—it's impossible to relax there. She prefers cats to dogs, which is almost worse than being a conservative. She's taken to wearing makeup and recently dyed her hair to cover the gray—Sadie says it's the influence of her latest man friend, a guy named Don Strauss, who believes aging people should "fight the good fight."

"Oh, please," John said, when Sadie told him this. And Sadie shrugged and said, "He's not so bad. He makes really good vegetable lasagna. He puts goat cheese in there."

"Well, that counts for something," John said, but privately he was thinking, **Right, I'll bet he's another vegetarian. Another Unitarian vegetarian who holds up peace signs at street corners every Saturday afternoon and aspires to live in a Mongolian yurt.** He waited for Sadie to say more about Don, but she didn't, and he didn't ask. Another unspoken agreement. He didn't ask about the men in Sadie's mother's life; Irene didn't ask about the women in his. Not that there were many to ask about. The last time he had a semi-serious relationship was five years ago, and that blew up when he wouldn't agree to lock his black Lab mix, emphasis on **mix**, out of his room on the nights she slept over. The woman complained that the dog snored and farted; John allowed that she did, too, and that was that. Festus died last year, and John thinks he's almost ready to get another dog. An Irish wolfhound, he's thinking, mostly because Sadie said she knows of a rescue group that recently took one in. "They're awfully big," John told her, and she said, "Exactly."

On the way to the airport, John looks over to see Sadie fooling around with her iPod. "Don't you dare put those plugs in your ears and disappear," he says. "Please."

"I'm not. I'm just getting it ready for the plane."

"I don't see why you young people can't step away from electronics for ten seconds of your life." **Young people!** Well, that's it: he's officially old now.

"Dad. I hardly used anything at your house the whole time I was there. I texted, like, twice."

John doesn't believe her. He saw the light under her door when he went past at night, and he heard the tap-tap-tapping. But he doesn't challenge her; at least she was courteous enough not to be constantly texting in front of him. He resents the very posture of people who are online, the way they bend their backs over their various devices, blocking out any possibility that they might engage with a real live person, who would never come with enough apps to satisfy them, let's face it. Virtual is so much more exciting than real. But only if you don't know how to look and listen, is what John thinks. He made Sadie sit out on the porch swing with him one night, just to hear the crickets and, later, to see the fireflies. He was gratified to hear her say, after about fifteen minutes, "Wow. This is nice."

Sadie puts the iPod in her backpack and zips it shut. "I'm going to get you one of these," she says. "I'll load it up with good music; you can see what I listen to."

"Sweetheart?"

"No, you'd like a lot of the songs! You really would."

"Okay, but no rap."

"Some rap. You'll see."

He stops for a red light and looks over at her. "You're an awfully pretty girl, you know that?"

She rolls her eyes.

"You're going to break some econ major's heart."

"Econ?"

"Veterinary medicine?"

"Better."

A great sadness comes over him, but he makes his voice light to say, "So! What's in store for the last of the summer?"

"Well. A challenge. A bunch of us are going rock climbing next weekend. **If** Mom will let me. So far she says no way."

"What are you going to climb?"

"Just Mount Tam, and only the lowest slab. Some people wanted to go to Mammoth Mountain, myself included, but that's a six-hour drive."

"Since when do you know anything about rock climbing?"

She shrugs. "I've done it a lot in gym class. Mom doesn't want me to do the real thing. You want to hear her pithy words of wisdom? 'Sadie, if you go rock climbing and you fall, you'll land on a rock.'"

She looks over at John, and he has to smile. That would be Irene.

"But I want to learn to do this," Sadie says. "And I'll be with people who know a lot about it. I have a friend who's been climbing with his family since he was six years old. He says it's great. He also says the only way to know yourself is to challenge yourself—in a hard way, so that you're really scared. He says what you do in times like that is what you **are**."

John nods. "I suppose there's some truth to that."

"You think?"

"Yeah."

"Have you ever done that? Taken on a challenge that really, really scared you?"

Marrying your mother. Didn't work out so well. "Not really," he says.

"Maybe you should try rock climbing."

"Yeah, not for me, I don't think. So are you going to need ropes and pickaxes and oxygen masks and all that stuff?"

"Dad."

"Well, what do I know?"

"It's not mountain climbing; it's rock climbing. All I need is climbing shoes. My friend gave me a pair of his sister's—they're almost brand new, and they fit just fine."

"I'll get you your own pair."

"Let's see if I like it first," Sadie says, and John feels a rush of pride in his daughter for being so practical and unselfish, for not taking him up on every offer he makes to buy her things. There's no doubt she understands that guilt is a pretty good wallet cracker after a divorce, even many years after a divorce, and she chooses not to capitalize on that. She was a child who would never dump a bowl full of Halloween candy left untended on someone's porch into her bag, or even take more than one piece. He used to worry sometimes that she was too good, and took an odd sort of comfort in the times she did act up.

"What you could do," Sadie says, "is talk to Mom and convince her to let me try this."

"Okay. I'll tell her it's fine with me. I'll tell her it's important that you take on physical as well as mental challenges. I think I can bring her around."

"Thanks. What's **your** next challenge?"

"There's an old building on Wabasha I'm trying to buy. I'm just starting negotiations. My God, the ceilings on that place are—"

"I mean a personal challenge."

"Renovation **is** personal to me. Since I was your age. Since before that."

"I know. I know all about your matchbox cities when you were a little boy, and how you tried to save your first old building when you were sixteen, and how you won first prize in the science fair for your city of the future. . . ."

"That was an incredible city."

"I'm sure it was. But I meant more along the lines of when are you going to date again? That kind of challenge."

"I'm fifty-six years old, Sadie."

"And?"

"I think I'm all done with that."

"You so are not!"

"I'm not really all that interested."

"Well, you should be. It's not good to be alone. To be honest, I worry about you a little bit, Dad. You don't even comb your hair half the time."

"I have a cowlick."

"Yeah, but you don't comb it half the time, either. And you don't eat well. I don't think you're uninterested in dating; I think you don't know how to go about meeting single women. Why don't you put an ad in the paper? That's what Mom does, and she's your age. Just write an ad, or go online, and see what—"

"Absolutely not. I am not dating someone I meet **online**." He will never admit that, one night, he looked around on Match.com. Sat before his computer in his shorts and T-shirt, drinking a beer, looking for someone who wasn't there. Not even close. Something occurs to him. "Are you meeting people online? Are you going **mountain climbing** with someone you met online?"

"**No, Dad.** And it's **rock** climbing. And I'm going with a whole group of people from school— if I even go. I'm just saying you should get **out** more. There's more to life than work."

"As I've been told. And told."

"Well, there is."

He signals for the exit to the airport. "I'll tell you what. If you climb a rock, I'll ask a woman out."

"Yeah, how will you meet her, though?"

"I have my ways."

"Name them."

"You'll see."

"You have one week," Sadie says. "That's when the climb is."

"Deal." He pulls over to the curb to let her out and puts the car into park. He lays his hand against the side of his daughter's face and sighs. Kisses her forehead. "All right. Get out of my car."

"I thought you'd never ask." She leans over to embrace him. "Don't **call** me all the time," she says into his ear, and he says, "Don't call **me** all the time," and then she is gone. Though she does turn back before she goes through the glass doors. Turns and blows him a kiss, and he waves back.

He pulls out into the traffic and blinks once, twice. Clears his throat. Then he turns on the radio and boosts the volume.

He thinks about whether or not he should make his next move with Amy Becker. Because what Sadie doesn't know is that he's already met someone; it was over a month ago. It was in a way he'd rather not share with his daughter. Or with anyone else.

2

On a cold November evening when Irene was fourteen years old, she was in her bedroom doing homework, and her mother was in the kitchen, making hamburger soup. It smelled so good, and Irene was impatient for her father to come home so they could eat dinner. But then the smell changed; something was burning. "Mom?" Irene called from her room. No reply, and the smell intensified. Irene came out into the hall. **"Mom?"**

She went into the kitchen and turned off the burner, then opened the back door to let the smoky air out. She saw that the light in the garage was on, and supposed that her mother had gotten caught up in cleaning something out there; she was always complaining about what a mess it was in the garage. "Hey, Mom!" Irene called from the doorway. She was in her stocking feet, and didn't want to put shoes and a coat on. But when her mother didn't answer, Irene did put on her shoes. She didn't bother with a coat—she'd only be a minute.

She pushed open the garage door and bumped into something: her mother, hanging from the rafter, a length of clothesline around her neck. Wearing her flowered apron. One shoe off, one shoe on. Irene backed away, ran into the house, and called her father at his office. "You must never tell anyone this," he said later. "And we will not speak of it again." Heart attack, they told everyone.

But then in college, Irene did tell someone: her roommate, Valerie. They were in their dorm room, studying, and Valerie was telling Irene about something they'd talked about in psychology class that day, having to do with children of abusive mothers. She said she couldn't understand how children could love mothers who treated them that way. And Irene began suddenly to cry, and then she told Val about finding her mother. When she finished the story, she was filled with a sense of panic, and with regret at having violated her father's trust, perhaps her mother's as well. She asked Valerie to promise that she would never tell anyone else, ever.

"I won't," Valerie said. "But—"

"That's all I want to say about it," Irene said. "I just wanted to tell you. But I don't want to talk about it."

"But don't you—"

"**Please**," Irene said.

And Valerie said okay.

After a moment, Irene said, "I mean it, about never telling anyone else."

"I won't."

"Even if we don't stay friends. Even if you think you **should** tell someone else."

"Okay."

"Promise me."

"I did."

"Promise me again."

"I **won't,** Irene. I won't ever tell **anyone.**"

"I shouldn't have told you."

Valerie reached over to touch Irene's hand. "Is it . . . ? Do you think it was your fault, Irene? You don't think it was your fault, do you?"

"I don't know. I guess for a little while I did. I kept thinking about one summer when I was six years old, and I used to run away all the time. Sometimes I went out to this big field behind our house. I would just sit there, in the long grass; it grew way over my head. It was peaceful. But mostly I went to the Mentzes' house. They were a childless older couple down the block, and they were always so nice to me. I used to run away to their house every couple of weeks or so—you know, pack my suitcase, show up on their doorstep. They always gave me some cookies and milk and then brought me back home; but I thought that secretly they wanted to keep me, they were just so **nice** to me. So I kept on giving them more chances to have me, until finally I gave up.

"But I know it wasn't my fault, what my mother

did. For one thing, it happened so many years after all that running away. I shouldn't have told you."

"Yes you should have," Val said. And then, "Irene? Can I ask you just one more thing?"

"What."

"What did your father say when he found out?"

"He got mad. He started swearing."

Val stared at her.

"Not at **me**."

Val's eyes were wide, her face a little flushed, and Irene thought she must want to ask a million more questions, say a million more things. She feared Val might move away from their friendship, because now she would think Irene was weird. But she didn't. She bent her head to her books, and after a while she asked Irene if she wanted to share a pizza.

They ordered a large sausage and mushroom and ate the whole thing. And then, at midnight, they heard there was a giant snowball fight happening on the quad, boys versus girls, and they put their coats on over their pajamas, slid their bare feet into their boots, and went out to defend their sex. They came back two hours later with snow down their backs, snow melting in their boots and caked in their hair, and even though it was widely held that you couldn't get colds from being cold, they both got very bad colds, which, in the way of the young, they rather enjoyed.

Irene sits in her bedroom recalling that night,

the details still so clear. She thinks of how, a month after she met John, she told him about her mother, too; he was the only other person she ever told. She extracted the same promise from him, not to tell anyone else. "I would never do that," he said. And he said nothing more, but he reached out his arms and she moved into them. All she heard for a long time was the sound of them breathing together, and the distant beating of his heart.

Irene snaps to, and turns to her computer. Now as then: forget the past; concentrate on the present. Here is the present: she is a woman in search of a man. Again.

She stretches her arms out, cracks her knuckles. How to approach it this time?

I believe in defacing books, she writes. **I think one's personal library should be full of books with broken spines and meaningful passages under-lined, with pages marked by chocolate or coffee or grease stains. If there are comments or questions in the margins, even better. I am otherwise a very neat person, as I believe that external chaos leads to internal chaos. Discuss. (Ha ha.) I believe in going to cafes in the afternoon and enjoying pas-try on a porcelain plate, even if it ruins your din-ner. This is a bit of an affectation, I suppose, as I only began doing it after I visited Paris and saw all of them doing it. "Them" being the French, of course, and who among us does not trust the French when it comes to food and fashion?**

I believe in bringing home rocks from every place I visited and loved, because I think rocks hold within them an essence of place, and that you can feel this essence—and therefore the place—if you hold the rock tightly in your hand. Naturally you must have patience, as well as an open mind and heart, and, like many spiritual things, it works better if your eyes are closed.

No. She deletes this last paragraph, then continues.

I believe in keeping my eyes closed at the dentist's and imagining Tahiti even though I have never been there. But I have seen pictures, and every time I go to the dentist I imagine me in those pictures with the blue, blue sea and the waves coming in. (As a kid I had a dentist who gave every patient a card for a free Dairy Queen cone after each visit. Devil or angel? I still can't decide.) I will never be thin again and I am interested in meeting a man who is just fine with that. Not that I'm fat. But I am average, and average is not thin. Average to zaftig, I guess would be more precise, and I still have very good legs if you care about that sort of thing, which I do. I believe in holding hands in the movie show when all the lights are low, and if you know and like that song, we're already off to a good start. I kind of hate writing these things, as I'm sure you can tell, but I understand and accept the need for them.

She rereads what she wrote, then gets up from

the little desk in the corner of her bedroom and moves to the window. She crosses her arms and sighs, leans her head against the cool glass. Across the street, an old Asian woman pushes a little cart full of groceries uphill. She has a brightly patterned scarf knotted under her chin, an open black coat, and she is wearing house slippers and nylon stockings rolled to the knees. Irene can see a baguette sticking out of one of the grocery bags, the fernlike tops of carrots, and what look like baby eggplants. She wonders what the woman will make for dinner. She wishes she could call out and ask her; she feels as though the information would comfort her. Would ground her. Life goes on. One makes dinner. One must eat. You are not alone, we are none of us alone, see how we all eat dinner? ☺☺☺☺☺☺!

Oh, it was a lovely day today, the sky a bleached turquoise color, no fog, only a few clouds that looked like clotted cream, placed as though by children's hands—oddly irregular that way. She wishes the dark weren't coming so soon.

This morning, Don Strauss called to tell her that he was getting back together with his ex-wife. "I'm so sorry," he said. "I was going to tell you to your face, but then I thought it might be less painful if I just called. Because what would we do after I told you to your face, you know? I mean, it would be so awkward for both of us. I want you to know I've not had any contact with her since I met you—this came out of the blue. She just now called, we had a really long, really honest talk, and we realized we're still in love with each other. And I think we have a chance to make it work this time. I'm happy for myself, but I'm sorry for any pain I caused you. I know you were a lot more invested in this relationship than I."

"What?" Irene said.

"I'm sorry. I didn't mean that the way it sounded. I just meant—"

"I wasn't more invested than you! What makes you think I was more invested than you?"

"Well, you did say a number of things that—"

"You know, you make that clicking sound with your jaw when you chew, and it just about drives me up the wall."

"Okay, Irene."

"Honestly, I don't know how much longer I would have been able to tolerate that. And did anyone ever teach you the virtues of using a toilet brush? Have you ever **heard** of a toilet brush?"

"I guess we're not going to be able to talk about this. I'm sorry for that. You're a wonderful woman when you're not outraged, and in fact I wanted to let you know that my friend Larry, whom you met at that art gallery we went to last week, was very taken with you, so if—"

Irene hung up. She called Valerie and got her voice mail and said, "Call me. Or if you can, come over. Minor crisis. **Minor**." She went to the refrigerator and looked in, closed the door. Opened it and looked some more, closed the door again. "Damn it," she said, quietly, and then, louder, **"Damn it!"** And then she cried, just a little, tears more of humiliation, of frustration, than of pain.

She flung herself into the kitchen banquette, and while she cried she looked through the Williams-Sonoma catalogue, and then she blew her nose and called to order the azure blue, three-and-a-half-quart Le Creuset oval Dutch oven, vowing to use it for the white bean soup recipe she's had taped to her refrigerator for months. After she placed the order, she almost reflexively called Don to tell him she'd gotten the pan—he'd told her she should buy it when she showed it to him after the catalogue arrived last Saturday. Yes, last Saturday, when Sadie had gone to see her father, and Irene and Don had made love in the afternoon and then they'd gotten up in a lovely golden light and she'd made them feta cheese and spinach omelets and Greek toast and served it with retsina and he'd said it was divine. But instead of calling Don—whose number **she had never memorized**, by the way—she'd gone over to her computer to compose yet another ad for the local paper that let you place personals of any length for free, so long as they were in the "Over 55" section. Mercy for the half dead. She'll write another damn ad—that's how she had met Don. She doesn't want to use online dating services, which scare her. She went on Match.com one day, surveyed the men in her specified age group, and felt a little blip of hope. A blond man who was an attorney, wearing a nice blue sweater and gray pants. An international businessman who was bald but still very attractive; he exuded a kind of Yul Brynner confidence. Then she surveyed the women close to her age, her competition, and immediately gave up. "**Why?**" Val asked when Irene told her that. "You're every bit as good as they are!"

"No," Irene said. "I'm not. Those women are all happier than I am. Healthier. Nicer. Richer, too."

"Irene, if you posted a picture, people would say the same thing about you. You look beautiful when you're smiling. You look happy and healthy, too. You're supposed to try to make yourself look as good as you can on those websites. That's what everybody does! Then, after a few dates, the warts come out. That's the way it works. You pretend you're perfect, and by the time they find out you're not, they hopefully like you a little, anyway. And you them."

"I like blind dates," Irene said. "And I like to show my warts first."

"It's a wonder anybody ever contacts you, with the ads you write."

"It's because I'm a relief from the usual love-to-walk-on-the-beach, that's why." That's what Don had told her.

And so here she goes, writing another ad. Back on the horse. Too many fish in the sea. No use crying over spilled milk. Et fucking cetera.

Maybe she swore too much. She does swear too much. But all her friends do, and then it just becomes sort of contagious. Don said "darn" and "gosh" and "heck," which she initially thought was charming—even trendsettingly retro!—but came to find annoying and possibly passive-aggressive. Recalling him using those pale epithets, she rolls her eyes and nods her head, as though she's the one who initiated the breakup and now she's confirming the vote.

"Eeeyup," she says, and then, alarmed, looks at her watch. Sadie's plane will be arriving in a couple of hours. Irene had wanted to go to the market and take some time selecting ingredients and then slow-cook a nice dinner for her daughter's homecoming, but instead they'll go to Hunan, which they both love. Over scallion pancakes, she'll casually mention that she and Don are all done. Sadie will make sure her mother is okay, and then she'll say she's glad, Irene would bet on it. She tolerated Don, but Irene knew she didn't see him as a proper match for her mother.

Sadie often understands things before her mother does. Babies always seem so wise when they're born, and both Irene and Valerie think Sadie has never lost that quality. There is something in Sadie's eyes that goes so far back. Valerie calls her "Buddha

Girl." For her part, Sadie calls Valerie "Gypsy Woman" for her long skirts and oversize hoop earrings and many bracelets; and she calls her mother "Betty," as in Crocker. Irene doesn't mind. In many ways, she's flattered. She thinks people who value creating a home and caring for children are vastly underrated. Vastly, vastly, vastly. Plus more vastly than that, and then some. What better thing than to have a skinned knee tended to by someone who feels the injury along with you? What deeper comfort after a bad dream than seeing a familiar silhouette at your doorjamb, feeling a familiar weight settling itself at your bedside? A table set properly, folded clothes, a stocked refrigerator. Who can say they do not appreciate the idea of home when it conveys such riches—not only appreciate it but also, in certain moments, grant it the elevated place it deserves?

Before she had Sadie, Irene was for many years a speech therapist. Sometimes her patients struggled so hard for words she could never understand, and this brought despair to both of them. But whenever Irene asked, "What do these things represent?" and showed them pictures of objects like a lit lamp next to a reading chair, a bathrobe hanging from a hook, a window box full of riotous geraniums, a pie cooling on the counter? Then! They might manage only **"Halk!"** but there would be that earnest look in their eyes, that light, and Irene would say, "Yes. **Home.** Good."

After Sadie started grade school, Irene went back to work part-time. But when she moved to San Francisco, there were no part-time jobs for speech therapists. So she worked for several years sharing a position as a receptionist at a temporary employment agency—she didn't want to work full-time until Sadie was in college; and with her own savings and alimony, she didn't have to.

A couple of years ago, a man named Henry Bliss called the agency, looking for someone to assist with making appetizers at a wedding that Saturday. Irene loves cooking, and she told the man she'd take the job herself. He ended up hiring her to work three, sometimes four times a week as a kind of culinary girl Friday. She does everything from shopping for groceries and general cleanup to food prep. By his own admission, Henry can be a bit of a challenge, but he adores Sadie; and the feeling is mutual. Sometimes he hires Sadie to help at events, too, and he pays her generously—mostly for hanging around and admiring him rather than passing trays of appetizers.

On occasion Henry has advocated for Irene's position when she and Sadie are having a dispute, and that keeps Irene mostly silent about what she would call the abuse she takes from Henry. In addition to that, she loves grilling eggplant, crimping quiche crusts, lining up three plump raspberries just so next to an artful squiggle of chocolate on a gold-rimmed dessert plate. She loves inhaling the aroma of the fresh herbs she is chopping. But her favorite thing is helping herself (when Henry isn't looking) to chunks of lobster or slices of exotic cheeses or spoonfuls of lemon curd or whipped cream or cake batter or cold blueberry soup. At her age, another job would be hard to find. She hopes to work for Henry full-time after Sadie starts college.

Irene stretches, then goes back to her computer. She stares at the blank page, then writes: **Yesterday, while waiting in line at the grocery store, I heard the woman behind me say, "Oh, I wish to hell they'd never even invented computers!" I wanted to turn around and hug her, but I didn't want to interrupt the conversation she was having on her iPhone, which I believe is a computer. This, I think, is the essence of a lot of the problems we face today. We need what we hate. And vice versa. Discuss. (ha ha)**

3

Sadie slides onto a stool at the airport bar and orders a Bloody Mary. "ID?" the bartender asks, and she laughs.

"I need to see your ID," he says, and she says, "Are you kidding me? I'm twenty-four. Twenty-five in a week!"

He stands there, his beefy arms crossed, and finally she gets off the stool and goes into the French Meadow café, where she orders a turkey-avocado sandwich and a cream cheese brownie and milk. After she eats, she goes to her gate. It's crowded there; only two seats are available, both next to businessmen blabbing loudly on their phones, and so she sits on the floor in the hall opposite the gate. She calls Ron Savage, and when he answers, she says, "Ready or not, here I come."

"Hey," he says, and she can hear the smile in his voice and she feels that little tornado low in her stomach. Practically everything Ron does gets to her: he can just stand there and she'll feel a zingedout kind of helplessness. It's so odd how long it took her to notice him. She knew him as a quiet member of their senior class: captain of the debate team; a pretty good actor, according to those who had seen him in plays; an excellent guitarist who sometimes played at parties; a good writer who contributed essays to the school paper, mostly having to do with a young person's take on current events, although occasionally he did a humor piece that was actually really funny. He hung with the arty crowd, she with the jocks, but then one day early in May she was behind him in the lunch line and they started talking and she thought, **Whoa!** She knows the line "Where have you been all my life?" ranks right up there with the cheesiest of clichés, but that's exactly what she felt, that day. She doesn't even remember what they talked about, but something he said or the way he said it made her really see him for the first time. Her best friend, Meghan, says it's pheromones, that that day in May was the first time Sadie had been close enough to Ron to smell him. "You can't fight pheromones," Meghan had said. "Or if you were together in a past life, you can't fight that, either."

Whatever accounted for Sadie's instant attraction to Ron, it was mutual, and they've been together ever since. She hasn't told her mother about him yet; he's too special to her. Sadie doesn't want anything her mother says or does to ruin things for her—Irene can be wonderful, but she can also be really strange. And Ron seemed in no rush to meet her mother anyway, or for Sadie to meet his. Sadie likes this, the way that what they have together belongs to them alone. Meghan covers for Sadie when she goes out with Ron, although she's starting to get tired of it, Sadie knows. The last time she'd called Meghan and said, "Ron and I are going out tonight, okay?" Meghan had sighed and said, "How much longer, Sadie?" And Sadie had said soon. Soon she'd tell both her parents about him. But not yet. Maybe when she's in school and Irene's hand isn't in every one of Sadie's pies. She can't wait for that kind of independence, which seems impossible to achieve when she's living under the same roof with Irene. She's heard that single mothers can do this—take helicoptering to a whole other level—but she's had enough. And it was Ron who helped her realize that. Not in a cruel way. Just in a matter-of-fact way. Like pointing to a kid who'd had training wheels far too long and saying, "Want to try to ride without those?"

So much about Ron is so different from any boy she's ever known. If this is love, she hates it and she wants more. She wants to hook up with him, but so far he won't. **He** won't! And he's not a virgin—he told her once he'd had his first sexual experience with a much older woman, when he was sixteen. She was a neighbor who lived next door to them for only a few months, a twenty-one-year-old whose husband was at war and who, after their encounter, stopped speaking to him, though she was the one who'd initiated everything.

Sadie is a virgin, though not inexperienced in oral sex. When she was a junior, she was at a party and someone dared her; and she'd gone into the bedroom and done it with the guy she was going out with at the time, Gary Stevens. She'd found it odd: maybe slightly erotic, but mostly **odd**. She'd told Gary that, and he'd offered to do the real thing, but she'd said no. She didn't see what the big deal was about either thing, actually; she thought of sex as a lot of fussin' and cahn' on about not much.

But now she thinks she understands what the big deal is, and she wants the real thing with Ron, she wants him inside her because she wants that closeness; she wants to say something to him that she cannot say with words. Once, when they were on the phone intentionally driving each other a little crazy, she said, "Honest to God, Ron, if we don't do it soon, I'm going to explode."

He made a sound she couldn't quite interpret, and she said, "Don't you **want** to?" The question made her blush to the roots of her hair, even on the phone; she instantly regretted asking it.

But then he said, "Of course I want to," and she felt better.

She made her voice low and soft. "Okay then, so why don't we—"

"It's **complicated**," he said. "I told you. Just let it be for now, okay?"

"Fine," she said. "Then let's stop teasing each other and talk about the Tet Offensive." She and Ron were doing summer reading for a history class they were both taking that fall when they started college at UC Berkeley. Learning about the sixties and the Summer of Love wasn't doing much to quell her desire for a certain type of exploration.

"How can you even **think** I don't want to?" he asked. "God! I can't wait to see those beautiful breasts and unzip your jeans and—"

"Okay," she said, laughing. "I'm hanging up." But then something occurred to her, a dark thought. "Ron? Can I ask you something?"

"What?"

"Do you have . . . a communicable disease?"

He laughed so readily and so loudly she believed him when he said no. It was something else, then. And she vowed to make it her business to disabuse him of whatever was holding him back. She wanted him to be the first. It was time, she was overdue, and she saw now why she had been waiting: it was for someone like him.

"How was your dad?" Ron asks.

"Same as always. He's such a good guy. Him, I want you to meet." She looks out into the crowd of people sitting at the gate, trying to find someone who looks like her dad. No one does. No one looks the least little bit like him.

"Maybe sometime soon I can."

"He's coming to San Francisco in a few months. You can meet him then, if you want." Her stomach tightens at the thought—not of her father and Ron meeting, but at the notion of her and Ron staying together that long. Things can fall apart so easily. Only last week Meghan had been dumped by her boyfriend Brian without one word of warning. Meghan came over with her face still swollen from crying half the night. She sat on Sadie's bed staring blankly at nothing and refusing Sadie's offers to do something, anything: a movie, shopping, a walk by the ocean, a little weed. "Are you kidding?" Meghan said. "That would make me feel **worse**."

"No," Sadie said. "It would put it all in perspective." But even as she said it, she wasn't sure it was true. She ended up just sitting quietly with her friend until Meghan got hungry, and then they went out to Octavia Street, to Miette bakery, where they ate the better part of a Tomboy cake.

Boarding begins, and she tells Ron, "I have to get on the plane in a minute. But I wanted to tell you I think our trip is on. My dad said he'd persuade my mom to let me go rock climbing. She almost always listens to him, even though she says she never does."

"Rock climbing?"

"Yeah, you know Tate Shiller and all those guys are going rock climbing. I said I was going with them. It would be pretty hard to get away for the weekend otherwise. I didn't want to ask Meghan to cover for me again; she's getting kind of tired of it."

"Your dad believed you?"

"Yeah. He trusts me."

For just a moment, Sadie feels bad about lying to her dad. But it's a little sin for a greater good; some-day it will be a funny story she tells about what happened in the very early stages of her and Ron.

"Upright dude. Are you sure you don't want to tell him the truth?"

"I can't tell him and not my mom. And if I tell my mom, she'll say I can't go." The gate agent calls out Sadie's group number. "I have to get on the plane," she says. She stands, shoulders her back-pack. "I'll call you when I land."

"Tell the pilot to hurry," Ron says, and she smiles and touches the phone where his voice came out before she hangs up. She stands in line behind a woman in a navy suit and a ruffled white blouse, on her phone saying goodbye to her significant other, apparently, for she says, "Love you, babe." She listens to something, then laughs, a deep, throaty laugh. "You first," she says. Sadie looks at the woman's left hand: an engagement ring, the diamond huge. Whenever Sadie sees engagement rings, she feels a strange mix of emotions: a kind of excitement mixed with a vague sadness. A longing for a specific kind of inclusion she both aspires to and fears. And, oddly, she feels a sense of failure, of shame. She knows it's nonsensical, but there it is, big inside her, this sense of having screwed every-thing up, of having lost something she never had.

After Sadie buckles herself into her window seat, a man sits beside her. He's overweight, round-faced and pink-cheeked, and making a mighty effort to suck in his gut. "How you doing?" he says, and immediately she knows he'll buy her a drink. Most guys she sits by on an airplane will, so long as there's no one else in the row with them. This plane is con-figured to have only two seats on one side, so Sadie's got it made. After the flight attendant explains the many things the passengers should do to save them-selves in the unlikely event of a crash (when what's really unlikely is that anyone will survive), Sadie will make her request: "Hey, if I give you the money, would you buy me a drink?" Usually the guys just wave her money away and pay for the drink them-selves. She lets them. The only bad part is if, later, they do things like ask her if she'd like to join them in the bathroom. In fantasies, the idea might intrigue her, especially if the guy is hot. The reality, though, would be something else. Sliding zippers down. The absurdly small space. How it would be to sit beside the guy afterward, his smell on her. The sad nothingness of an encounter like that.

While people shuffle slowly down the aisle, shove their bags into the overhead, and take their seats, Sadie stares out the window. She thinks of her father putting his hand to her cheek before she got out of the car to go into the airport. She thinks of how, when they ate dinner one night, she asked if he'd ever consider moving to San Francisco. He was silent for a long time. Then he said, "I don't think so, Sadie."

They ate with their heads down for a while, the sound of their forks on the plates amplified in the sudden silence. Then, "Would you ever consider moving here?" he asked brightly, almost in a jokey way, and she said maybe. She said it as if she had never thought about it before, as if, having thought about it now, she might really do it. "May**be!**" Then they both felt better.

She thought of how she'd come upon him making her bed for her one morning, and she'd said, "Dad, I can do that!" and he'd held his hands up and said, "Okay, okay!" and then had made her bed the next day, too. Made her bed and placed her old stuffed animals on it, just so. She thought of how he was sitting in the kitchen before breakfast that morning, his head down, his hands clasped between his knees. He didn't see her, and she tiptoed back upstairs, then came down again, making a lot of noise this time. She found him at the cupboard, digging out his cast-iron pan to make her his famous hash browns. "You want two slabs and two staring up to go with this?" he asked.

Two slabs and two staring up. A line that the character of Grover, from **Sesame Street,** once used when he was a waiter ordering bacon and eggs over easy from Charlie, the short-order cook. John and

Irene and seven-year-old Sadie had all been hud-
dled together on the sofa and watching the show
when Grover said that. Her parents had burst
out laughing, and then explained to Sadie what
the terms meant. They were under a flannel quilt
John's aunt had made for him when he was a little
boy, drinking hot chocolate. Outside, a blizzard
that had canceled work and school dumped eighteen inches of snow on the ground.

After dinner, Sadie and her parents went into the
backyard and built three snowmen and a snow
house for them to live in. Later, after they'd tucked
Sadie in, she saw John grab Irene in the hallway
and kiss her. And then they went to their own bedroom and she heard those sounds that at first she'd
thought meant pain but had learned did not.
Those were the days when Irene laughed loudly
and clasped her hands under her chin at the funny
things Sadie's father said; when she hummed folding laundry and licked cake batter from her fingers
with outsize relish. It was when she made homemade birthday cards for both Sadie and John, and
decorated every single room of the house for
Christmas—even the dog wore a little ornament
on his collar. In those days, Irene used to answer
the phone every afternoon around four-thirty and
tell John what they needed, and sometimes she
said, "Just you."

The plane starts to taxi, and Sadie watches the
runway move past faster and faster. She always likes

to watch the takeoff and the landing, not only likes to but feels she must. It's as though she's in charge, as though it's her powers of concentration that will let them become safely airborne and then earth-bound again at the end of the flight. It seems to her that a lot of people on planes feel the same way: she sees people attend to takeoffs and landings as gravely as she, and is often tempted to ask if they're doing what she is. But she never does. You don't ask some things. People hide.

"Headed home?" the man next to her asks.

Sadie holds up a finger. "Just a second." The ground blurs, there is the scooplike lift upward, and then everything below turns miniature. It always brings a feeling of peace to Sadie, that sudden detachment, that sense of no going back now. Done. Decided.

As she looks down, she honors another ritual and searches for her father's house. She never finds it, but she always looks for it just the same. She doesn't know why; seeing it would only make her sadder. There would be the roof of his house, his sidewalk and backyard and car in the driveway, and then would come an image of him, missing her. Sitting out on the front porch steps, maybe, leaning back with his elbows supporting him, his long legs stretched out before him, calling hello to everyone who passed by. Or down at the nearby park, where he liked to watch the little kids play T-ball.

Last night, while they were sitting out on the porch, he told Sadie that he'd been approached again about coaching, but he didn't think he could deal with the parents. "Shouldn't allow them anywhere near the field," he said. "All they do is ruin the game with their big fat egos."

"You used to come to my games," Sadie said. And he said, "Yeah. Where I sat and watched you play and kept my mouth shut."

"Except when I scored," Sadie said, and he laughed and said, "Right. Except when you scored." He looked at her then and his face changed and he said, "I used to love watching you play." She wondered if he was thinking of her mother then, too, missing her, maybe; but of course she didn't ask him that. She couldn't ask him that. She'd tried once, when she was around ten years old; she'd asked him if he missed Irene, and he'd shrugged and said, "Ah, well, you know," and then changed the subject. And she'd understood that if he'd answered yes, she'd have felt terrible. If he'd answered no, she'd have felt terrible. And if he'd been noncommittal, suggesting he rarely thought about Irene at all, she'd have been devastated.

As the plane rises higher, she looks to the west to see if she can find the lake two blocks from her father's house where he used to walk Festus every day and where he taught her to do the breaststroke and the sidestroke and the backstroke all in one day, then rewarded her with a triple ice cream cone, most of which Festus ate because she dropped it. Her dad offered to replace it, but Sadie refused, saying it wouldn't be the same, and she was full, anyway.

"What are you looking for?" her seatmate asks.

"I don't know," she says. "Nothing."

"Ladies and gentlemen, we'd like to ask you to cease all conversation and put down your reading materials," the flight attendant says, and Sadie sits still, waiting, her pain and therefore her want growing more intense. Her knee starts to jiggle and she makes it stop. She'll get the Bloody Mary mix. He'll get the vodka. In the unlikely event that he doesn't get it for her, she'll cease all conversation, put away her reading materials, and sleep.

4

It was at the end of June that his friend Stuart had urged John to go to a divorced parents group. They'd been out at O'Gara's, watching the Twins screw up a close game against the White Sox on the big-screen TV. After the game was over and they'd finished the postmortem, Stuart told John that his wife, Angie, had suggested the group for John— she'd read some story in the paper about it. "Right away, you'd have something in common with all those people," Stuart said. "You could make some friends, maybe even find another woman. And you want a divorcée, you don't want a widow or someone who's never been married. If you get a widow, she's always going to be mooning over her husband. If you get someone over forty who's never been married, you're looking at a whole **world** of trouble."

"I almost didn't get married," John said, and Stuart lowered his chin and looked over his glasses at his friend.

"What, you think I've got problems?" John asked.

"Aw hell, who doesn't have problems." Stuart signaled to the bartender that he was ready for the check. Then he said, "Listen, I don't want to make you feel bad, but you're getting a little weird. I mean, I'll bet you walk around talking to yourself."

"You don't talk to yourself?"

"Not as much as you do. You talk to yourself way too much."

"How do you know?"

"Don't you?"

Silence.

"Hey," Stuart said. "Don't think I'm . . . I'm just saying I think people are meant to be with people. You suffer in a marriage; but alone, you suffer more. Did you ever read that Mark Twain book **Extracts from Adam's Diary**? Adam thought Eve was a real pain in the ass, talking too much, looking at her reflection in the pond all the time, getting them expelled from **Paradise,** for Christ's sake! But what he said at the end was that he was better off living outside the Garden with Eve than inside it without her."

John said nothing, took a last pull on his beer. It occurred to him to say that Adam didn't have ESPN, but he got the point. He got it.

"I think you should give it another shot, that's all. Go to this group and just sit there and listen. If nothing else you hear some stories other than your own. Maybe you meet somebody to have a meal with, to bounce ideas off of."

"That's what you're for."

Stuart put his coat on, turned up the collar. "Yeah. But I can't be the one to do it all the time. You know? You need more than me."

For so many years, Stuart had been filling in the gaps, propping him up, and John supposed Angie had grown tired of it. So he agreed to find such a group, and Stuart told him there was one meeting the next night, at a Unitarian church not four blocks from him. John knew the building—he'd often admired the architecture.

"How do **you** know about that meeting?" John asked, and Stuart shrugged. Meaning, John realized, that Angie had found it because they'd been talking about him. **Poor John. Gotta do something about John.** It was embarrassing, like someone telling you far too long after the fact that your zipper was open.

At ten of seven the next evening, John was in the dimly lit basement of the church, searching for the right room. There were a number of things going on, including a cooking class that was filling the hall with the scent of chocolate. He'd taken some care dressing, finally settling on a casual look: white shirt, jeans, black sneakers. A khaki jacket against a light rain. After he arrived at the church, he'd gone into the bathroom for a leak but also to make sure his cowlick was down. Then he came out and walked slowly down the hall. He stopped to read some of the notices on a bulletin board: he didn't want to be the first one in. He was intrigued by an ad featuring a photo of a well-preserved Karmann Ghia, and even wrote down the email address; maybe he'd go and have a look at it, even though it was a god-awful yellow. He saw ads for volunteering at a walk-in ministry, a room for rent with kitchen privileges, classes in Japanese. There was a flyer for a stay at a monastery, but he figured his own life lately was close enough to that.

He wondered what he'd talk about in this group. What were the things divorced people talked about? How they and their exes came together? How they came apart? How the children suffered, despite their best intentions and no matter what their ages?

The first time Sadie stayed with him for her week in August, when she was eight, she got out of bed in the middle of the night and stood before him until he woke up. "What happened?" he said, and she said, "Nothing."

"You okay?" he asked.

"Yes."

He sat up. When he reached for the light, she said, "Don't turn it on. I'm going right back to bed. I just wanted to come in and see you."

"Well, I'm glad you did. But should I turn on the light, and we can go downstairs to the kitchen and have a chat? Share an orange?"

"No, that's okay."

"Happy to do it. Or . . ." He wasn't sure about this, but he asked anyway. "Do you . . . Would you like to come in bed with me for a while?"

"No," she said. "I'm too old. I just wanted to see you. We can talk in the morning. Good night."

She went back to bed. He checked on her about fifteen minutes later: sound asleep. He stayed awake until four-thirty, then got up to make coffee and sit on the front porch, waiting for the sunrise.

Then there was the time Sadie was two and wearing her white patent leather shoes, which she had loved. She'd stepped into mud and then looked up at him, dismayed. The ease with which he could fix this problem suddenly juxtaposed itself against the fact that it would not always be so. The world would break Sadie's heart and try her soul, whether she deserved it or not, because she was of the species **Homo sapiens,** a bipedal primate living most definitely outside the Garden, and nothing he did could protect her from that. And the realization had gotten to him. Later that night, after Sadie was in bed, he'd told Irene about it. She'd sighed and said softly, "I know. Sometimes I just look at the size of her sweaters, and it kills me what she's headed for. It isn't fair. And I know life isn't fair. But it isn't **fair**."

He wouldn't tell either of those stories. He wouldn't say anything, unless he had to, and then he'd keep it neutral. "Just here seeing if I can learn something," he'd say. And it would be in a friendly, low-key way that suggested he was not desperate, only curious.

The next time he looked at his watch, it was six minutes after, and he started walking quickly down the hall—if he recalled correctly, the room was just two doors away. A woman rushed past him to go into a classroom where there was a circle of about fifteen folding chairs occupied by mostly middle-aged people, more women than men. **Here goes,** he thought, and followed the woman in.

She turned out to be Amy Becker, a blonde with a charmingly off-kilter smile. He was instantly attracted to her, wildly attracted, in fact, in a way that both surprised and invigorated him. She had brown eyes, and he loved that combination, a blonde with brown eyes: Angie Dickinson, who didn't love that combination? She wore very little makeup, if any. She was younger than he, he thought, but not that much younger. She had a nice figure, and was dressed in a flowered skirt and a simple white blouse, pearl studs. She wore red, low-heeled shoes, which the woman she sat next to complimented her on, saying, "Oh, look at the **flower!**" He heard Amy say, "Thanks. I just got these and I was worried that the flower was silly. But then I thought, well, even if it's silly, that's okay. Silly is fun. Especially on shoes. And hats, of course. So I bought them. Actually, I bought two pairs. The other pair is green, the most beautiful green, like grass." John looked down, smiled to himself. He liked women who put on inadvertent little shows like this. It was something that had initially attracted him to Irene; she could be very much like this woman seemed to be.

Amy pushed one side of her longish hair back behind her ear, took in a breath, and looked around the group. She froze for a moment when she got to John, and he figured it could be because he was new, but he hoped it was because she found him attractive, too.

"Okay, last call," a man, obviously the leader of the group, said. "I'd like to invite you all to help yourself to something to eat or drink before we get started—we've got refreshments tonight courtesy of Mike Stroger." A thin, fast-talking man with an overly prominent Adam's apple and what appeared to be recent hair plugs said, "Yeah, my ten-year-old daughter made those; she was all proud and wanted me to bring them." John joined a few others at the small table against the wall and grabbed a cup of coffee and a chocolate chip cookie, bit into it, and took one more. He got back into the circle just in time for the introductions. He was positioned to be the last to speak, and he was glad, especially when he found out that he'd accidentally gone into the room not for divorced parents but for bereaved spouses.

"I'm John Marsh," he said, when it was his turn to speak. "This is my first time here, and I guess what I'd like to do is just mainly listen." He hung his head a little in the way he thought a recently bereaved man might. He told himself that he **would** just listen, then never come back to the group again. He also told himself that he'd invite Amy to coffee afterward and immediately confess his error.

He did one of the three: the third time he went to the meeting, he invited Amy to have coffee with him afterward, and she said yes, conditionally. "I'd love to, but let's not get coffee. Let's get a drink at Frost's; and let's avoid saying **one word** about our spouses or grieving or death. Let's leave all that for the group."

"Okay!" he said.

What they did talk about was gardening. Amy had a big vegetable garden, and John volunteered to help her care for it—he told her he liked working in the dirt, as he did.

"Do you mind worms?" Amy asked, shuddering a little, and John said, "No, worms? I **like** worms. I've got a worm for a roommate." Amy laughed and said she wished she didn't mind them, she knew their worth for aerating and hydrating and fertilizing the soil, but they had creeped her out ever since some kid in grade school had chased her with a whole bunch of worms hanging from a stick.

"Well, yeah. Because he liked you, right?" John said.

She nodded.

"I once beaned a girl with a snowball so hard, I knocked her down. I was **nuts** about **her**."

They talked about dogs, because each of them was contemplating getting one. They talked about Amy's job as a producer for an afternoon show at WCCO. Then they moved on to his job, and his ideas about what architecture really was, how he wanted to focus on building beautiful things that would last, and Amy watched him talk, her chin in her hand, smiling. Then they decided to move from the bar into the dining room for some dinner, and he thought, **This is going well,** and then damned if she didn't **say** that very thing. She looked over at him, her head tilted, a little smile on her face, and she said, "Well! This is going well."

"I was just thinking that," he said, and the happiness he felt at that moment was something that . . . what? Unloosened him. That's how he'd put it. If he were to say it. Which he wouldn't. He was more of a snowball man.

And then, after the fifth meeting, she came home with him. She took off her blue dress in the dim light of the bedside lamp, and she sighed so sweetly when he entered her, he nearly wept. Her innocence. His deceit. How to make it right. And something else. The same feeling that had plagued him the last few times he'd had sex, that ineffable sadness. For a while, he wondered if he was just coming to terms with getting older, if he wasn't feeling some bittersweetness in making love because the writing was on the wall in terms of how much longer he'd be able to land the dart on the board. No more beating on **this** breast, pounding out his invincibility. No, the time had come when he was paying reluctant attention to the ads featuring silver-haired couples soaking in hot tubs together, smiling their triumphant little smiles. But this particular sadness wasn't about being past his prime, about preparing himself to offer embarrassed excuses to some flush-faced woman who would say it was okay, it didn't matter, no, **really**. He didn't know what the hell it was, but it wasn't that.

He pulls into a gas station. He's lucky he and Sadie made it to the airport; he hadn't realized the tank was so low. Irene never let the tank get lower than one third full, which was ridiculous, but it did prevent them from ever running into trouble. Gaswise, anyway. While he watches the numbers click higher and higher, he decides his deception has gone far enough. He'll call Amy and ask her over tonight, and he'll tell her the truth. He hopes she'll still want to see him. If not, well, there's always the group he was meant to go to in the first place. Or he can go back to the ease of solitude. It's really not so bad, being alone, never worrying about what has to be done for, or with, or in the interest of another. It's like you let your mind stay in its pajamas all day. What's wrong with that? The only one he really has to answer to, the only one he owes anything to, is Sadie. Although, as she is fond of reminding him on a nearly daily basis, she can take care of herself.

5

"No," Irene says. "I don't care what your father says. Your father is not your primary caretaker. I am your primary caretaker, and I do not feel it is safe for you to go unchaperoned with a bunch of kids to spend a whole weekend rock climbing."

Sadie draws lines with her chopsticks through the black bean sauce left puddled on her plate. "What are you so afraid of?" There is a half smile on her face that does little to mask her frustration.

"Oh, boy. Where to start?" Irene cracks open a fortune cookie, unfolds the slip of paper, and reads aloud: "**Grace falls from unexpected place.** Hmm. Plus how to say 'thank you' in Chinese: **x-i-e, x-i-e.** How do you pronounce that, I wonder."

"I'm really good at climbing, Mom. And I'll be with even more experienced climbers. I'm not an idiot. I won't do anything risky."

Irene sits back in her chair, exasperated. "I just don't understand this sudden desire to spend so much time climbing! Why do you need to go and hang off the side of a rock? Isn't life dangerous enough?"

Sadie raises an eyebrow, stares directly at her. Irene knows that now she has said too much. Now she's moved from what might be seen as reasonable concern into her own neuroses, a bad habit of hers. Why should she make her naturally athletic and incredibly responsible daughter a victim of her own multifarious fears? Just because Irene would never go rock climbing doesn't mean Sadie shouldn't.

An hour before Sadie landed, John had called, ostensibly to brief Irene about his and Sadie's time together, to offer his usual glowing assessment of their daughter, the one thing they still had in common. But he'd also made a case for Irene letting up on Sadie, and Irene knew he was right. Sadie will be leaving home very soon, going off to live in a dorm at college, and, rather than getting used to the idea of her daughter's independence from her, Irene realizes she is resisting it more and more. "For everything, there is a season," Valerie had told her recently, and Irene had said, "Yeah, well, how do you know for sure what the season is?"

Val had laughed. "You look at a **calendar.** So to speak." Then her face had grown serious and she'd said, "Irene, try to look at this objectively. It's a good thing for Sadie to grow up! Won't it be kind of nice to have the place all to yourself? If you want a little afternoon delight, no problem. You can turn on all the lights in the middle of the night. You can play all your music all the time. If you don't want to shop for groceries, you won't have to. You won't have to **cook**."

"I like to cook!" Irene had said.

"Fine. Make ten thousand cookies to send to the dorm. Irene, Sadie is going to leave you, no matter how you feel about it. Don't make her feel guilty about what should be a really exuberant time of her life. She's going to college! Be proud of her! Be glad she's grown into such a lovely and responsible young woman! She's ready to be on her own! **Trust** her!"

"Yeah, you can say that, Valerie. Because when your kids went off, you weren't left alone."

"That's true," Valerie had said. "Still. You've always tried so hard to be a good mother, Irene. Don't stop now."

Now Irene throws her napkin onto her plate. "All right, Sadie. Go rock climbing. But would you . . . ? I would like you to call me when you get to the top. And then when you're down again."

"Mom."

"I mean it. I don't care how weird it makes you feel that you have to call your mother. Find a way to do it."

"**Okay**."

Irene signals for the check. She crosses her arms, imagining Sadie clinging to a toehold, having lost her footing, someone above her saying, "Hang on!" Then she imagines Sadie standing up on a bluff, looking out over a view so beautiful it makes her chest hurt. "Maybe I'll try rock climbing," she says.

"Yeah, okay, Mom."

"So . . . how was Dad?"

"Good. Great."

"Is he . . . Is he okay?"

"What do you mean?"

"Just . . . generally. Is his work going well? Is he happy?" **How does he look? Is he seeing anyone? Did he ask about me? Did you tell him anything about me?**

"Yeah. Dad's always happy."

Sadie's phone rings, and she ignores it, not easily.

"We can go," Irene says. "Auntie Vee's coming over."

"I'm going out," Sadie says quickly.

But Irene already knows. What else do you do when you're eighteen, have been away from home for a while, and have just gotten back? Go out again. See your friends. She remembers **some** things.

After they get home, Sadie throws her bags into her room, tells her mother she's going over to Meghan's, and all but runs out the door. A few minutes later, Valerie arrives. "So what's the crisis?" she asks, and Irene goes into the kitchen and takes down the extra-large martini glasses.

"Uh-oh," Valerie says, slipping into one of the benches at the banquette. "You said **minor** crisis."

"Don's gone back to his wife."

"Jeez. That was fast."

"Well, you know what? Actually? Not fast enough."

Valerie says nothing at first, just sits watching Irene make the drinks. But then she very quietly says, "Are you okay?" and Irene says, "Yeah!" in a self-evident way, as though Valerie had just asked if people had noses.

Irene puts their drinks on the table and sits heavily on her side of the banquette. She and Val clink glasses, and sit drinking, each lost in her own thoughts.

Then Irene says, "I'm . . ." Her voice is tremulous. "I'm just . . ."

Valerie nods. "I know." She reaches across the table to lightly squeeze her friend's arm.

"And I've been listening to Ray LaMontagne."

"Oh, **no**."

"You know the part in 'Jolene' where he says, **'Still don't know what love means'**? I still don't know what love means, Val."

"Yes you do. And haven't I told you a **million times** not to listen to Ray LaMontagne when you're sad?"

"Well, in full disclosure, I listened to Lucinda Williams, too."

"Oh, my God. I hope you had suicide prevention on speed dial." Valerie's hand flies to her mouth. "Oh. Oh, Irene, I'm sorry, I'm sorry I said that."

"It's okay."

" . . . Can I ask you something? Do you ever think about her?"

"My mother?"

Valerie nods.

"Yeah. Sure."

"What do you think about?"

"I think about a lot of things: how she looked, things she said. Times she was actually tender to me; she used to cut my cinnamon toast into the most perfect little triangles. But mostly I wonder how she felt when she went out to the garage that day. I wonder how it sat in her that she wouldn't be coming back in. It must have been the loneliest feeling in the world."

"So you forgive her."

"Yes. I forgive her. I learned a long time ago that the bargain she must have struck that day was between her and something much bigger than me or my father or the life she lived with us. She was a woman who could neither give nor accept love. It must have made being here awfully hard.

"Anyway. Ray and Lucinda. Ray and Lucinda! I like to listen to sad music when I'm sad. It seems honest. It makes me cry, and sometimes a good cry is the only thing that can make you feel better. But you know, it's not even that I'm sad so much as . . . I feel like I'm too old, suddenly, for so many things I guess I thought I'd have forever. I'm just, you know, **tired**. You know what I mean? Not in my body. In my heart."

"Oh, sweetheart."

"Plus, I'm a little mortified."

"Yeah, I know you are."

"Why do I keep doing this, Val? Why do I keep trying to find someone?"

"Because you don't want to be alone."

"Yes I do," Irene says. "I do now. I'm done. There is no hope. I'm worn-out. Used up. My body is a freak show." She drains her glass. "I'm having another martini. You?"

"No, I'd better not. I . . . Oh, all right. Might as well. I've gone this far. I'm starting to lose feeling in the roof of my mouth. Now I'll have to take a cab home. I hope I get a nice driver and not one of those hostile ones." She hands her glass to Irene, then says, "And your body is **not** a freak show."

"It is," Irene says. "And so is yours."

"It is not!"

Irene says nothing. Takes a big sip of her drink, then another. Then, "Let me see it," she says.

"See what?"

"Your body."

"You've seen my body a million times."

"Not lately. Not for **years**."

"Well, I'm not showing it to you. Really, Irene!"

"Seriously, Valerie, I need to see another older woman's body. Compare and contrast. I'll bet Don went back to his wife because of my body."

Valerie rolls her eyes.

"Come on," Irene says. "I just want to see if I'm normal."

"Fine. You show me your body, and I'll tell you if you're normal."

"How will you know?"

"How will **you**? And anyway, if you want to see naked women, just go to any gym's locker room."

"Valerie. I don't belong to a gym, you know that. Every time I join a gym, I go six days in a row and then never again. I hate gyms. They're evil. They're like Las Vegas. I mean, they're going to win: you'll pay, but you won't go. They know that. If everybody who paid went to the gym, there'd be no room. I'll bet for every person there, there are fifty who never come. Or a hundred!"

"Okay, Irene. Calm down."

Irene takes in a breath, stares out into space. Then, "How about this," she says. "Let's both take our clothes off and just be really, really honest with each other. Although for you it won't count."

"Why not?"

"Because you're married."

"Just because I'm married doesn't mean I don't care about my body!"

"I didn't say you didn't care about it. But you don't have to use it. Sexually."

"Of course I do!"

"You don't have to use it to **attract**."

"Again. Of **course** I do."

"Yeah, but not like I have to."

Valerie considers this. "True," she says.

"So get undressed."

Valerie looks around the kitchen. "You mean . . . Here?"

Irene goes to the window and shuts the blinds. Then she goes back to the banquette to sit down. Drums her fingers on the table. Raises her eyebrows.

"**I'm** not going first," Valerie says.

"Well, I'm not, either."

"It was your idea!"

"Yeah, but you're married."

"Oh, for God's sake!" Valerie takes another drink, then stands and takes off her top and her skirt, her tights. "I can't believe I'm doing this! I'm leaving my underwear on. I am not taking my underwear off."

Irene leans back and appraises her friend. "What kind of bra is that?"

"Chantelle."

"Nice. Looks like it gives good support."

"It ought to, with what it costs."

"I'd pay a lot for a bra like that."

"So go and get one."

"I will. But take it off. And your underpants, too."

"Irene. No."

"But I can't see really important stuff!"

Valerie puts her hands on her hips. "Like . . . ?"

"Like if you'd trip over your boobs without your fancy bra or if you're thinned out down there. You know? I mean, I look positively **denuded**!"

Valerie stands thinking, then clasps her arms and shivers. "It's cold in here."

"Only if you don't have clothes on."

"This is ridiculous." Valerie pulls her tights back on, her skirt and top. "I have to leave soon."

"That's okay. I saw what I needed to."

"What?" Valerie slides back into the banquette. "What did you see?"

Silence.

"Irene. What did you **see**?"

"I **saw**, Valerie, that you have no petechiae. Which means I'm not sure we can be friends any longer."

"What the hell is petechiae?"

"They're these gross little red spots. Something about the integrity of your blood vessels being compromised when you age. They're on my boobs and my stomach. Little red spots."

"Let me see."

"No. It's gross."

"I showed you my body!"

"Some of it."

"So show me some of yours!"

"Fine!" Irene leaps up and removes all her clothing. "There!" she says. "There it is! All of it!

See? I'm horrible. Tell me the truth, I'm horrible, aren't I?"

"Oh, Irene."

"What?"

"You're not **horrible**."

"Well, I'm certainly not attractive. Am I?" She spins around in a clumsy circle, then, a little dizzy, sits back down in the banquette across from her friend. "Ew. This leather feels weird against bare skin."

"It's leather?" Valerie says. "I thought it was vinyl."

"Oh, right," Irene says. "It's fake leather. But it still feels weird." She stands up and starts to get dressed, hoping Valerie will find something to praise, something that, up until now, Irene herself has not seen, or noticed, or understood was attractive. But what her friend says is, "Sweetheart. This is not the time of our bodies." Her voice is sad.

Irene stands there, her white cotton, waist-high panties in her hand like a flag of surrender.

"I mean . . . Don't you keep the **lights off**, anyway?" Valerie says.

And then, alarmed, they both turn to the sound of the front door opening. "Forgot something!" Sadie calls out and comes into the kitchen to find her mother holding a pile of clothes up against her naked body.

"Whoa."

"Hi, Sadie," Valerie says.

"Hey."

"We're just comparing bodies."

"Uh-huh. Okay. I gotta get my phone, I forgot it. See you."

Neither woman moves until Sadie goes out again. Then Irene dresses silently. When she sits at the table again, she says, "Well, there you go. Eight weeks of income for some therapist, easily."

"I don't think so," Valerie says.

"Really?"

"I don't think she cared."

"Really?"

"You know what it's like when you're that age. You don't think of anyone but yourself."

"If I were eighteen and came home and found my mom naked in the kitchen with her best friend, I'd care plenty."

"So you'll tell her later what we were doing. She'll get it. She's a good kid."

Irene sighs. "I know she is. Hey, she's going rock climbing for a whole weekend, unchaperoned. What do you think?"

"I think it's great."

Irene says nothing, but her face says, **Wrong answer.**

"Do you remember what **you** were doing at eighteen?" Val asks.

"Probably still playing with dolls."

"Noooo. As I recall it, you were screwing the drummer in that awful band every hour of every day."

"Not every hour of every day."

"Well, it sure seemed like it."

"It was a different time. Not so dangerous. And sex was . . . it was like a handshake.

"You know, I'd play dolls now if anyone would play with me. Want to play dolls?"

"Nah. Paper dolls, I'd play. Because I'm only interested in changing their outfits. Remember those little hats paper dolls had, with the slits you put over their heads?"

"You can change outfits on real dolls, too."

"Too much work. I liked the tabs. Easy on, easy off." Valerie looks at her watch. "Listen, I have to go. Forget about Don. You'll write one of your dopey ads and be seeing someone in a week. I just wish you'd write a real ad, sometime."

"I do write real ads!"

"No, you write facetious ads because it's so hard for you to say anything serious when you feel something deeply. And also so, if you get hurt, you can say, 'Ha, I didn't mean it anyway.'"

"Thank you, Dr. Val. Will we be seeing you on the Oprah Winfrey Network soon?"

"It's true that you do that! And as long as I'm being Dr. Val, don't worry about Sadie. She doesn't have to listen to you anymore, anyway. Legally, I mean."

"I know. Don't tell her."

"Believe me, she knows. And you know what else? You need to let her do some serious hating on you."

"What do you mean?"

"I mean she needs to feel free to hate you. Otherwise, she'll never free herself from you."

"Yeah, easy for you to say. You have sons."

"Well, sons do it, too! My sons had to hate me so they could leave and grow up. And they still hate me sometimes. They really hurt my feelings, sometimes! I've told you about stuff they've done. Come on, Irene. You know that's the way it goes. Kids are cruel to their parents. You did it, too. When your father used to come and visit, you'd be mean to him, if not in deed, then in thought. Then after he left, you'd be racked with guilt because you loved him."

"Who said I was so mean to him?"

"**You** did!"

"Well."

"I have to go, hon."

"I know."

Valerie comes over to Irene and hugs her. "Oh, buck up, bucky, things aren't so bad."

"Yeah. Thanks for coming over. And for the burlesque show."

Irene watches from the kitchen window as Valerie walks down the sidewalk and rounds the corner. She dumps out the remains of both her and

Valerie's glasses. Turns on the TV and walks away from it. It's only the sound she wants, the illusion that someone is in the next room.

At nine-thirty, Irene climbs into bed and opens the cookbook Henry Bliss assigned her to read. She's to pick out the most enticing-sounding appetizers and make copies of the recipes. "Make sure they're exotic and beautiful!" he told her. That's what he always tells her. Last time she gave him recipes, he held one up between two fingers and far away from himself, as though it were not only distasteful but malodorous. "**Pizza** loaf?" he said. "I ask for elegant appetizers, and you bring me a recipe for **pizza loaf**?"

"I tried it!" Irene said. "It's good! And it has pesto and tapenade! Isn't that a little exotic?"

Henry said, "Irene. Everyone in San Francisco knows about pesto and tapenade. They're like salt and pepper!"

"Well, I don't think everyone knows what tapenade is," Irene said, and Henry closed his eyes and shook his head. Then he said, "You're a Minnesotan. Your people just discovered that lemon juice doesn't have to come from a green bottle. But that doesn't mean **everyone's** so benighted!"

One of these days she's going to hand him the recipe for pigs in a blanket. For Lipton onion soup dip, which she happens to think is divine.

By the time Sadie comes home, Irene has fallen

asleep with a cookbook opened to a page with a recipe for glazed tofu that calls for yuzu peel and shiso leaf and dashi kombu. She awakens to the sound of her daughter's voice, and gets out of bed to go and stand before Sadie's closed bedroom door. She knocks gently. She hears Sadie say, "I'll call you back," then, "Yeah?"

"Can I come in?"

"Yeah!"

Irene pushes open the door and stands there. She's not quite sure why she's come. Maybe she's still asleep. "Okay," she says. "Good night." She starts back to her bedroom.

"Mom?"

Irene turns around.

"Is something wrong?"

"No. Well, yes. I was going to tell you at dinner, but we got off on rock climbing. I've . . . Don and I are not going to be seeing each other anymore."

"Oh. I'm sorry. Should I be sorry?"

"You mean, was it his idea?"

"Well, yeah. Was it?"

Irene leans against the doorjamb, crosses her arms. "Yes, it was. Uh-huh."

"But . . . Why?" Sadie asks. "Do you want to tell me why?"

"I don't know, really. He said he was getting back with his wife. But also I think it was that he just wasn't that attracted to me. So, when you came home, I'd just asked Valerie . . . I just wanted her to give me an objective opinion of my body."

Sadie looks down.

"I know you must have felt like . . . Anyway, that's what it was. I'm sorry you had to walk in on it."

"It's okay."

"So how's Meghan?"

"Good."

Irene stands there, smiling. She looks around Sadie's room, at the poster of Paolo Nutini taped to her wall, the many photographs of her friends. On her dresser is a book that both John and Irene used to read to Sadie when she was a little girl; it was her favorite one. It's called **Paper Boats,** and it's a poem by an Indian writer named Rabindranath Tagore, about a little boy who writes his name and where he lives on paper boats to float down the stream, hoping that someone will find them and know who he is. Sadie sees her mother looking at the book and says, playfully, "Want me to read you a story?" and Irene says, "Not that one."

After she goes back to bed, she lies awake for a while, remembering how John used to read aloud to her, and she to him. It was in bed, most times, but occasionally they would do it in the living room, on the sofa, sitting side by side in their stocking feet. What a lovely thing that was. How safe it seemed, how sweet an offering. She still has never done that with anyone else. A guy she dated a couple of times asked, once. He pulled a book off his shelf and said, "Let me read something to you."

"May I?" Irene said and took the book from his hands. "Show me the passage. I'd rather read it myself."

6

Sadie waits until she hears her mother close the door to her own bedroom. She counts to one hundred, slowly. Then she calls Ron. "Hey," she says. "Are you asleep?"

"Nah. Hi. What are you doing?"

She turns onto her side, pulls the quilt up over her head. "Nothing. Just thinking of you."

"What a coincidence."

"Six more days till Saturday," she says.

"A little over a hundred and thirty hours."

"That makes it seem longer."

"You still feel okay about it, right?"

"Yeah." Mostly, she does. She doesn't like lying to her parents. But neither would ever let her go away for a weekend with a boy, especially one they'd never met! And she doesn't want them to meet him until . . . Well, she doesn't know when. She supposes she wants them to meet him when she's sure of him. When he's sure of her. When nothing can threaten what feels so important to her, so vital. And so fragile.

She looks out her window at the moon. It's full tonight; it was beautiful in the park. They'd gone over to Golden Gate, and he'd kissed her so many times, and he'd pressed her against him closer, closer, until she'd gasped for him to stop. And he did, just like that. He sat up and smiled down at her. "You okay?" he asked, and for a moment she got almost angry at him. Why wasn't he all . . . asunder? Why was he so calm and cool? Didn't he **feel** any of this? He said he did, but he sure didn't act it. There he was, breathing normally, the only sign of their fierce near coupling a bit of hair out of place at the back of his head. And she was still breathing so hard, her jeans embarrassingly (and uncomfortably) damp, and her heart beating so hard she felt sure it must be visible in her neck.

"I feel stupid," she said.

And then his expression changed and he lay down beside her and turned her head so that she was facing him. "No. You're not stupid. I feel everything you do. It's just that I . . ."

She waited, holding her breath, but he said nothing more.

She sat up. "You what?"

He held his arm up over his face, creating a shadow. "Whoa, that moon is **bright**, isn't it? I've never seen it so bright, have you?"

"What were you going to say?"

He looked puzzled. "You mean . . . When?"

She sighed, rested her forehead against her knees, and looked at the ground below her. The grass was silvery, the blades all individuated. She wished she didn't care quite so much for him. But she did.

He sat up then, too, and rested his palm on her back. "It isn't time," he said. "That's all. You just need to trust me. Will you try to trust me?"

"I do trust you," she said, but she didn't look at him.

"Sadie?"

Now she did turn to him, and there he was with that smile, so what could she do? She smiled back. He kissed her lightly, then stood and reached for her hand. "We need to get you back home."

"I don't want to."

"I know. Me either." But he pulled her to her feet.

He dropped her half a block away from her house so that they wouldn't be seen, though he watched her walk all the way to the door of her building, making sure she was safe. He was old-fashioned that way; he'd opened the car door for her until she asked him to stop. (And then, oddly, she missed him doing it.)

She flips her pillow, turns onto her side. "Am I going to see you tomorrow?"

"Not tomorrow."

"Why not?"

"I promised I'd help my mother move some furniture around. And then I have to start packing stuff up in my room. She's going to turn it into an office when I go to school."

Sadie can't imagine this, not with the way her room has been preserved for her in her father's house in St. Paul. She supposes she's been expecting Irene to do the same thing with her room here. How would it feel if Irene didn't do that, if she seemed as eager for Sadie to leave as Sadie was to go? Strange to contemplate; impossible to!

"How about Monday, then?" Sadie asks.

"Not Monday, either. I can't tell you why. It's a surprise."

"Really," she says.

"Really."

He does not say, "Let's do something Tuesday," and she's not going to say it, either. These are the times her heart takes a nosedive, times when he says or does something that makes her think it could all go away, just like that. And then, if her parents knew about him, it would be awful. Irene would try to help, coming in and sitting at the side of bed and saying, "Do you want to talk?" and it would only make things worse. And her father. He would say, "**Who** was this guy?" And then he'd try to cheer her up like he used to when she lost a game.

"Please believe me, Sadie."

"I do." Only she doesn't, not completely. Oh, it's awful to care about someone this much.

"Anyway," she says. "I just wanted to say good night. And . . . I don't know. Nothing. Good night."

"Good night." His voice is soft, sleepy-sounding. It makes her curl her toes. Why won't he say something about Tuesday? Is he beginning to grow tired of her?

But now he says, "Sadie? You know those songs, those stories, that talk about how people feel they were made for each other? I feel that way about you. I feel like . . . I don't know. Like we are the exact right people for each other. I don't know why, or at least I can't say why right now. But . . . Sleep with that, okay?"

"Okay." Now she feels better. "I guess I should hang up." She says this in a way that she hopes will make him say, "No. Let's talk until morning." But he doesn't say that. He says good night, and then he is gone.

She holds the phone over her heart. She has just been with him, she has just talked to him after having been with him, but she feels bereft. She lies still for a while, watching the play of shadows against her bedroom wall, listening to the faint sounds of the traffic outside. She thinks of her father, who must be sleeping now; she imagines him in his T-shirt and pajama bottoms, and she misses him. It unfolds in her chest: she misses him. He's a nice guy. He's such a nice guy! He's smart, he's funny, he's creative. He's nice-looking. If her mother were to meet him now for the first time, she'd love him. The irony.

She hears her mother's bedroom door open, then the sounds of the toilet flushing, the water running. She thinks about her mother asking Valerie to give her an objective opinion on her body. God! She needs to stop trying so hard. Sadie could actually teach her a thing or two about men, if her mother would listen. Which she wouldn't.

Sadie has learned a lot of things not to do, in her efforts to help her parents. But what **to** do? She feels sorry for them, both of them. Sometimes she looks at her mother standing at the stove making something for dinner, and what is it that she sees? She doesn't know, but it kills her. Her mother's forehead wrinkled with her efforts. Her dumb apron, her socks falling down; she buys silly socks all the time, then holds them up before Sadie saying, "Aren't these cute? Kind of funky, huh? I thought they were so cute." Now and then Sadie still brings her mother presents, like when she was a little girl. A gift for no reason: A cupcake. A scarf. A book. And her mother is always so grateful. Too grateful, like a dog. Then Sadie gets angry that she gave her anything, yet she'll go out and get her more.

She looks over at the book on her dresser, the one she offered to read to her mother and her mother promptly declined. Sadie knows why. She was sorry the moment she suggested it. The memories it would bring back of the days when they were still together, and her mother didn't need to sit scowling at the calculator when she did her taxes, when her father got to eat homemade pie at his own kitchen table instead of buying those pathetic single slices entombed in plastic.

People are stupid. Why are they so stupid? There is an algorithm for the way humans were designed: love and be loved. Follow it and you're happy. Fight against it and you're not. It's so simple, it's hard to understand.

Sadie closes her eyes and sees Ron's face, his long lashes, his full mouth, the way his hair slides over one eye. His long legs, the slow way he puts his jacket on. It makes her full of a feeling that's close to tears, a desire that is in large part frustration. Her feelings for him are so huge, so complicated, so demanding.

"I trust you," she whispers. Sometimes saying it makes it so.

7

On Monday evening, John and Amy are sitting at his kitchen table, finishing dinner. John made a chicken cacciatore of which he is not unreasonably proud (a generous pinch of cloves is the secret). At one point, Amy gestured to her own chin to let John know he had something on his, and he liked how natural the moment was between them. Amy pointed, he wiped it away: done. Say all you want to about the grand and glorious aspects of a heady romance—lengthy and poetic recitations of love, Sturm und Drang, kissing in the windswept rain— what John likes best are the small and undramatic moments that make for a kind of easy comfort, for a feeling of being grounded in a relationship. A feeling of being **off duty**. You show up on your first date with your best shoes on, hoping to get to a place where you keep your shoes off, is what he thinks.

Amy takes a last bite and then folds her napkin beside her plate. "Thank you. That was delicious."

"You're welcome. I'm glad you liked it."

"May I have the recipe?"

You may have the cook! pops into his brain, but he doesn't say it, of course not, it's much too soon for such pronouncements. "I'd be glad to give you the recipe," he says.

"Hey. Know what happened to me today?"

He sits back and crosses his arms, smiles. "No. What happened to you today?"

"Well, I decided to take the bus to work instead of driving? And I got on and I sat behind this woman who started crying. She was very quiet about it, just every now and then she would reach up and wipe away a tear. She had this kerchief on her head, this ratty old flowered kerchief, but it was clean and it was tied very neatly, you know. And she had her purse on her lap and she was holding on to it like it was hands. At first nobody else seemed to notice she was crying, but then everybody around her did. And it got very quiet. And then finally this man got up from the back of the bus, and he came up and sat next to her and put his arm around her, and he didn't say a word, he just stared straight ahead with his arm around her and she kept crying but it was better now, you could tell, she kind of had a little smile even though she was still crying. And I don't know if he even knew her! I think everybody was wondering the same thing: Does he even know her? I guess he must have known her; otherwise she probably would

have leaped up and started screaming or something, but you never know! You just never know, it
might have been someone whose heart went out to
her because she was crying. And he decided he
would comfort her. And she let him. And I think it
was a kind of miracle. A living parable or something. Plus it was so interesting! I thought, **I'm
going to take the bus every day! This is great!** And
I also thought, **See? This is all it is, people need
each other.** And it seems like we are always our best
selves when we **admit** ourselves to each other, our
needs. I think everybody around that woman felt
like cheering, we all felt great because she felt better. Of course we didn't cheer, that would have
been . . . Well, that would have been like one of
those movies where, when you see a scene like that,
you just roll your eyes and want to walk out and get
more popcorn. But anyway, nobody cheered,
nobody even looked directly at this couple except
for this one young woman who kind of had something wrong with her and she was just staring right
at them and muttering to herself. But the whole
thing made me think . . . Well, I got this over-
whelming feeling of . . . I don't know. We're all
one. We really **are** all one."

John leans forward. "I see the LSD in the red
sauce is kicking in."

Amy flushes, puts her hand to the side of her
face. "Oh, God, I talked too much, didn't I? I
always talk too much. I don't mean to, but it's like

all these thoughts start bidding for placement—
pick me, pick me!—and I don't know what to pick,
and so, you know, I pick them all and then I just
talk too much. And then I can't stop, I just keep
going. As you see. Although sometimes I remember that I talk too much and then I don't say **anything**. Which is also bad. Though probably not as
bad. Oh, look at this, logorrhea central, I'm sorry,
take out my batteries."

He laughs, and leans over the table to kiss her
forehead. "I love to hear you talk. And I know what
you mean. I know exactly what you mean." He gestures to the front porch. "Want to go out and set a
spell?"

She nods happily. "Let's wash the dishes first."

"No, no; you're the guest. I'll do it later."

She hesitates, then says, "I don't want to be the
guest. I want to help you clean up. Okay?"

"Okay." But something shifts in him. He's nervous, saying it, and he thinks she hears it; and then
he regrets that he has altered the mood in this way.

Together, they clean up the kitchen, she pointedly silent, now, a dish towel tucked into her skirt
band. They work well together, and he feels himself
beginning to relax. He likes her a lot. He really likes
her. A woman who talks too much and admits it,
how refreshing. And it's nice how much she talks,
it's a welcome relief from taciturn women who
maintain that cool and blaming reserve. Irene was
cold like that, at the end. A few days before she left,

she sat stiffly on the sofa beside him, and he asked her, "Where do you go, when you're here?" They'd been watching **Meet the Press,** a show they used to enjoy, and they'd even relished the commercials because that offered them time to talk excitedly about what they'd just heard. They were aligned politically, and it reinforced their closeness to carry on together about what they saw as gross errors of the government. Toward the end, Irene no longer talked with him during the commercials but instead continued to stare straight at the screen. They both did. They watched, with apparent interest, something in which neither of them had any interest at all. They sat unmoving, unspeaking, like mannequins, but their faces were absent even of the barely there expressions those storefront figures wore.

On that day, when he asked her the question about where she went when she was there, she rolled her eyes and walked away, and he watched the rest of the show alone. He was aware of a familiar ache in his gut, and he realized everything in their marriage had come to either sadness or anger. He tried to think of when it all started, but he couldn't point to a time. He tried to think of what the reason was, but there wasn't one, really. It had just happened. It was an old story, and it had happened to them: a particular kind of erosion started, was inadequately treated, grew, and finally could not be treated.

When John was in junior high school, he was in a play, Edgar Lee Masters's **Spoon River Anthology.** John's role was that of Fletcher McGee, and his first lines were "She took my strength by minutes, she took my life by hours." He was troubled by those lines, as he was by those of another character, Mabel Osborne (played by Jill Santos, a radiant brunette on whom John had a huge, hopeless crush). Mabel, speaking about a geranium planted over her grave, says, "Everyone knows that you are dying of thirst, yet they do not bring water! They pass on, saying: 'The geranium wants water.'" During the weeks of rehearsal, when John heard those lines over and over, he would wonder how people once in love could come to such things. If he could just get Jill Santos to notice him, he would marry her and they would never be like that. They would be so happy, and they would have a bunch of handsome children chasing each other across the front lawn, laughing. Later, when his marriage with Irene became so completely unraveled, he understood all too well about a neglected geranium. A thing like that becomes ugly pretty quickly, and then you just want it to finish dying so you can get rid of it.

But Amy. Another good thing about Amy is how she dislikes travel, and would not badger him about going here or there all the time. Irene did that, and it always made him feel like home with him would never be enough for her, she wanted to go to Italy, she wanted to go to Africa, she wanted to buy a summer home so they wouldn't be **here** all the time. She said that last looking out the window at the back-yard one rainy day, and he wanted to say, "What are you seeing when you say that, Irene? The grass that we finally got to be heaven on bare feet? The little vegetable garden with the chicken wire Sadie labored to install and then photographed, in her pride? The blueberry bush that you yourself insisted upon? The rope swing under the elm tree? Or maybe the double hammock, in which one night, while Sadie slept in her room upstairs, we crept out and made love most adroitly?" He didn't ask her that. He did ask her why she always wanted to leave home, and she gave him a withering look and said, "People go on **vacations**, John. People **need** to go on vacations." Well, he didn't need to. He didn't like to, really. All that pack-ing and unpacking. Those awful stacks of mail upon return, the forgotten milk turned sour in the fridge. Amy was a woman who apparently shared his con-victions, a woman who saw the vacation in going nowhere at all.

It's more important than ever that he reveal the truth to her about him not being a widower. He has to do it tonight.

Just after they are settled out on the porch with their glasses of wine, Amy suddenly sits up straighter in her chair. "John. I have a confession to make."

He laughs. "Funny you should say that. I do, too."

"Can I go first?"

He gestures expansively: **Be my guest.**

She looks down at her lap, tucks a piece of hair behind her ear, speaks softly. "This is about my husband, about when he died. I think I told you he died at home." She looks quickly over at John, and he nods.

"Well, on the last day, I was sitting beside him and I had been up all night—again—and I was so exhausted, all the way down to my bones. And he was such a **mess** by then. I'm sorry to say it that way, but he **was** a mess—that's the way he described himself, too. We even laughed about it one day. He'd asked for a mirror, and he looked at himself in it, and he got real still; and then he just started laughing, and I did, too. Oh, that was such an odd and dear moment.

"But anyway. He looked nothing like himself. And the room reeked from him. It did, it just reeked all the time, nothing I did helped. But that day I was sitting there with him, and he all of a sudden started having trouble breathing, he was gasping and snorting and . . ." She pauses, gathers herself. "He wasn't able to talk at that point, but I knew he was having trouble breathing. And I knew what to do to help him; I'd done it before. I'd readjusted him, I'd suctioned him a million times. But that time, I didn't do anything. I just sat there. And he died."

She looks over at him, her eyes full of tears. "The

doctor had told me he didn't have much longer, maybe another few days, but I let him die then. I never told anyone this. But in those last moments, he looked over at me, needing help, and I did nothing. I think he was aware that I was choosing to do nothing. And all that was in his eyes . . ." She swallows hugely. "All that was in his eyes was love.

"I was wrong to do that. I was so wrong. And I see that day over and over. I wish I'd helped him. But I didn't. You must think I'm a terrible person. I killed him."

"Amy."

"I did!"

"**Cancer** killed him."

She says nothing, wipes a tear from beneath one eye, then the other.

"I wonder if he wasn't grateful to you."

"I don't think he was **grateful**." Her torso jerks, holding back a sob.

"Well, want me to tell you what I think?"

She nods.

"I think the last thing he saw was a wife who loved him and did not want him to suffer any longer. He knew he was going to die. I suppose one way he might have died is after having become unconscious. Or alone, after having suffered more. Instead, he died looking into the face of the person who loved him best, the one he loved best. To me, that's a good death."

"But it was about **me** not suffering any longer!"

John waits to speak, weighing the silence between them. Then he says, "You know, a few years back, I read a story in the paper that I'll never forget. It was about a man who shot his wife in the back of the head. They were old, almost ninety, and she had Alzheimer's; he'd been caring for her for years. I imagine it was beyond difficult. One day, she had a moment of absolute clarity. And it was in that moment that he shot her. He confessed immediately, called the cops over right away. At his trial, all his children were there. All of them in full support of him. At first I thought it was because in that moment of lucidity, she must have asked him to let her go. But then I decided it might have been a lot more complicated than that, she might not have asked him at all. It might have been that seeing his wife as herself again sent him over the edge because he knew it would not last, and he couldn't bear losing her again. Or it might have been that he wanted her to be aware of what he saw as his final gift to her. In any case, it seemed clear to me that what he did was an act of mercy and not of malevolence. And I think his children thought that, too."

Amy is quiet. Then she says, "Well, I just needed to say that to someone. I know it doesn't absolve me of anything, but . . . I just needed to say it to someone. To you. I needed for you to know it about me."

"I'm glad you told me."

She leans back in her chair, sighs. "So. What's your confession?"

He hesitates. Is it a terrible time to tell her? Or will it add some welcome levity to the situation? He's not sure.

"Never mind," he says. "Not now."

"Oh, no," she says. "You have to tell me. It can't be as bad as what I told you."

"I'll tell you another time."

"Tell me now."

"Oh, all right," he says. "Okay, I'll tell you. So, what it is . . . Well, I kind of met you under false pretenses. Not false. Accidental. I'm not a widower, Amy. I'm divorced."

Her brow furrows. "What?"

"I'm not a widower. I'm divorced. My ex-wife is in San Francisco. Irene is her name. I came to the church that night looking for the divorced parents group. But I saw you, and—"

"Oh, my gosh. That's why you never talked! You were just . . . cruising!"

"No, it's not like that. I mean, I didn't follow you knowing you were going to **that** meeting. I followed you thinking you were going to the divorce group."

"But you must have realized right away that you were in the wrong place!"

"Well, yes. But by then, I . . . Well, I was very interested in you. So I just stayed. I meant to tell you right away, but—"

She stands. "I have to go."

He gets out of his chair, moves to stand before her. He starts to put his arms around her, but she steps away from him.

"Amy. Look, I know it must seem like I'm—"

"I have to think about this. I just really have to go home now."

"Okay, but please understand. I was so attracted to you. It was such a surprise, I hadn't felt like that for so long, and I didn't know what to do. And the time to tell you the truth never seemed to come."

"You listened to so many people talk about such private things!"

He hangs his head.

"They **trusted** you!"

"I know."

She goes into the house—for her purse and sweater, he suspects. Yes. Here she comes again, her car keys in her hand.

"I wish you wouldn't go."

"I have to."

"Let me walk you to your car."

"It's right in front."

"I know, but let me anyway."

"I'll be fine." She descends the steps, walks quickly down the sidewalk.

"How about I call you later?"

No answer.

"Amy?"

She turns around. "I just need some time, John. Okay? I'll call you, if . . . I'll call you."

She disappears into her car, drives quickly away.

He looks over at the chair where she was sitting. At her wineglass, still half full. He drinks the wine, overly aware of the lipstick stain on the glass. Aware too, now, that the Twins should still be on, and hateful of himself for having that thought even occur to him. But. There you go.

He goes into the house and turns on the television. Damn it. She could have been a contender. He looks at his watch, as though gauging how long **this** one lasted. Damn it.

He turns his attention to the screen. "Low," he says. **"Out."**

8

On Saturday morning, Irene rises early to make Sadie breakfast before her daughter takes off for rock climbing. She prepares oatmeal with raisins and dried apricots and walnuts, wheat toast spread with peanut butter, a bowl of cut-up cantaloupe, strawberries, and bananas. When Sadie comes into the kitchen, clumsy with sleep, she stops dead at the sight of the feast.

"Never mind," Irene says. "You'll need to be well nourished, making that climb."

"Yeah, but I don't need—"

"If you don't want it all, don't **eat** it all."

Sadie slides into the banquette, pushes her hair off her forehead. "Don't get all pissed off."

"I'm not pissed off."

Sadie blows on the oatmeal, spoons a bite into her mouth. "Are too."

"Don't talk with your mouth full."

"Don't be so **pissed off**!"

Irene sits down at the table. "I'm sorry." She

reaches over and pulls a strawberry off the top of Sadie's bowl of fruit and eats it. **I have a bad feeling about this,** she wants to say. **I feel so strongly that something bad is going to happen.** Instead, she says, "I guess I'm just nervous about your doing this."

"You **think?**"

"It is dangerous, Sadie."

"It really isn't. We're climbing up a little rock, we're camping out overnight, the next day, we're climbing down the rock."

"Who's going, again?"

"Kids from my class, Mom. You don't know them. What's the point in my reciting their names again?"

"Okay." Irene goes over to the stove and begins scrubbing it. For a while, there is only the sound of that and the clinking of Sadie's spoon.

Finally, Irene comes back to the table and sits down. "I know I'm overprotective," she says.

"Yeah, you should have had more kids. Ten or eleven. Kind of spread out the anxiety."

Irene smiles. "Maybe so."

"I'll be fine. Honestly."

"Okay, but just . . . Will you please call me, and let me know you're okay? Just a quick call when you get up there, and one when you get down. You don't even have to talk. Just call and say 'Me,' and hang up. Whenever you can. How's that? If I don't answer, leave me a message."

"Are you working today?"

"Dinner party today at some mansion; tomorrow we have a brunch over on Sea Cliff."

"Wow. I think movie stars live over there. Is it a movie star's house? Do you get to serve canapés to a prima donna?"

"It's some executive. The only prima donna will be Henry Bliss."

"Poor Henry," Sadie says, popping a piece of cantaloupe into her mouth.

"Poor Henry?"

Sadie shrugs. "He's an artiste. He's only annoying because he cares so much about his work. Anyway, you love him, you just won't admit it." She stands and arches her back, stretching. "Okay, thanks for breakfast."

Irene looks at the nearly full bowl of oatmeal, the untouched toast. "What, that's it?"

"You know I'm never hungry first thing. You do know that, right? I mean, thanks for making this, but I'm just not hungry yet."

Irene nods. **Don't get all pissed off.** "Do you want to take some PowerBars with you?"

"I have one in my backpack." She looks up at the kitchen clock. "I'm going to take a shower and get ready. Don't take anything away; maybe I'll eat more when I come out."

The oatmeal will be cold by then, Irene thinks. And Sadie, reading her mind in the way she sometimes does, turns around to say, "Microwave."

Irene goes to stand at the kitchen window and look out at the day. A lot of fog today. Just here or everywhere? It will burn off. Please let it all burn off. Sadie in a heap, someone saying, **I don't know; I guess she couldn't see.**

The phone rings, and when Irene answers, Henry sighs and says, "I knew it. Why are you still **there**? Why aren't you out shopping? All the good produce will be gone."

"Henry," Irene says. "It's eight o'clock in the morning."

"My point."

"I'm feeding my daughter breakfast."

"She doesn't feed herself?"

"Ha, ha." She hears Sadie turning off the shower. Shortest shower in the world. She just can't wait to fall off that rock.

"So when are you leaving?" Henry asks.

"In about fifteen minutes."

"Well, add something to the list."

Irene goes over to the junk drawer and takes out a pencil. "Okay. Go ahead."

"Do you have a pencil?"

"Yes, Henry, I have a pencil. Also, it's in my hand."

"Okay, so write this down."

Irene rolls her eyes.

"Marcona almonds. Get a pound."

"Got it. See you soon."

"Wait a minute. That's not all."

"What else?"

"Piment d'Espelette."

Oh, God. She hates it when she has to ask. Before she met Henry, she considered herself a pretty sophisticated cook. No more. "What's that?"

He sighs.

"Just **tell** me, Henry."

"It's a **chili** powder, very coarse, made from Espelette peppers. You've honestly never **heard** of it?"

"Shocking, I know." What she does not add is that she has no idea what Marcona almonds are, either, but at least she knows they're almonds. And now that she thinks of it, she remembers that they are Spanish almonds, very tender, and she knows exactly where they are in the store.

"What are we making with almonds and chili powder?" she asks.

"Popcorn."

"Are you kidding me?"

"No, Irene, I am not kidding you." She can see just him standing there, a little Napoleon wearing a perfectly executed bow tie, a shirt so white it hurts your eyes, knife-pressed black jeans, a black-and-white striped apron, and his chic black bifocals. "It happens to be fabulous."

"I'm sure."

She hears Sadie calling her and tells Henry she has to go.

"Wear your hair up," Henry says.

"Don't I always?"

"Well," he says, in his snotty voice. "**Sort** of."

"All right," Irene says. "I'm on my way."

"Well, wait, since you're already late, you might as well go over to the cheese shop and get some washed-rind Gorgonzola, five pounds of that, and then just two pounds of Ubriaco. Oh, and a new Girolle."

"How many pounds of New Girolle?"

He speaks slowly. "A Girolle is a **tool**, Irene. Used with the tête de moine **Swiss** cheese, to make those little **rosettes**. Remember?"

"Oh! Yes. So . . . one Girolle."

"Yes. All right, I'm going over to the house. I'll see you there. Go to the back door. The kitchen door."

"What, I shouldn't ring the front bell and say, '**Gollllly! This here sure is a big house! What all do y'all** do **in such a big house? Sheeeit!**' "

"Remind me to yell at you when you get here; I don't have time now."

"Oh, you won't need me to remind you."

"Kisses and hugs!"

She hangs up.

9

Sadie stands shivering at the corner where she is to meet Ron. He's late, and Sadie is pissed. It isn't a good sign, she's thinking. This is the kind of carelessness Meghan's boyfriend displayed before he dumped her: showing up late, not calling as often. And Meghan just took it. Later, she said she wished she'd done something back to him: gone out with another guy, not shown up somewhere they'd agreed to meet. She thought she'd been too nice, a doormat, in fact, and that that had been a major turnoff, inviting abuse. "You can't let them take you for granted," she said.

When Sadie tries Ron's phone, all she gets is his voice mail; she has also texted him twice with no response. She's hoping his not being there on time has to do with the surprise he said he'd have for her; maybe when he presents her with that, whatever it is, she'll forget all about him being late.

She checks the time, and sees that she's been

waiting twenty-seven minutes. Almost half an hour she's been standing there! She looks up and down the street; no sign of his car, or of any car, for that matter; they purposely chose a quiet street. And it was on this corner they were to meet, she's sure of that. She supposes it's possible that he won't come at all. And then what? Going back home would be lame, and anyway, what if, for some reason, her mother is still there? She doesn't want to have to come up with excuses for why she is home. And she can't go rock climbing as she had said she was going to do—by the time she got there, it would be too late to join the group, they'd already have started up. She stands there shivering, trying to think of what to do.

A car pulls up, and Sadie sees the driver inside gesturing to her. She steps closer, and he rolls down the passenger-side window. "Am I anywhere near Sally Ann's Breakfast? The address I was given was wrong."

"You're about six blocks away." She gives him directions, her arms wrapped tightly around herself. "Get the stuffed French toast," she tells the man. "It's got raspberries and cream cheese, and it's really good."

"Oh, I'm not going to eat; I just want to look at the place. I'm a location scout."

"Oh. Cool." She nods, shivers harder, and looks up and down the street again for Ron. Nothing.

"Thanks!" the man says and starts to pull away. But then he stops, rolls down the window again, and says, "Excuse me, but . . . You okay?"

"Yeah!"

"Can I give you a lift somewhere? Looks like you're freezing out there! Tell you what: How about I buy you some breakfast?"

"No thanks," she says, but she's thinking, **Such thick hair, great eyes.**

"Just a coffee? Maybe you could give me some other recommendations for good diners."

Again she declines, but as soon as the man drives off, she shouts after him and he stops. Sadie walks quickly toward the car. What the heck, she'll go to Sally Ann's and have some of their famous hot chocolate and warm up. Let Ron sit and wait for her, and see how it feels. She figures when she comes back, he'll see her getting out of the guy's car and ask, "Who was that?" and she'll just say, "A friend who came by and saw me standing there. We went for coffee." She doesn't like that kind of game playing and she hadn't wanted to do it with Ron, but maybe men really are all alike, at least in some respects.

When she reaches the car, she pokes her head through the open window, aware that, as she does so, the top of her blouse falls away to reveal her breasts; aware, too, that the guy is classy enough not to look directly at them but still sees them. An older guy, who knows about not being so obvious;

and he is **hot**. "If you don't mind, I changed my mind. I'll go to Sally Ann's with you. There are other diners I can tell you about, three really good ones, all close to here."

"Great! I'd appreciate it. The locals always know best."

Sadie looks up and down the street for Ron one more time. Then she says, "Just one thing, can you bring me back here right after? I'm supposed to meet someone."

"Absolutely," the guy says, and he actually gets out of the car to open the door for her. At least **someone** is taking care of her, respecting her.

"I'm Seth Goodman," he says, as they drive away.

"Sadie."

"Sexy Sadie."

"Yeah, right. So, you turn left at the next corner."

He goes straight.

"Uh-oh, missed it. You did want to go to Sally Ann's, right?"

He laughs.

"You know what?" she says. "I'm sorry. I changed my mind. I really shouldn't leave when my friend is coming. I'd better go back. Or you can just let me out here."

But he says nothing, keeps driving. She looks ahead to see if there are any stoplights coming up. No. But there is a stop sign at the top of the hill. She puts her hand on the door handle, ready to leap out when the car stops. Only it doesn't stop. He blows that stop sign, then the next, then guns the engine and heads in the direction of the Bay Bridge.

"I can't do this," she says. "I have to meet someone."

He checks the rearview and accelerates.

"Can you let me out?"

"Relax."

"I said I want out! Stop this car! Right now!"

He looks over at her. "Don't make me mad. Really don't."

"Come on," she says, lowering her voice, changing its tone to annoyed but mostly friendly, as though they are friends just joking around with each other. As though he has her in a loose headlock at somebody's keg party.

He doesn't answer, drives on.

She tries the door handle, despite the speed they're going. It's locked, and apparently under his control. "Please let me out." She keeps her voice low, calm.

"In time," he says. "Relax."

He is not relaxed. His knee is jumping like crazy. He's wearing black jeans, a white shirt, a brown leather jacket. His eyes are a light blue, slightly asymmetrical. High cheekbones, black hair. She thinks, **Remember everything**. Black Nikes. Little ears. Thick wrists. A large circular stain on the floor mat. She looks away from him and tries to calm down.

When they are on the bridge, she asks, "Where are we going?"

He takes one quick look at her. "What did I say? I said '**Relax.**'"

Her phone rings: Ron's ring tone. She grabs for it; the guy pulls the phone out of her hand and throws it out the window. She sees it briefly flash in the sun before it hits the pavement.

"I have to go to the bathroom," she says. It's true.

"Yeah, right."

"I really do."

He shrugs. "Piss yourself."

"You want me to ruin your car?"

"Be my guest."

A car pulls up even with them, and Sadie leans forward slightly and tries to engage the driver. But he is staring straight ahead, bobbing his head to music. She reaches over to try to lean on the horn and Seth slaps her hand away, hard. "You know what? You sit there and you don't move. And you don't talk anymore, either." He pulls a box cutter from his jacket pocket and shows it to her. "Perhaps you recall the power of such a seemingly innocuous instrument." He makes a small cut on his own wrist. "**Ouuuch,**" he says. He smiles. "See, the thing about me? I don't care. I don't care about **anything.**"

She watches small beads of blood rise up at the

incision line. She does not move. She does not breathe. Her heart drums inside her, her mind races, she feels herself growing dizzy. She takes in a breath, holds it.

There. Better. And now some outrageous force rises up in her: **Do something!** But what? What can she do? She feels her eyes fill and rapidly blinks the tears away. She rubs her lips together, rubs again, again.

Don't cry, she thinks. **Pay attention.** She is starting to shake, and she's aware of some slight grunting sound coming from her with every exhalation. She sneaks a look over at the guy, to see if the sound is annoying him. He seems not to notice. He's driving along as though he's preoccupied with his own thoughts now, as though she isn't even there.

She stares straight ahead, thinks of herself standing at the corner, only minutes ago. She thinks of Ron pulling up there, looking for her, and a small sob escapes her. She clears her throat to cover it, and makes herself go blank.

In the hills of Berkeley, he pulls over at an isolated spot. She turns to face him. "Now comes my favorite part," he says. "Take off your blouse."

"No," she says, and he slaps her face, then slaps her again. She gasps at the sting, feels an earring come loose and fall.

She grits her teeth and pulls her blouse off over her head, then holds the fabric against herself. She's wearing a bra her mother doesn't know she has, a lavender one she bought at Victoria's Secret, and she is wearing matching panties. She preened in the mirror when she tried them on, imagining what Ron might say when he saw them.

"I'm going to wrap your blouse around your head," the man says. "If you fight me, I promise you'll regret it."

He yanks the blouse from her and ties it tightly over her eyes. She opens them when he is done, to see if she can see anything. No. "It's too tight," she tells him. "It hurts."

The car takes off again.

"Are you . . . Why are you doing this?" she asks. Her voice is small, tremulous.

"If you let me out now, I won't tell anyone. I promise."

He says nothing, but she can feel him listening. Emboldened, she says, "I can understand how you might get this idea and—"

"All right, that's it!" He slams on the brakes, and she feels the cold of metal against her throat.

"Don't, don't, don't," she says. "Please don't." Her voice is trembling; her chin, too.

"You don't want me to cut you?"

"No."

"Then shut the fuck up!"

She shuts up. She sits still. At first, she tries counting turns, but then she gives up. They can't stay in the car forever. When he shuts off the engine, she'll scream bloody murder as soon as she gets out. And then she'll run.

When he does cut the engine, though, he grabs her arm so tightly she cries out. Then he half-drags her to a building and thrusts her inside. "I'll be back with your new best friend," he says. "I want you to be really, really nice to him. **Creative**. You do that, and then I'll let you go." There is the sound of what she guesses are locks, two of them. She hears footsteps, then the engine turning over and the car driving away. And now there is nothing but her own ragged breathing.

She takes the blouse off her head and puts it back on, her hands shaking so bad she can hardly work the buttons. **"Oh, God,"** she keeps saying. She stands trembling, weeping, looking around at the dim space she is in.

It is a shed no more than ten by ten with a concrete floor, no windows. A bare mattress on the floor, nothing else. She goes into a far corner of the shed and stoops down to relieve herself, watches the little river of urine forming and considers that this might be the last time she ever pees. As she is finishing, a spider descends before her on a quivering strand of silk, and she cries out, leaps up, and quickly zips her pants.

She moves to the other side of the shed and counts to one hundred to make sure the man is far enough away, then begins yelling, so long and loud she nearly loses her voice entirely. She hears nothing back but the faint sound of birds. She bangs with her fists and her feet on the walls of the shed, hoping that its small size and elementary construction will make it possible to knock the thing down. But no. She digs at the thin line of dirt at the edge of the concrete foundation with her fingernails, then takes off her bra and tries to dig with the underwire. She flings herself against the door so many times she fears she will break her shoulder.

She still has her backpack; and now she sits beside it and looks inside for something that might be of some use. A wallet. Keys. A few pairs of underwear. Three PowerBars! Where did they come from? Sadie had fibbed when she told her mother she had one. Her eyes fill, thinking of Irene slipping them in, assuming she was just adding a little extra, **just in case,** as was her way. She must have done it while Sadie was in the shower. It seems miraculous to have food, now; she is so grateful. She digs deeper, and finds what she was hoping for: a bottle of water, also added by her mother.

Sadie eats a PowerBar, has a bit of water, and then stands. She cries out for help with what little voice she has left again and again. Then she slams herself into the door again: once, twice, three times. Again. Again. Other shoulder, same thing. She kicks at the door with one leg, then the other. Then she lies on the floor and kicks with both legs.

Finally, her body aching, she lies on the bare, fusty-smelling mattress and stares dully upward.

All those times she read in the newspaper or online about women being abducted and later killed. She would stare into their faces and try to imagine how it happened, what it might have been like, if they were in some way responsible. She would look at them and feel so bad for them and for those who loved them. But she would also feel as though these events happened in some kind of parallel universe. Such a thing would never happen to her. She would look at those women's eyes, their hair, the shapes of their mouths, the necklaces they might be wearing, and she would wonder, **How did they feel?** Well, now she knows. She is both terrified and angry, more at herself than at the man. She let this happen. She fell for a stupid ploy, she got willingly into the car. She lies there, alert for any sound, trying to think of what else she might do.

He said he was going to get someone he wanted her to be nice to, and then he'd let her go. She doubts he'll let her go. She wonders if he really is bringing someone or if he himself will come back. Or not. She knows nothing about him, really. She could not gauge the caliber of his personality, she did not know what kind of approach to take with him, what kind of psychology might work in her favor. She has a way with people, she can almost always find a way into their affection, but not this time. As soon as she got in the car, the man's eyes went flat as a fish's. She doesn't think anything she might say or do will reach him. And what of the person he is supposedly bringing back? Anyone complicit with the man who took her will not be interested in listening to Sadie's pleas for help.

So it's possible she will be used, and killed. She feels it as a horrible abstraction; she can't imagine that it will really happen to her. But if it does, she hopes it's quick. She hopes she can make a picture in her mind of something beautiful to see when everything happens. She hopes that, in her last moments, she will be able focus on what else there was in her life, things separate and distinct from this awful day.

But she **might** survive. She **might** be able to convince them to let her go, when they are done with her, or even before. She'd read once in the newspaper about a woman who awakened from a sound sleep to a man who had broken into her house with the intention of murdering her (as he had several other women). She offered a simple question— **What do you need?**—and the man broke down before her, collapsed to the floor and began weeping, pressing his fists against a face over which he'd pulled a nylon stocking, and then he pulled the stocking off. She said she saw him then as a dangerous but wounded animal, and she spoke kindly to him, thinking that, if he killed her, at least her last act would have been one of compassion.

"What a **California** reaction," her mother had

said, with some measure of what Sadie read as con-
tempt, after she, too, saw the story. But Sadie felt
she understood that woman's response. When your
life is so close to being over and you know it, isn't it
possible you might offer your greatest act of gen-
erosity?

When her ancient cat, Shadow, died recently,
Sadie asked her mother not to take him to the vet,
since it was clear the time was nigh. "Are you sure?"
Irene asked, and Sadie said yes, she was sure. She
told her mother, who stood weeping in the hall,
that she wanted to be alone with him, was that all
right? Irene nodded. Sadie took the cat into her
bedroom, under the covers with her. She spoke
gently to him, petted him, rocked him. She felt a
kind of shift as he started to go, and she watched as
one of his pupils fully dilated. Before the other
pupil dilated and he stopped breathing, he looked
up into her eyes, and he lay one paw gently on her
breast. All the pain he'd been enduring up to that
point, and it was considerable, seemed to vanish.

She hopes, if she dies today, she can feel the way
he seemed to. Or like Meghan's grandfather, who at
the last moment of his life sat up in his hospital
bed, looked across the room at something no one
else could see, and said, "Is that you?" He smiled a
glorious smile and died. Just like that. "It was like a
movie," Meghan said. "It was really weird but also
really beautiful. It made me not afraid to die. I
mean, for a while, at least." She and Meghan had

talked a lot about death that day, lain on the floor eating leftover fancy cheeses and crackers that Irene had brought home from a party and talked about what dying might be like for them, what it really meant. Could it be true, as some religions suggested, that life was only what you had to slog through in order to reach the afterlife? Sadie had always taken offense at such a notion, and so had Meghan. As her friend had put it that day, **How can you look at a sunset and suggest that this life is meant only to be endured? Or, you know, a baby?**

Sadie stares at the ceiling, slows her breathing. In an odd way, relaxes. If she dies today, she got to live. And now she'll see what happens next. She hopes she can come back and tell others not to worry.

And if she is allowed to live, she . . . What? She imagines herself walking away from the shed, whole and uninjured, released back into her life. She imagines walking in the door to their flat and seeing Irene in the kitchen, imagines calling out, "Mom?" and Irene turning to see her, her face lit up like it always was when she came home, then changing when she saw that something had happened. Or maybe she wouldn't tell her mother. Maybe she would keep it to herself instead of feeding Irene's fears. Maybe there would be something noble in that, turning the tables and protecting Irene, for a change. And so now she imagines walk-

ing in, making excuses to her mother for her
absence, making her believe that it was a mini-
rebellion, and she was sorry for any worry she'd
caused, then going into her bedroom and sitting at
the side of her bed and holding her old stuffed animal rabbit against her middle, smelling her child
self at the top of its head.

She thinks if she does get to live, if she does get
to walk out of here like that, she will forgive the
man, so that she can unburden herself as much as
she can of everything that has happened today. She
will forgive him so that he does not own any part of
her life. She knows how to do that.

When Sadie was in seventh grade, her best friend
turned against her. It was for no reason Sadie could
discern; the girl just chose suddenly to make Sadie's
life miserable. When Sadie visited her dad not long
after all that abuse started, she told him about it.
He listened, lying on the floor of her bedroom as
she lay in bed. It was always her favorite time with
him, when they talked before she went to sleep.
And when she had finished talking, he told her
about how kids could be really vicious at that age,
especially girls, and that what her friend was doing
had way more to do with her own self than with
Sadie. He said, "I know you feel bad about it, but
here's what I want you to do. Create an imaginary
box. Into that box I want you to put all the wrong
things Isabel did to you. Put all those things in
there, and put your hurt feelings about those things

in there, too. And then put the box high up on an imaginary shelf. Just put it away. You don't have to deny anything, but you don't need to have it out, either. Just put it away, and maybe someday you can look at it again and see it another way. Most of all, remember this: You didn't do anything wrong. It's just the way things worked out between the two of you. For now."

Once more, Sadie moves to the wall and strains to see something through the cracks of the little shed, but it's no use; all she can make out is a narrow line of green. She goes back to sit on the mattress and puts her head in her hands. Her eyes are swollen from crying. She has no idea where she is. She has no idea what time it is, and regrets the fact that she no longer wears a watch, that she relied on her cellphone for that. She hears a noise outside and stiffens, but apparently it was an animal; there are diminishing rustling sounds, then silence. A mountain lion?

She lies down and closes her eyes and waits, her body straight. Waiting is all she can do, and so she does it as well as she can.

10

Saturday afternoon, John sits on the patio at W. A. Frost, waiting for Tom Meister to show up. They're going to have lunch and talk about financing John's latest idea for refurbishing the hotel on Wabasha. Tom is the only mortgage banker John knows who's a bit of a sentimentalist, a practical romantic, really; and that's exactly the kind of banker he needs for this project. He's worked with Tom before, and he likes him. They've developed a casual friendship; whenever a client gives Tom tickets for a Vikings or Twins game, he invites John to come along. For his part, John occasionally meets Tom for a drink and provides an ear for the man's woes with the opposite sex. Tom is a thirty-seven-year-old womanizer who can't settle down, but he likes to think the problem is much more complex than that. John just lets him talk. Tom's got a good sense of humor and perspective; he's not one of those guys sitting at the bar all hunch-backed and damp-eyed, blubbering into his beer. A few weeks ago, in fact, when he told John about his latest disaster, he slid onto the barstool beside him, loosened his tie, and began singing the lyrics from a country-and-western song: **You done stomped on my heart/And you mashed that sucker flat.** Then he ordered a boilermaker and some buffalo wings and said, "Okay, ready for this one?"

Tom is chronically late for most appointments, but every now and then he shows up on time, so John always feels compelled to arrive at the appointed hour. Ordinarily, he brings a book or a newspaper, but this time he has forgotten. He could peruse the menu in the overly studious way people sitting alone do, but he already knows what he wants: the fried egg BLT and the curried carrot soup. He supposes he could check his email, but he did that not fifteen minutes ago, just before he came into the restaurant. He was looking for a message from Amy, which he did not find. He'd thought of sending her one, but in the end decided against it, not sure if he was honoring the need to give her or himself space. It had hurt when she left the way she did; but then, suddenly, it had not.

He leans back in his chair, watching people come onto the patio with the benign interest of a cat stretched out on a window ledge: **Pretty girl. Nice briefcase. I know that man from somewhere—an actor at Dudley Riggs's Brave New Workshop?**

At the table next to him, two women sit down and begin talking in low tones with their heads practically touching. He'd bet anything they're engaging in the time-honored practice of man-bashing. He discreetly moves a bit closer and hears, "Oh, please, she's always been sensitive about that. And everything else! She's such a little drama queen. If he had a functioning brain cell, he'd dump her."

Well. So much for assumptions. He thinks again of emailing Amy, speaking of assumptions. It could very well be that her behavior the last time they were together embarrassed her, and she's waiting for him to make the first move toward reconciliation. Probably he should wait awhile longer, though. Best not to rush these things.

He watches an older couple eating their lunch, and their ease and enjoyment in each other's company is obvious. He bets they've been married for over fifty years, although the last time he thought that, he asked the guy, whom he met in the rest-room, how long he'd been married to the woman he seemed so happy to be with, and the guy said, "Oh, hell, we're not married. Why do you think we're jabbering like a couple of jaybirds? This is just our second date!" John looks for wedding rings on this couple's hands: yes. And so he decides that they've been happily together since their twenties. They fought, but they fought fairly. They under-stood and believed in commitment. It did happen.

He looks at his watch. Tom is now half an hour late; John will wait another five minutes and then give him a call. He looks up into the trees to see if he can spot any birds or, even better, nests. He used to pay Sadie a quarter for every bird's nest she spotted. He wanted her to be skilled in the art of noticing, and he liked teaching her about the ingenious architecture of those tiny abodes. She liked the Baltimore oriole nests most of all, she told him, on the day he showed her one, and when he asked why, she said it was because they seemed the hardest to build. Always after a challenge, that one. It was a good quality, so long as it was not taken to extremes.

She'll be rock climbing today, presumably is doing it right now, in fact. He wishes he were with her. He's missed out on so much of her life, and he resents it. But Irene was hell-bent on moving to the coast, and he doesn't want to live in San Francisco. There's too much **there,** there. He is put off rather than charmed by Lombard Street and the trolley cars and Fisherman's Wharf. He dislikes the gawking tourists, carrying on about the Golden Gate Bridge and how they wish they could live in such a place as this.

What he likes is the subtler style of his own town, the nonblaring treasures that abound: Mickey's Diner and Manny's Steakhouse. The alcoves at the St. Paul cathedral, the houses tucked into Crocus Hill. The gigantic international grocery store on University and Dale; the venerable used bookstore on Snelling, the omnipresent lakes. He and Sadie both love the annual Minnesota State

Fair, the tractors and the quilts and the blue-ribbon cakes and the engaging patter of the men selling Miracle knives. They like the sight of the 4-H kids sleeping next to their cows and the towering Clydesdale horses that are dressed up in bells and hand-oiled, brass-trimmed harnesses to pull the Budweiser wagon. Every year, they join the throngs of admirers who stand before the sculpted-from-butter heads of Princess Kay of the Milky Way and her attendants. These are displayed with a noticeable lack of irony in refrigerated cases. Best of all, they like the church tent, where stout, kindhearted women wearing faded floral aprons serve meatball sundaes.

St. Paul spawned the Wolverines, a band whose members wear threadbare tuxedos and play 1920s and '30s jazz songs, many of which they scored themselves by listening again and again to old records. It has Garrison Keillor's Common Good Books. There's the conservatory at Como Park. The James Hill House. The Mississippi River Boulevard and Summit Ave. Even the cold winters and the humid summers of St. Paul, John likes them, too. In part it's because—he smiles ruefully, thinking this—they are a challenge.

He checks his watch again, and when he looks up, he sees a woman coming out onto the patio. It's Amy, and she's with a tall, good-looking man, who is laughing loudly at something she just said. She hasn't seen him, and so while she has her back to him, he leaves his table and asks to be seated inside, in a far corner, so she won't pass him on the way out. As soon as he is reseated, he begins drumming his knuckles on the table. When he sees Tom come in, he calls out his name and rises to wave him over.

"Hey," Tom says, pulling out a chair and sliding into it. "Sorry I'm late." He folds his sunglasses, slips them into his front pocket. He looks around the room, raises his chin to the young woman a few tables over who's waving at him. She's lovely, with thick blond hair that hangs down to her waist.

"So, Tommy," John says.

"Get this," Tom says. "That blond woman who looks like Barbie? That's her name! **Barbie!** Hey, how come we're not out on the patio? It's dark in here. And it's beautiful outside."

"It's quieter in here," John says. "So as I told you, I'm thinking about a residential hotel, and here's the beautiful thing. An extended-stay hotel runs about three thousand a month. Renting an apartment costs about a thousand a month, but it's empty, and it provides no services. I'll be the place in between, for about eighteen hundred, so I've got a competitive edge already. But by putting it there on Wabasha in that great old hotel, I'll have virtually no competition. I want a restaurant in there that can service both the public and the residents, and I want a rooftop garden—there'll be a view of the river from there. I've already talked to a structural engineer—putting it on top of eleven stories won't be a problem."

Tom blinks. "Hello. How are you? Did you order yet?"

"Sorry." John hands him a menu. As soon as they've placed their orders, John starts in again. "Think of the guys who come here for business for six, eight weeks. They're displaced from their homes and their families and friends. They need a comfortable place, they need the companionship of others like them. I'll give them that. And more. For example, they won't have to incur the cost of every-day maid service, but I'll offer someone to come in and tidy up whenever they want."

Tom nods, thinking. "How many rooms?"

"One hundred sixty-five."

Tom stares into space, doing calculations in his head. John knows him well enough to see that he's not immediately enthusiastic about the idea. He'll need to personalize it more. He leans back while the server puts his lunch before him, takes a bite and waits for Tom to do the same—he, too, ordered the fried egg BLT.

"Damn, this is good!" Tom says, after he takes a bite.

"Yeah," John says. "So, listen. This idea isn't just for businesspeople who travel. Let's suppose your girlfriend dumps you."

Tom's fork stops midway to his mouth, and he looks at John.

"Suppose you've been living with her and she all of a sudden gives you the heave-ho."

"Yeah, I'll try to imagine that," Tom says.

"All right, so you're out of there and you've got nowhere to go except maybe your sister's pull-out sofa. But you don't want to be in your sister's house with her asking what happened **this** time and the nieces and nephews rifling through your duffel bag and asking you to play Candy Land every five minutes. You don't want to see your sister and her husband sitting and watching a movie at night all cozy and getting bowls of ice cream for each other. You don't want to crash with your friends for nights on end, either, you're too old for that bullshit. You're not sure what your next move is; you just need some time alone to think."

Tom nods. "Yup."

John leans back in his chair. He might pretty much have him, now. "You come to my hotel and there's a comfortable room, and you can be alone if you want to. But there are also other people so you don't have to be alone. Might even be some other people who've been dumped."

"Some guys to talk to," Tom says.

"Not just guys," John says, and he can tell by Tom's face that the deal's all but done.

"So what are we looking at?" Tom says. "Eight, nine million?"

"Nine point five."

"I'll talk to Bill Montgomery this afternoon; we

might be able to get you in for a meeting by mid-week."

After lunch, John goes out to the parking lot, and there is Amy again: the guy has just opened the car door for her. And now she sees him, too. She is startled, but then she smiles and waves. He waves back, unsmiling, then dives into his car and takes off.

11

Sunday mornings are given over to God, as Irene understands him. Which is to say that, on Sunday mornings, Irene attends open AA meetings. She is hurrying to one now. Then she'll head over to the brunch she's working today.

Irene is not an alcoholic, but one of her friends, named Carl Palmer, is, and a few years ago, she attended her first meeting with him. They had made plans to go to Angel Island one Sunday, but Carl said he had to go to his meeting first. Irene asked if she could come along and he said sure, this was an open meeting. Irene had been curious about those meetings for a long time. A few people she knew went often, and seemed to profit immensely from them.

The meeting was held in a classroom of a church in Presidio Heights. Irene and Carl arrived late, and sat in the back. A young woman was standing at the front of the room, speaking, and Irene had to lean forward to hear her. Her voice was ravaged-sounding, and Irene thought that she would make a good blues singer. She had dirty blond dreadlocks, and she wore an oversize navy hooded sweatshirt over blue jeans and work boots. She held a cup of coffee in one hand, and there were rings on every finger. "So I was home that night," the woman said, "and the kids were sleeping—they're two and three—they'd been sleeping for a couple hours, and I was trying to watch TV, but it was starting, you know, I just needed a drink so bad, and I had nothing in the house. I started pacing around, and finally I just couldn't stand it, I busted out and went to the bar at the end of the block. I told myself I'd just get one quick drink."

There was a kind of murmuring among the crowd, a lot of knowing **uh-huh**s.

"I know, right?" the woman said

Busted out? Irene thought. **You left your two- and three-year-old children** alone?

"Anyways, I got home at one o'clock in the morning. And I right away went into the kids' room and they were okay, they were sound asleep, but I sat on the floor and just fell over crying. That was my low point, and the next day I went to my first meeting.

"And I'm doing good, I haven't had a drink for over a month now."

The woman was applauded, but Irene sat stiffly in her chair, trying to think of how she might climb over the people who had come in after she, and get out of there. She wanted out of there. That woman had left her children alone! For hours! And come back drunk! Irene looked left, then right, trying to see which was the best way to go. Carl grabbed her arm. "Sit tight," he said quietly. "You don't walk out when someone's presenting." He wasn't angry, but he was firm, and so Irene sat still.

The woman said, "This morning, my son told me about a dream he had last night. I'm not going to tell you his dream, even though it was a good one. But him telling me his dream? It made me want to tell you mine. I know most people don't like to hear other people's dreams, but I would like to share this one. Hope it's okay. It's **short**," she added, and the crowd chuckled.

She drew in a big breath. "So what it was, is I dreamed I was at the head of this birch-bark canoe, same kind we had when I was a kid growing up on a lake in Wisconsin. But I wasn't in a lake, I was at sea, and it was real foggy and the waves were really high, and the water was so black. I was scared to death. And I couldn't move my hands to row, I couldn't unclench my fists. I thought, **My God, I can't move, I'm going to capsize.** I didn't know why I hadn't capsized already. I looked behind me, and I saw that the boat was real long, I mean **real** long, like I couldn't hardly see the end. And it was just packed with people. I didn't know 'cause I'd been sitting with my back to everybody. But the boat was packed with people. And **they** were rowing.

"Like a lot of you have said before, I was so ashamed to come here the first time. I was so afraid to admit to my weaknesses and my wrongdoings. One thing is, they were so bad. Other thing is, if I admitted to them, I'd have to do something about them. But that dream reminded me that **a lot of us are in the same boat,** right?" She joins in the laughter, then says, "Okay, I'm done, but I just want to end by saying I can't wait for my hands to start working so I can row someone else. And also I want to say that I think it's our salvation that so many of us are in the boat together."

Some man on the other side of the room called out, "Our **salvation** is that there's nobody who's **not** on the boat!"

Carl looked over at her then, and Irene nodded.

12

Sadie starts awake. Outside, there is the distant sound of a dog barking. The night has passed; sunshine is pushing through the cracks of the shed. It's cold.

He didn't come back.

"Help!" Sadie cries. She gets up off the mattress and goes to the door of the shed. "Help!" She presses her ear to the door: nothing. She pounds on the door, kicks at it. "Help! Help! **Heeeeelp!**"

The word seems ridiculous. **Help.** She's said it so many times, it's starting to lose its meaning. "Help!" she says, one last time, and then laughs. Laughs!

Maybe she's starting to crack up. People do crack up, under circumstances like these. She has to get a grip. She can't think about the fact that no one will find her. She can't think that he is coming back. She has to make her thoughts small and immediate.

She goes to the corner of the shed she peed in before, and pees again. Not much there; she's not had much to drink. And she'll need to ration what little water she has left, just in case. It hurts, thinking again about Irene putting that water bottle in her backpack, taking care of her in spite of the fact that Sadie keeps pushing her away. If she gets out of here, **when** she gets out of here, she'll make it up to her mother. Somehow. Although she's said that before, that she'll make things up to her mother, and then has done no such thing. Has, in fact, made things worse, in the ongoing and escalating battle that has developed between the two of them. She tried to talk about this to her dad, but he seemed only to want to defend Irene. To the extent that Sadie said, at one point, "Well, why'd you get divorced, then?" He started to respond, but then did not. And she did not press him. Him, she does not press.

But. Now is not the time to pile on guilt. Now is the time to think practically.

She tries to remember what she learned about how long people can go without water: Three days? A week? She won't drink any water yet. She'll wait until she is even thirstier.

So. She has peed. Now what? If she were home, she'd shower and brush her teeth. She rubs vigorously at her face, checks the corners of her eyes for sleep. She gets out her toothbrush and toothpaste and brushes her teeth, then spits in the corner where she peed—the bathroom, she supposes. She thinks about using a little water to rinse her mouth but decides not to waste it. Instead, she uses her index finger to run across her top teeth, then her bottom, then sucks the paste off her finger. Next, she shakes her hair around and runs her fingers through it, combing it as best she can. She feels a pressure in her bowels, and tries to ignore it.

She goes back to the mattress, sits down and holds her knees to her chest. Pulls harder. Exercise. She stands and begins doing jumping jacks, she'll do one hundred, and then she'll do sit-ups and then she'll do push-ups. Then she'll have a bite of PowerBar, only one bite despite the fact that she's really hungry.

Sadie is beginning her push-ups when she hears something outside. Footsteps?

She rushes to the door, starts to call out, then stops herself. It could be him. She holds her breath, listening. Nothing, now.

She feels a great drop into despair, into helplessness, but then just as suddenly feels a great rush of anger. "Let me out, you asshole!" she shouts. "I'm not afraid of you! Let me out! LET ME OUT!" Nothing. She stands there, panting. Waiting. Nothing.

"Are you there?" she says. And then, "I'm sorry. Could you let me out?"

Nothing.

She will not cry. She will not. She goes to her backpack and takes the tiniest sip of water. The tiniest. Puts the cap back on tightly. What if it spills? She puts the bottle in her backpack. Takes it out again. Takes everything out of her backpack and then puts it all back, neatly. Housecleaning. She puts the backpack in the corner opposite the bathroom.

She goes over to the mattress she slept on and brushes the dirt off it. Maybe it's cleaner on the other side? She lifts the mattress, then drops it. Shudders. Definitely not, definitely not cleaner on the other side. She sees a weed growing at the edge of the shed and goes over to examine it. She strokes the tiny green leaves. A pet? Art? Something she might be able to eat? What if it's poison? What if someone comes to rescue her and she's dead because she ate something poisonous?

If she picks it and puts it on the mattress, she can look at it through a little hole in her fist and it will be like her bed is covered in vines and will be pretty and that will cheer her up. But then it will die.

So the weed will be a pet, another live thing, stuck in the same place as she.

"Help!" she yells, but it is not very loud. Useless, really.

She might be able to chart the passage of time by the angle of light that makes its way in. When the light seems overhead, lunchtime. Maybe there won't be a lunchtime. Maybe she'll be rescued by then. Or the other.

13

"What have we here?" one of the party guests asks Irene, taking a cocktail napkin from her and surveying the platter she is holding.

"What we have here is grilled flatbread with za'atar," she says. She rights the platter, which had begun to tip sideways.

"And what is za'atar?"

What **is** za'atar? She thinks for a moment, then recites: "It's a mix of thyme, marjoram, and ground sumac. Oh! And sesame seeds!" She adds this last a bit too loudly, then, more quietly, adds, "It's a North African spice mix."

He takes a bite, nods. "Good!" he says, and little crumbs fly out of his mouth. His face colors slightly, which Irene finds charming. "Sorry," he says.

"It's okay." He's a good-looking man: tall, blond hair and gray eyes. He hasn't been a great mixer; mostly he's been availing himself of whatever Irene brings out and then going back to stand in the corner of the massive dining room to fool around with whatever device he's holding—who can keep up? He and Irene have struck up a kind of makeshift friendship. Each time she brings out something new, she offers it to him first.

Irene is passing appetizers because two of Henry's staff members are sick. Normally she likes to stay in the background and work in the kitchen. She hates passing appetizers. She doesn't like the way guests usually treat her, especially at the high-end parties, the way they act as though they're patting her on the head when they take something from her. As if she cares! If they don't eat the appetizers, well, then, the staff will. Henry is good at letting his employees take home any leftovers the host doesn't want. And at the more lavish parties, the hosts don't usually want anything but the leftover liquor. "Oh, no—you go ahead and take that," they say, puffed up with their magnanimity. But there is always some sort of hawk-eyed proprietary glance at any tray of food they're giving up, too. As if they're being generous because their mommy is making them be.

"What's coming next?" the man asks. And then, "My name is Jeffrey Stanton, by the way. Since I've talked to you more than anyone else at this party, I might as well introduce myself."

"I'm Irene."

"Irene . . ."

"Marsh." For a moment, she worries that Henry will come flying out of the kitchen, saying, "No! No!

No! You do not give your **last name** to the **guests!**"
It prompts her to spell her last name, too. Which
prompts Jeffrey to spell his, and Irene laughs. This
makes her tray shift, and a few flatbreads fall onto
the floor. Jeffrey quickly picks them up and puts his
fingers to his lips. "Nobody saw," he whispers.

"I'll take them back to the kitchen and dump
them."

"Oh, don't do that. Go and offer them to that
guy over there." He points to a man who has his
back turned. Silver-haired. Imposing, even from
behind.

"Who's that?" Irene asks.

"My boss. Emerson Cummings. Spelled **A-s-s-
h-o-l-e.**"

"Ah," Irene says.

"Actually," Jeffrey says, "I wouldn't want you to
give him dirty flatbread. I wouldn't want you to
give him anything."

The swinging door to the kitchen cracks open,
and there is Henry Bliss, giving Irene the Look.
"Gotta go," she says.

When she gets back into the kitchen, Henry
can hardly contain himself. "What are you **doing?**
We've got pork belly skewers that have to go out
right **now;** they're getting **cold.** And you need to
pass the **bresaola.**"

"What bresaola?" She puts down the platter of
flatbreads, and eats one that hadn't fallen on the
floor. She thinks.

"The **bresaola** with shaved **brussels** sprouts and **horseradish**. It's over there, Sandy's just putting the orchids on the tray. We need to get this stuff **out**, Irene!" He puts his hands on his hips. "I swear, I hate to fire people, but I think maybe I'm going to have to fire you."

"You know what, Henry? No need. I quit." She'll go back to speech therapy. Or she'll find something else. She's had enough.

"Oh, stop it." He walks away from her to open the oven door and waves the warm air toward his nose, closing his eyes and inhaling deeply. "I'm going to need the walnut vinaigrette for these beets really soon! Irene, go help make it. Hurry up."

"No, Henry," she says, speaking loudly. "I **quit**." The other workers in the kitchen fall silent: Tommy, the handsome young Asian man who almost never stops giggling. Linda, the aspiring pastry chef who lives in fear of Henry but also worships him. The self-named Cayenne, who's pierced everything she can and now is after Irene to get herself a nose stud.

Henry comes over to stand before Irene. "Keep your voice down. And you **can't** quit now. You know I'm short today. Those sesame balls are going to come out of the deep fryer in exactly seven minutes, and they have to be served **immediately**!"

Irene takes off her apron and lays it on one of the massive granite counters.

"Oh, for . . . **Irene**! We're going to serve dried fig **souvlaki**! You **love** that! And lobster salad! With corn and basil and zucchini! Look, I'll . . . You can take all the leftovers home. **All** of them. I'm **sorry!**"

"I'm not," Irene says and walks out the back door, where the sun is shining and the birds are calling and several hours of daylight remain. She's abruptly quit jobs twice in her life: once, when she was a waitress at an ice cream store and they screamed at her for her uniform being too short— the uniform they had given her to wear, for the record. The other time was when she was a secretary at a company where the sexism was rampant, and her boss closed her in his office and pressed her against him and when she resisted he told her she'd better learn to play the game. She went to lunch that day and never came back. She'd forgotten how good it felt to seize one's own life back into one's own hands.

She almost throws her car keys up in the air, but she'd probably miss when she tried to catch them. Instead, she simply picks up the pace, and by the time she comes around to the front of the house, she's practically skipping.

On the stairs leading from the front door, she sees Jeffrey Stanton. He holds up a hand. "Hey!"

"Hey."

"You're leaving?"

"I quit. I just quit my job." She shrugs. "Ta da!"

"Huh! Want to go and get a drink and teach me how to do the same thing?"

She laughs.

"We can take my car," he says. "It's right here."

Oh. He means it. She sneaks a look at her cell-phone to see if her daughter has called yet. No. Oh, what is the matter with Sadie? Why has she become so resistant to nearly everything Irene asks of her? The little Val that lives in her brain says, **Because she needs to separate from you, remember? Let go of her life and worry about your own!**

"Okay, I'll come," she tells Jeffrey, and she gets a little zip of feeling straight up her spine.

Val's right. The hell with worrying over Sadie. Let go, let go, let go. Sadie wants to be so independent? Fine. Let her be. Irene will turn off her phone and hope that Sadie calls and gets **her** voice mail. Hopes, in fact, that Sadie comes home before Irene gets back and has to wonder where **she** is. Irene will step **way** back, in fact, and then let's just see how independent Sadie really wants to be. Ordinarily, Irene would leave Sadie a message, saying where she was going, when she might be back. Not this time. Nope. And look: it's not as hard as she thought. She's fine. It's a relief not to have to constantly report your whereabouts. A relief that, Irene acknowledges ruefully, Sadie longs to feel, too. But! Sadie is eighteen! Irene is . . . not eighteen!

Maybe if Sadie is not home when she gets there, she'll put Joan Baez on the stereo. Loudly. Bette Midler. The Glenn Miller CD she loves so much that Sadie can't abide. (Mom, **it sounds like moth-**

balls smell!) She will make dinner for a most emphatic **one**. If Sadie comes home hungry, oh **well**. Two can play at this game.

Irene walks over to Jeffrey's car, and he opens the door for her. A Prius. Light green. What an excellent man.

"How about the Top of the Mark?" Jeffrey asks her, after they've both buckled themselves in.

"Really?"

"No good?"

"No, that's great," she says. "Let's go." **Cougar,** she thinks. And then she thinks, **No. Not a cougar. I'm too old to be a cougar. I'm an old lioness, stretched out in the sun, not much interested in chasing prey anymore, but not above accepting an offering. Due an offering. Yes, a lioness in the sun, who has earned the right to stop running after things that don't want to be caught.**

14

On Sunday afternoon, John goes to a movie so vacuous he has forgotten it by the time he gets to his car. He supposes it's another sign of aging that he's gotten so cranky about movies, but must they all be so simpleminded? Must a movie be in some language other than English for it to linger in the mind, to invite further thought and conversation? Not that he has anyone to converse about movies with. Suddenly. Even Sadie hasn't answered her cellphone in the last couple days.

He goes to the cleaners and chats about the weather with the friendly Korean woman who works there, avails himself of one of the lollipops she keeps on the counter. He likes this woman for her unalterable cheerfulness, her neat blouses and cardigan sweaters, even—oddly—for the way she remembers his phone number but never his name.

He stops at the hardware store, which he always enjoys doing, in part for the memories it brings back of him going to those stores with his father.

His dad seemed able to answer any question John asked about any tool or part, seemed to know immediately what bin to go to for any size nail or screw or hook or washer. There was a confidence Sam Marsh exuded in those places that John enjoyed seeing; later, he thought that it was a way for his father to mitigate the loss of his wife, of his son's mother. In the hardware store, things made sense. There was an answer for every problem. In this world, at least, his father knew without question what to do when things broke.

John's final stop is the grocery store. Here, listening to the Muzak version of "Raindrops Keep Falling on My Head," he pushes his cart listlessly up and down the aisles, selecting too many items from the produce section, as usual. There is a kind of virtuous feeling he gets, loading his cart with heads of broccoli and cauliflower, bunches of carrots, but then he always ends up throwing a good half of them away. There is such a vast distance between the fantasy of him making his own curried carrot soup and the reality of him holding up a carrot so limp it bends nearly in half, then tossing it in with the used coffee grounds. He supposes he should join the single set, the men and women who stand at the ready-made counter in their work clothes, selecting dinners for one, but something about that depresses him. He wants the illusion, at least, that he is capable of cooking for himself. That he is a man who dons a striped apron, puts opera on the stereo, and sings along as he exuberantly adds red wine to the pasta sauce.

When he gets home, he sees that Amy's car is parked in front of his house, and she is sitting in it. He stands in the driveway holding on to his bag of groceries, waiting for her to come over to him. And though he fears that she has come to collect a bracelet she left, one he found on the floor of the bedroom, he is also thinking about what he bought that he can whip up into a dinner for two. He tries to read the expression on her face, but can't.

"Hi," she says, when she reaches him.

"Hi."

"Okay. I came to tell you something. I miss you. But I'm still mad at you. I think it was really wrong, what you did."

"I think so, too. And I'm sorry."

"It made me question your character."

He nods. "I can understand that." He wants to say, again, that it was never his intention to deceive her, that he just got in deeper and deeper, and then didn't know the right way to tell her the truth. But he senses that the best tactic now is to keep his own talking to a minimum.

Which does not exactly work, because Amy turns around and heads back to her car.

"Amy! Could you . . . Can we talk some more?"

She opens her car door.

"Give me another chance!" he yells loudly, embarrassing himself. Anyone at home on his block is now privy to the vicissitudes of his romantic life. Perhaps anyone in his city.

From the front seat of her car, Amy pulls out a basket with a bouquet of flowers he recognizes from her garden, and a bottle of wine. She walks back up to him. "One more chance. But, John— please, don't lie to me again. The truth is always better."

Her cheeks are flushed, her lipstick fresh. She's wearing a necklace with a pearl that lies in the valley between her collarbones, a flowered dress with a thin black belt, open-toed heels. She is such a lovely woman.

"I know," he says. "I won't lie to you again, I promise."

"I mean about **anything**," Amy says.

"What if you get your hair cut and you're really happy about it but I don't like it?"

"You must man up and tell me. Also you must tell me if something makes me look fat. If I am careless with someone's feelings. And especially if you're angry about something—you must tell me about it before you get **too** angry. Look, let's keep it simple: If I ask a question, you answer it truthfully, no matter what it is. And I'll do the same. Okay?"

He thinks about this. He wonders if declarations of truth aren't more important than declarations of love. He thinks they might be. He takes in a breath and says, "Deal."

She laughs. "You know why I believe you?"

"Why?"

"Because you thought about it for **so long** before you answered."

"Well, it's an important question. Listen, I just went to the grocery store. As you can see. You want to have some dinner with me? I can make vegetables and vegetables. And fruit."

"Yes. And I want to tell you that the man you saw me with in the restaurant is my brother. I just took him to the airport, and on the way there, I told him about you. His advice was that I beat it over here as quickly as I could."

"Good advice."

In the kitchen, John puts down the bags and turns to face her, then lifts her hand to kiss it.

"You are such a sweet man," she says.

"I only did that so you would peel the carrots."

She comes closer and lightly kisses his mouth. "I'd love to peel the carrots. And I'd love to have dinner with you, but I have to tell you, I'm not starving. I could wait a while. If you wanted to . . . you know, wait a while."

"I'm so glad I got nonperishables," he says, taking her hand and leading her upstairs.

It is nine-thirty by the time they come back down, and they are both ravenous. They forgo making dinner and eat peanut butter and jelly sandwiches, then a hastily concocted fruit salad. And then Amy goes to get her purse and pulls a piece of paper from it. "Are you ready?"

"For what?" He tightens the tie of his bathrobe, leans forward to see what's on the paper. He feels an odd rush of trepidation, as though everything that just took place between them is bogus, and now she is going to present him with something suggesting she wants out of their relationship after all.

But when she lays the page down on the table, he sees that it's a computer printout of the image of a puppy—the image is not clear, it but looks like a mixed breed, one ear standing straight up, the other down.

"I think I found something," she says. "Do you want to go and look at him with me and see if you agree?"

"Sure."

"I think we should agree. I mean, he'll be my dog, but he'll probably be around you a lot, too. Right?"

"I hope so."

She studies the photo, then looks at him, and the overhead light catches her face in a way that makes her seem older than her years, but lovely. He thinks he knows how she will age, what she'll look like in ten years, even twenty. More important, he thinks he knows what she'll be like. After they made love, they spent a long time talking and he was again struck by her optimism, by her kindness. Before he met Amy, he had resigned himself to thinking he'd probably be alone in old age, had told himself that he'd be better off that way, but now some light has slipped under that door.

Amy slept briefly, and he lay beside her, deeply comforted by her presence: the warmth of her body, her measured breathing, the scent of the perfume she always wears, the notes of which he cannot identify but somehow reads as **green**. He lay in the dimness of evening, listening to cars going by, to the sounds of children playing, to the repetitive calls of the robins that have nested in the tree between his and the neighbor's house. He thought of Amy sitting in her own bedroom during her husband's last days, how her heart broke a million times over, watching him leave that way. And he thought of the decision she'd made that would haunt her for the rest of her life. So much can be done to a life with one impulsive decision.

"Leave, then!" he'd told Irene. "I want you to. I've wanted you to for years!" And Irene, pulling a suitcase out of the closet, weeping, saying she hated him and couldn't wait to be gone. And then she really was gone, she and Sadie both.

After they drove away, eight-year-old Sadie looking out the window at him standing helplessly on the front porch in his stocking feet, his fists clenched, he'd gone upstairs and knelt before the toilet, because he thought he had to throw up. But nothing happened; he'd hung his head over the bowl, his mouth open, aware of the circumscribed coolness of the tank water, the little ripples caused by his exhalations, and nothing had happened. After that, he'd sat bewildered on the bathroom floor, staring straight ahead, unblinking. Then he'd called Stuart.

John closed his eyes against the memory, then reached over to gently touch Amy's hair, and she opened her eyes and smiled at him. And he smiled back, immensely relieved to be back in the present.

"So you'll go with me, tomorrow, maybe around ten?" Amy says, of the dog whose photo she just showed him.

"Yes," John says. "Will you stay with me tonight?"

"Yes." She nods, tucks a stray hair behind her ear, and nods again.

He thinks, **I knew she'd do that, nod twice**. It sits solid in him, how well he knows her already.

15

Wearing mismatched pajamas and her bathrobe, Irene sits before her computer. She stares at the screen, and tries to think of what she might say in yet another ad but can only think of how short-lasting was her gay disregard of her daughter. The truth is, she's frankly worried about Sadie now. She may have resented having to call Irene, but she would have called. Wouldn't she? Does Irene suddenly not know her own flesh and blood? Well, it's five after eight, not that late. Too soon to get frantic. She'll save being frantic for her late Sunday evening activity.

She takes a drink of tea, and the last bite of the beet dish that she made herself for an early dinner. Then she begins typing again, quickly. **Are you eating dinner and reading this ad?**

No.

When I was a little girl, I used to want a bracelet that would prick me if I were doing

something wrong. A kind of external conscience. But then one day when I was on the swings at my elementary school, it came to me that I was full of envy of Cynthia Hamilton, whose shoe box for Valentine's Day was stuffed to the limit. And I was full of rage at Mrs. Monroe, my math teacher, for being a math teacher. And I was full of guilt for having found a dollar on the floor of the church we attended which I knew was intended for the collection plate but which I kept for myself. I thought, if I had a bracelet like I wanted, my wrist would get so perforated, my hand would fall off.

Irene sighs. Maybe Val's right. Maybe she should stop with the wacky ads, and try to be sincere. Although she was sincere about wanting that bracelet! And she is sincere in suggesting that maybe a conscience that punishes with physical pain isn't such a bad idea!

She starts yet again. She writes: **Woman in search of** . . . The cursor blinks. In search of what? A forty-three-year-old man? She doesn't think so. Jeffrey Stanton told her over what turned out to be a lengthy lunch that he was very much attracted to older women, always had been. He used to fall in love with his teachers routinely, one quite seriously. When he was a senior in high school, he had a torrid affair with his fifty-year-old art teacher. "Fifty!" Irene said.

"That's when women start getting interesting," he said. He told her he dated almost exclusively older women.

"Hmm," Irene said. Part of her was flattered; part of her was thinking, **Boy, is this guy screwed up**.

"May I ask you something?" she said. "It's kind of personal."

"Please," he said, putting down his fork to give her his complete attention.

"Do you do this because you're afraid of having a relationship with someone your own age?"

He answered her in what seemed to be an honest way, saying, "I've asked myself that question. But I don't think so. I think it's that the character of women has changed. I don't particularly like the so-called modern woman."

"I'm a modern woman!" Irene said, offended.

"You're a modern woman with an old-fashioned heart," he said. "Aren't you?"

She supposed she was.

"Look," he said. "I don't want to talk you into doing something you're uncomfortable with. I just thought we kind of hit it off. I'm . . . between relationships, as they say, and I'd really like to spend more time with you. I think you're interesting and I think you're beautiful."

Tears sprang to Irene's eyes, and she blinked them away, embarrassed. Then she laughed. "Sorry," she said.

"Been a while since someone's told you that?"

"Been a long while."

"But you are, you know. You're beautiful."

"Well. Thank you."

"You don't believe me."

She looked at him, full of things to say but unable to formulate a single sentence. Did she find herself beautiful? Of course not. And yet sometimes she thought she looked nice. Sometimes she thought she looked really nice.

"When I say you're beautiful, you think, **Not anymore.** Right?"

She shrugged. "It's the truth. One doesn't hold on to beauty."

"Is that what you think?"

"Well . . . **yes.**"

"Are you familiar with the Japanese word **shibui**?"

Irene shook her head no.

"It refers to a certain kind of aesthetic. It's about balancing simplicity with complexity, and it's about being aware of subtle details. That way, you don't get tired of what you see. It's also a way of constantly finding new meaning in beauty. Which, incidentally, is not compromised by the years going by, but enhanced by it."

"Well," Irene says. "I think the concept works with inanimate objects, maybe."

Jeffrey got out his wallet and Irene thought, **That was fast.** She thought she'd offended him.

But it wasn't that. He pulled out a small photo of a painting. It was of an older woman, maybe in her early sixties, nude, sitting in a chair, a blue silk robe pooled at her feet.

"This was my greatest love," he told her. "She represents what I'm trying to explain to you. She had a beauty that resonated because of what was inside. That's really important in trying to understand **shibui.** It sounds simple, like a cliché, really; but it's true: a woman is most beautiful when she is herself. The Japanese call it a beauty with 'inner implications.' It's not a show-off kind of thing, some peacock display of clothes and makeup and demeanor. It's quiet. Subtle. And here's the most interesting thing: **Shibui** relies on the ones looking at a person or an object to make something for themselves out of what they see; in that way, it makes an artist out of the observer. It's counterintuitive, I suppose, a kind of two-way equation. I wish I could explain it better."

"No, I think I understand." Irene looked at the wash of sun on the side of the woman's face, the prominent knuckles of her hands. And then, of course, her breasts, her belly. And for the first time, she saw an aging woman's body in a different way, having nothing to do with competitiveness or fear or revulsion or herself. She looked simply at the fact of it: skin, bone, eyes. Lines, angles, planes. Light and shadow. And yes, beauty. The woman's hair was completely gray, but quite long and thick, parted on one side, wavy.

"What happened?" she asked.

"Cancer."

"Oh," Irene said, and she looked again at the painting, seeing more, this time. "I'm sorry. How long were you together?"

"Eight years."

"That's how long I was married."

"That's how long we were married, too."

"She was your wife?"

"She was my **life**."

Irene looked at the painting again. "Who did this?" she asked, and Jeffrey said, "I did."

"You paint?"

"Another surprise, huh? There's more to me than managing people's portfolios."

By the end of the meal, she'd agreed to go to the opera with him, to a performance ten days away. Irene liked that it was relatively far away. It would give her time to get out of it, should she change her mind.

Whatever she decides, her conversation with Jeffrey has made her think she should keep herself in the game, and so here she goes again, dropping yet another line in the water.

Irene carries her plate and fork into the kitchen and puts them in the dishwasher. On the way back to the bedroom, she passes the hall mirror and stops to regard herself. Is it really the company of a man she wants? She thinks about the girl she used to be: lying on her belly beside a narrow creek, her hand cupped in the water to catch the tadpoles, her summer shirt riding up in the back. Holding her mother's hand as they climbed the wide steps to the library, then settling deliciously into bed that night, surrounded by books holding stories that would take her away. She remembers straddling the top rail of the backyard fence to play cowgirl, one of her mother's scarves around her neck, the black velvet hat she wore to church transformed in her mind into a Stetson, a folded towel serving as a saddle.

She remembers going to junior high on the first day of classes, wearing a black tight skirt for the first time, with a hot pink blouse that refused to stay tucked in. In high school, playing Ike and Tina Turner in her bedroom at a volume so low she could hardly hear them, because her father found the singers vulgar.

In college she met Val, for which she will be grateful every day for the rest of her life. Then after school came her years as a speech therapist, when she dated everyone from doctors to men who worked construction to coffeehouse musicians. Every time she met a man she liked, she would tell Val, and every time a relationship crashed, she would tell Val. And relationships crashed continually.

But then came John. And then Sadie: the cool

gray morning she delivered her daughter, the strange awkwardness between her and John afterward, the way they seemed not to know quite what to do with each other, though clearly each was independently besotted with their child. How frank was the tenderness and joy in John's eyes when he looked at his daughter, how different it was from the way he looked at his wife. "Good job!" he told her after Sadie was born, and he clapped her on the shoulder. The people in the delivery room just stared, expecting, Irene supposed, that what he should have done was at least embraced her. Well, he didn't. Nor did she embrace him, not then, anyway. She did hug him before he left the hospital that night, but even in that embrace was an impenetrable distance. Somehow, even at the height of their love for each other—and they did love each other, in those days—they could not cross the divide.

Once, early on in Irene's marriage, when she told Val that she and John never said "I love you" to each other, Val said, **"Why not?"** And Irene said she didn't know. "Well, just say it!" Val said, but Irene didn't. And didn't. And didn't. She never did, and neither did he. They did other things, they offered gifts both tangible and not, but neither spoke those words, except to Sadie. About a year before they divorced, when she and John went briefly for marriage counseling, the therapist ferreted out of them that neither had had parents who expressed love, at least not verbally; neither had grown up hearing "I love you." The therapist asked John and Irene to face each other and say the words. They faced each other, and neither spoke, neither was willing to go first, and finally Irene laughed, and John did, too. "Okay," the therapist said, unamused. "I'll pick one to go first. Irene, tell John you love him."

"I love you," she said, obediently.

"Look at him when you say it," the therapist said, and Irene looked at John and said, "I love you."

"Now you, John," the therapist said, and John looked at Irene, took in a breath, and said quickly, "I love you."

"How did that feel, saying those words?" the therapist asked.

Neither answered.

"Irene, can you say how it felt?"

"Um," Irene said. "It was . . ." She wanted to say it was nice. But she also wanted to say the truth, because they were in trouble then, and she thought, if ever they were going to be out of trouble, they'd need to tell the truth. And so she said, "It was like the words were these big wooden blocks, and they were hard to get out of my mouth."

"John?" the therapist said.

"It was sad," he said.

"Sad?" the therapist said.

John looked over at Irene, and she looked away. That was their last time to go for counseling.

Irene comes back to her desk chair and looks around her bedroom, idly massaging one elbow. How did she get here, living in this two-bedroom flat in San Francisco, California? She would never have predicted this for herself. But then it seems to her that life is learning that you can never quite fully put in to one port, for the way that things are always changing, including oneself. Oh, in some respects, people stay irrevocably themselves (truth be told, Irene would still like to be a cowgirl, never mind that the skills required are not her own), but mostly the only thing one can rely on is unreliability.

And so for now here she is: a fifty-six-year-old divorced woman, writing ads to ask for something that is not what she really wants. What she really wants is to feel a part of the world in a way she has never quite been able to do, to feel **among** and not apart from. She pushes her glasses up onto the top of her head and rubs her eyes. "No more," she says, her voice seeming overly loud in the empty room. She shuts off her computer, closes the lid, and vows not to waste her time doing this again. But she knows she will. There will come one of those empty times, one of those lonely evenings when she looks at the clock and despairs of it being only 7:10, and she will once again sit under the lamplight in her robe, trying to sell herself in a neighborhood newspaper.

She hears a sound at the front door and smiles. There's Sadie; she didn't call as Irene asked her to, but at least she's home safe—and a day early! But the sound is a knocking, and therefore is not Sadie, unless Sadie lost her keys. Irene goes to the door, looks out the peephole, and sees Henry standing there, his arms crossed tightly over his chest. She moves quietly away. She'll pretend she's not home. But he has seen or heard her, for he knocks again, saying, "Come on, Irene. I know you're there."

Reluctantly, she opens the door. "What."

He raises his brows, regards her obliquely. "You're not even going to invite me in?"

She steps aside, and he goes into the living room and takes off his jacket. "Cold outside," he says. Irene stands stiffly as he lowers himself into one of the armchairs, places his jacket over his lap just so.

"Oh, sit **down**," he tells Irene, and she perches stiffly on the edge of the sofa. She wishes she weren't in her nightclothes.

"Look, I'm **sorry**," he says. "It was a little tense at that party."

"It's tense at every party, Henry. Every party, every event, everything we do."

He nods gratefully. "Right. So you can understand—"

"No, I mean, **you** make everything tense. It doesn't have to be that way."

He sits staring at her, arms crossed and one eyebrow raised, as though she's a painting he's about to negatively critique. Finally, he says, "Are you really quitting?"

"Yes, Henry. I'm really quitting."

"Even if I give you a raise? And increase your hours?"

The phone rings, and Irene excuses herself. Finally! She hopes her daughter has a lot to tell her, so she can beg off to Henry. But it's only a marketing call, and Irene bangs the phone down and returns to the living room.

"Well! I guess you're mad at more than me. Aren't you?"

"I'm worried about my daughter. Who was supposed to call me hours ago and hasn't yet."

"Where is she?"

"Rock climbing."

"Alone?"

"No, with a group of kids. For the weekend."

He waves his hand. "She's fine. She doesn't want to call her mother when she's with a group. It's **embarrassing**, Irene, come on. I remember wanting to go on a camping trip to Yellowstone with a bunch of guys when I was seventeen and my mother told me I could go if I called her every day. I could just see myself thrashing through the woods every day to find a pay phone. So I didn't go and I'm still talking about it in therapy. Just relax; Sadie will call you when she's ready. Or she'll just come home without calling, and that will teach you the lesson she wants you to learn."

"Sadie's not like that. She wouldn't not call. She just wouldn't **do** that." Irene's getting annoyed. Henry didn't come here to talk about Sadie.

"Anyway," Irene says. Pointedly.

"Yes, anyway," Henry says. "So that's my offer. I'll let you work full-time. And I'll give you a raise."

"No. I don't want to work for you, Henry. It's very unpleasant, actually. You're a very rigid person."

"**I'm** rigid! What about **you**?"

"I'm not rigid!"

"Oh, you **so** remind me of that woman on **Project Runway** who said she wasn't a manipulative person after Tim called her out! And she was the **personification** of manipulation! Irene, trust me. I'm saying this not only as your employer but as your friend. And don't you make that face; we are friends and you know it.

"Look," he says. "Think of this as a mini-intervention, and believe me when I tell you that you are rigid. And controlling."

"Uh-huh," she says. "Anything **else**?"

"Well, a bit unyielding. Since you asked. Plus it appears you're pretty good at holding a grudge."

"**I'm** unyielding? Are you kidding? My life with you has been nothing **but** yielding. And I'm tired of it! And I quit! So why don't you just . . . You should just leave, now. Please."

Henry points to a pink stain on her robe. "What's that?"

"What." She looks down at her lapel. "Oh. Beets."

"With feta cheese and caramelized onions and pine nuts?"

She says nothing.

Henry goes on. "The recipe which you got from **me** and, as I recall, have made several **times**? And **enjoyed**?"

"So?"

"So you **like** working for me. I just need to . . . Look, I get it, okay? I need to tone it down a little. Or **you** need to toughen up a little, because I probably **can't** tone it down. It's a problem, I admit it. I am too involved in my work. As a matter of fact, James just left me because of that."

He adds this last quietly, almost nonchalantly.

"Really?" Irene says. "Are you . . . **Really?**"

"Oh **well**."

"But you've been together for . . . what?"

"Ten years," he says. "Ten years and four months and six days. If you count today, which, technically, I do."

"And he left? As in, took his clothes and moved out?"

"Not all of them. He'll be back to get his stuff when he's found an apartment."

"Well . . . **Henry**. I'm sorry. I really am."

He stands. "I made him ricotta pancakes with pecan syrup for breakfast. And he ate them, knowing he'd be dumping me right afterward. What kind of person does that?"

Irene doesn't answer.

"Honestly? I think he might change his mind. I think he might go and have his little hissy fit **with all that that entails,** and then come back. But he might not. So could you please not quit yet? Don't quit yet. Just . . . you know, ignore me. I mean, do what I **say,** but ignore **me.** My attitude. I don't mean anything by anything."

"Yes you do," Irene says. "You're a snob and you're all the time trying to make me feel inferior."

"You make **yourself** feel inferior."

"Nooooo. I'm not just walking along, feeling inferior. **You do** something and then I feel inferior."

"All right, Irene. Here it is. I really need you. I got a call from someone with tons of money and zero taste who wants a retro party with the most ridiculous recipes. I mean, **gelatin** molds."

"Oh, I have the best one," Irene says. "Strawberry pretzel salad."

"Oh, God."

"You use a stick and a half of butter. And strawberry Jell-O. And frozen strawberries and canned pineapple. It's so church social. She'll love it. You know what else is in there?"

"Please don't tell me."

"Cream cheese and Cool Whip."

"Oh, God. I'm putting you in charge of this whole affair. I'm not even going. You take care of everything. And don't bring any of my cards to this event."

"I didn't say I'd do it. As of now, I am not in your employ."

"Irene. I am what I am. Okay? So. Do you want to quit or do you want to accept a twenty-five percent raise and more responsibility and keep working for me? It's not going to be so easy for you to find another job, by the way."

"Thirty percent," Irene says.

"Fine."

"No, wait, forty percent."

Henry looks at her.

"No?"

"Thirty." Henry is heading for the door when his cellphone rings. He takes it out of his pocket and checks to see who it is, then looks triumphantly over at Irene. "It's him. He's come to his senses. I'm not even going to talk to him. Let him just wonder where I am. And you stop worrying about Sadie. She's the most responsible person I know. And to be honest yet again, maybe she's just taking a little space that she needs—and **deserves**, Irene."

"Right," Irene says. But what she feels is not that Sadie is taking a "little space" but that she is in trouble of some kind. It is true that she has worried about her daughter unnecessarily in the past. But there was also the time when Sadie was five and had gone on a field trip with kindergarten class—they were going to a u-pick farm for strawberries. Irene was out weeding the garden when an ominous feeling came over her. She went inside and checked to see if anyone had called. No. She shrugged off the feeling and went to the sink for a glass of water. She'd almost finished drinking it when the phone did ring. Sadie was in the ER; she'd been brought there after having been bitten by a dog. Irene called John and arrived at the hospital just after him. She found him sitting with Sadie, whose hand was wrapped in a big white bandage, and John was praising her for being so brave. "I got stitches but I didn't cry," Sadie told Irene. Irene did, though only a little. She and John locked eyes over their daughter's head, and despite the circumstances, what Irene was feeling was an immense sense of gratitude for their circle of three.

She goes into her bedroom and sits at the edge of the bed. It occurs to her to call John, but she is reluctant to sound the alarm, as placing such a call would do. She looks at the clock: it's almost nine. She tries Sadie's cell: no answer. Maybe she turned her phone off when she started the climb and has yet to turn it back on. Irene supposes the group could be having a celebratory dinner, after which Sadie will finally call her; surely she will remember by then that she was supposed to let her mother know as soon as she completed the climb. Irene regrets not having asked more questions, written down the names of people Sadie was climbing with, where they were going, what the exact timetable was. How could she have let her go, knowing so little? But she was chastised for the few questions she did ask. And the truth is, unless Sadie's in school, Irene is often ignorant of where she is. "I'm going to a movie," Sadie says. Or "I'm going out with Meghan."

Meghan! Irene knows her number; it's on her cellphone from a time Sadie was with Irene and had forgotten her own phone and needed to call her friend. She scrolls down the numbers, finds what she thinks is Meghan's, and calls it. She gets Meghan's voice mail. Where **is** everyone?

With some trepidation (**Mom!** Sadie will say), she leaves a message: **Hi, Meghan, this is Irene Marsh. I'm trying to find Sadie, and I'm not having any luck. Just wondered if you knew where she was. Please call me if you do. Or ask her to call me.** She stretches out on the bed, picks up the novel she's reading. A few chapters, and maybe by then Sadie will have called. If her phone is on and she sees that her best friend is calling, she'll pick up. Meghan will say, "Your mom called; better call her back." The first thing Irene will say to Sadie is, "If you **say** you're going to call, **do** it."

Some time later, Irene wakes up with the book still in her hands. She checks the clock. Eleven! "Sadie?" she calls out. Nothing. She goes into her daughter's darkened room and turns on the light. Not there. She goes back to her own bedroom and tries Sadie's cellphone once more: nothing. The police? She doesn't think they'll do anything until Sadie is gone longer. And anyway, what would she say? **My daughter went rock climbing with a bunch of people, none of whom I know, and she's not home yet.** The police will ask, **Your daughter's age?** And she'll say eighteen, and they'll look at each other and then tell her that Sadie is free not to report in to her mommy. And she will say, **But you don't know my daughter.** Now, though, she wonders if it's she who doesn't know Sadie.

She goes into the kitchen to the bread box and shoves a piece of sourdough into her mouth. Then another. A kind of clock ticks louder and louder inside her. She calls Valerie to ask if she thinks she should call the police. No answer. Then she remembers that it's movie night; Valerie will be out with her husband seeing two movies, between which they'll have dinner. She goes to the window, to see if there is anyone coming down the block. All she can see is her own helpless face, looking back.

She sits in the banquette, folds her hands on the

table, and feels herself beginning to relax. This is always the room in a house that brings her comfort. When she was looking for a place to live in San Francisco, it was the kitchen she always went to first. "You're quite the cook, I gather," the real estate agent finally said. And Irene murmured something that could go either way, because it was too hard to explain. Irene loved kitchens not because she was such a good cook but because the kitchen was always the place where a need was unambivalently expressed and met. Hunger. Food. When her mother died, Irene crept into the kitchen in the middle of the night with a blanket and a pillow. She lay beneath the kitchen table, where she finally slept.

She gets up to make a cup of chamomile and reaches into a high cupboard where she keeps a china tea set from Tiffany's. John gave it to her one year for Christmas, and at the time, she wondered why. She didn't drink tea, then. When she opened it, the look on her face expressed a kind of puzzlement that comes when you are given a gift you didn't expect or want. "I can take it back," John said, and Irene said, "Oh, no, it's beautiful. It's just a surprise."

She uses it often, now, at times when she feels she needs to take a little extra care of herself—times when she's hurting, or discouraged, or feeling the kind of weariness that cannot be cured by sleep. As she rinses out the teapot with hot water, she realizes she never really thanked her then-husband for what was, especially at that time, an extravagant gift. "John," she says. "Thank you." Saying his name out loud makes it almost seem as if he is there, now. If only he were.

16

Every so often, Sadie gets up and feels her way around the now pitch-black space, tries in vain to see out, calls out. She believes it is Sunday night, and tomorrow, when she can see, she will make two scratches on the wall. Also, she will periodically mark the movement of light across the walls of the shed, and in this way fashion a rudimentary clock. Just before darkness descended, she dug a deep slit in the bathroom corner, into which she defecated. She covered this with dirt, wiped herself off with dirt; then, in a similar manner, tried to wash her hands with dirt. After that, she wept a little: for the humiliation, for the hopelessness, for the pain she has in her shoulders from throwing herself against the door.

For a while, she let herself blame her mother for this happening. If Irene weren't so uptight and overbearing, Sadie wouldn't have had to lie to her about going away with Ron. She would have felt safe to introduce him to her mother, and none of this would have happened.

Then she remembered something.

Not long ago, Irene had an appointment for a physical, and she was furious by the time her doctor came into the examining room, because she'd had to wait for nearly an hour and a half, counting the time in the waiting room. Dr. Miller had come in and greeted Irene by saying distractedly, "How are you?" And Irene had said, "I'm angry! This is too long to **wait**, Dr. Miller!" The doctor had acknowledged that this was true, and said she'd gotten to the clinic late because she'd had an emergency at the hospital, and then there were two emergency phone calls to take care of when she arrived at the clinic. She'd looked into her pocket, where something was buzzing, and said, "And it looks like someone else is paging me now." Irene said the doctor had stood there, staring blankly, and then she'd said, "I'm so tired." "I thought she was going to cry," Irene said. "And I all of a sudden **saw** her, and she had lost so much weight and she had big circles under her eyes." They started talking about how the doctor had gone into medicine because her father was a doctor and she loved medicine, she loved helping people. But now. Now she was constantly over-worked, being assaulted by insurance companies until she felt, as she described it, "like raw meat." She was seeing way too many people in not enough time, and so many of her patients were depressed because of the economy, because of the ongoing escalation of violence everywhere, because of political polarization and extremism and hopelessness. Her mother said she'd told the doctor to hop up on the examining table and Irene would have a look at her. The doctor had laughed, and then Irene had hugged her and told her to go home that night and eat a bunch of mashed potatoes and butter, and then Irene had gotten examined.

That was Irene. Right when you were ready to scream, she'd ingratiate herself with you. That was what Henry said about her mother, and it was true. That was what her mother said about Henry, too; and it was equally true.

Sadie gets up and stretches, calls out once more in the darkness. Like evening prayers, she thinks.

Finally, she is tired again, and she lies on the mattress and feels herself descending into sleep, a little mercy.

Sometime early the next morning, she is startled awake by the sound of a car door slamming. She scrambles to her feet, puts on her wrecked bra, straightens her blouse. Is she rescued? Oh, God, she is rescued! "Hello?" she says. Her voice is so hoarse, she can hardly hear herself. "Hello?" she says. Nothing.

He's back. And he has brought someone else. She hears the sound of two men's voices. Here it comes. It is coming and she sees that she has deluded herself in the most spectacular and ridiculous of ways. She is afraid, and that is all. She is not ready to forgive, she is not ready to die, she is not ready for anything. She is only afraid, she can taste it, she can smell it, and now she feels the back of her throat begin to tighten so that she can hardly breathe. "No," she says, in what little voice she has left. "Please."

"Stand back!" she hears, and the door is broken in and there before her is a police officer, who says, "I'm Officer Dickinson. Are you Sadie Marsh?"

She nods, squinting in the sudden brightness, astonished at how wide outside is.

"I'd like you to come with me. I have to ask you some questions."

She is helped into the back of a squad car, where she is given a bottle of water and asked if she feels ready to talk. "Yes," she says. She hears her own voice newly. She is aware that the girl she was when she left her house on Saturday morning is not the girl she is now. She doesn't feel like a girl at all, anymore. She feels like a member of a species living for an indifferent amount of time on the planet Earth, a species in which most members assume a false security nearly every day of their lives. She is no longer among that group. She has been singularly and irrevocably educated.

17

"Want some of this?" Valerie asks. She's standing at the stove in her flowered robe, flipping bacon in the pan and drinking her first cup of coffee. Irene had come over at eight, when Valerie and Ben were still in bed.

Irene doesn't answer. She's hardly slept. Early this morning, she went to the police station to file a missing person report, which she told Valerie was such a surreal experience. The endless and heart-breaking questions. The way she had to describe Sadie's eye and hair color, the little birthmark on her chest, which, as a toddler, she used to try to wash off. When she described the clothes Sadie had on when Irene last saw her, she'd begun to sob. "Most times, these things turn out fine," the cop had said. "No reason to get yourself all worked up until there's something to be worked up about. Most times they turn out fine."

"I told him thank you," Irene said, "but what I was thinking was, **What about the other times?**"

She told Valerie she couldn't wait to get out of there and get back home, she kept thinking she should never have left home, but when she finally did return, when she opened the door and called, "Sadie?" no one answered. When she checked the landline, no one had called. When she pushed open the door to her daughter's bedroom, it was just as Irene had left it: the bedside lamp on, the covers turned back in anticipation of a daughter who, after she was good and yelled at, would surely need sleep. She sat in her living room for a while, then bolted over to Valerie's and burst into tears.

Valerie had been sympathetic, but Irene sensed that her friend disapproved of her going to the police, thought she'd jumped the gun. When she asked Valerie that very question, Val said, "Well, to be honest? Maybe so."

Now she comes to sit at the kitchen table with Irene. A shaft of morning sunlight lies wide on the tabletop, and Irene thinks that, under other circumstances, she would find this beautiful, the way the light bisects a vase of flowers. "Do you think I should call John?" she asks.

"Why?"

"Because Sadie is missing!"

"I'd give it one more day."

"Well, if she lived with John and she were missing, I'd want to know. Why is no one taking this seriously but me?"

"Okay, Irene, you know what? This is Sadie's

declaration of independence. It's here. And it's been coming. You know that. You know you're too close to her. I swear, you're the only mother I know who used to get **sad** when school started. She's not calling you because she **shouldn't have to.**"

"I just wanted to know that she was safe, Val! She's not on a class trip to Paris with thirty-five chaperones and looking at art, she's **rock** climbing."

"She's done it before."

"In a gym. And if she wasn't going to call me, she wouldn't have **said** she would. That's the thing. That's the real thing."

"If she had said she wouldn't call, you wouldn't have let her go. Right?"

Silence.

"Right?"

Valerie goes back to the stove to turn the bacon again, pops some bread into the toaster. "Eat some breakfast. Then you'll feel better. Then go and find something to **do**. She'll be home before you know it. And then you can yell at her, won't that be nice?"

Irene stares at her hands.

"Ben and I are taking the day off and going to Carmel."

Irene nods.

"You want to come?" Valerie asks, but Irene knows a mercy invite when she hears one.

"No, I've got a lot to do at home." What? What does she have to do at home?

"How do you want your eggs?" Valerie asks, moving back to the stove.

"On top of Sadie's head."

"I'll make scrambled, okay?"

"Fine." Irene picks up the miniature Magic 8 Ball Valerie keeps on the table. "Is Sadie all right?" she asks. She upends the ball, then holds it upright to let the message float up to the viewing window. **Better not tell you now.**

"What did it say?" Valerie asks.

Irene tells her, and sighs.

"Irene?"

"What."

"It's an **8 Ball**."

"It's always right. I think it says so right on the box."

But when Valerie puts a plate of buttered toast and eggs and bacon before her, Irene starts to feel better. She'll go downtown. She'll go to a movie. She'll go over to Mill Valley and take a walk down the Tennessee Valley Road to the ocean. There's a massive three-hundred-year-old oak tree she likes to look at on that walk. She's seen people stand before it and pretend it's a god of some kind. Lots of people do that. Maybe they know more than she does.

When she gets back, surely Sadie will be there, then. And everyone can say I told you so.

18

After she leaves the police station and gets into Ron's car to go home, Sadie says, "I can't talk about it right now."

"I understand," he says.

He drives slowly, carefully, and Sadie wipes away the tears that keep gathering and falling. She thinks about what happened at the police station in order not to think about other things. The shed. The man.

Sadie was interviewed by a female police officer named Maria Sanchez with a very bad perm but a kind demeanor. Sadie woodenly recounted the sequence of events, then answered a few questions, most of which seemed designed to do two things: one, make sure she'd suffered no physical harm, and two, put the fear of God in her about ever getting into a car with a strange man again. As if she needed to be told! Next she was interviewed by a state's attorney named Marilyn Woo, who told her she would not have to come to the bond hearing but would have to come to the trial—she would be notified as to when it would be held.

After she signed the complaint form, the attorney asked if Sadie would like to call someone to come and get her. Sadie called Ron.

"Would you like to call your mother, too?" Ms. Woo asked.

"Do I have to?"

The attorney shrugged. "You don't **have** to call your mother. You're eighteen."

"Okay, well, no, then," Sadie said.

The attorney cocked her head. **No?**

"Not right now."

Attorney Woo leaned forward. "Any trouble at home? Anything you want to tell me?"

Sadie laughed. "Only that I don't want to cry in front of you. My mom will start crying when I call her. And then I will. She's a very emotional woman. That's why I didn't call her to come and get me, she'd be so wound up she'd be a danger to everyone, including herself. But I'm going to use my boyfriend's phone to call her as soon as I get in the car."

Marilyn Woo rose and put her hand to Sadie's shoulder. "Take care. And understand that it will take a while to get over this. It may creep up on you in unexpected ways. You might need a little help getting through it."

Did the woman not understand what fortitude

she had exhibited in getting through this experience? Sadie wondered. Did she notice how Sadie had not wept, and had answered every question calmly and thoroughly?

"I'm pretty strong," she said.

"I know you are." The attorney looked at her watch. "You're free to go, Sadie."

Sadie sat still for a moment, then bolted from the room and into the hall, where she sat on a wooden bench to wait for Ron. She thought about what would happen when she called Irene, about the histrionics that would surely follow, the blame, too. **You got into a strange man's car?** She knew her mother must be worried, but Sadie needed a little time to think about what all this had meant— or not meant—to her and her alone. She didn't want Irene to translate the experience for her, to tell Sadie what it meant, and how to deal with it. Awful as it was, it belonged to her and not her mother. She felt that, if there were a way to come to peace with it, it meant seeing it not so much as something that happened to her but as a confluence of random events. That was something that was gently intimated by Marilyn Woo, who said, "Unfortunately, things like this happen all too often. I don't want you to be thinking it was your fault. You need to accept responsibility for getting into the car, but not any blame for what happened afterward. **He's** the bad guy, right?"

Maybe Sadie could ask the attorney to call her mother and let her know she was all right, and on the way home. Sadie went back into the office where she had been interviewed. It was empty now. But in the room next door was a woman sitting at a desk, working on a computer, a sweater over her shoulders, glasses perched at the end of her nose. "Excuse me," Sadie said. "May I speak with Marilyn Woo? I forgot to tell her something."

"She's left for court," the woman said. "But I can give her a message."

Sadie hesitated, then said, "No, that's okay."

She went back out into the hall. She would call Irene herself, when she was ready.

Now, Sadie asks Ron, "Where **were** you? Why didn't you come? I waited on that corner for so **long**."

"I know, I know, I'm sorry. I was at a doctor's appointment and it took way longer than I thought it would. I got some news. Anyway, I came to where we were going to meet just after you got into that guy's car. I didn't know what was going on; I was pissed, and I followed you. I tried calling, but you didn't answer. Then I started thinking maybe you were in trouble or something; it wouldn't be like you not to answer, and besides, the guy was driving like a maniac; I knew I was going to lose him. So I called the cops and gave them his license plate number."

"I know; they told me. You saved me. You really did."

Ron stops at a light, and she feels him looking at her. "You okay?" he says, and she nods.

"Did he hurt you, Sadie?"

"Mostly he scared me, is all. He locked me in a shed, and said he was going to bring somebody to me to . . . be nice to."

"Are you kidding? I'm going to kill him."

"He was crazy, that's all. He . . ." Something rises up in her. "That's all I want to say right now."

"Okay. But do you need anything right now? Anything."

"No." **Just you.** She closes her eyes, and thinks about how, when she came out into the hall of the police station, she'd caught a glimpse of the man who'd taken her. He was in handcuffs, being led away, and he didn't look so powerful or fierce now. He looked sad and sort of ridiculous. She considers the fact that this whole thing might have been not anything like human trafficking but rather some sort of elaborate hoax. But the box cutter. That would have been going too far, wouldn't it? And his throwing her phone out the window. Maybe he'd been high, and irrational in the way that some drugs made you be. Maybe he **was** dealing in human trafficking. She supposes she'll find out at the trial.

She opens her eyes and looks out the window,

and nothing she sees seems to make its way into her. "Ron," she says.

"Yeah."

She starts to speak, then stops. There is too much in her brain; she doesn't even know what she most needs or wants to say. She is still afraid, there is that—just now, when they were stopped at a light, a man passed close by Sadie's side of the car and she gasped and grabbed the door handle. She thinks it will be a long time before she trusts strangers again, and she'll never have the blind trust she had before today.

"Can you pull over?" she asks, and Ron goes into a parking space that has just opened up.

"I think . . . I'm not ready to go home."

"You're not?"

"No."

"Why not?"

"I'm just . . . I'm not ready to face my mother yet. I'm not ready to tell her about everything that happened. I have to think about what I want to say, and how to say it."

"But she must be so worried about you! Maybe you should at least call her and let her know you're okay, that you'll be home soon."

" . . . Yeah. I guess."

He takes his phone out of his pocket, offers it to her.

Sadie punches in all but the last number, then

hangs up. "Ron, I can't. I just can't yet! I mean, there's too **much**. She doesn't even know about you. I'll have to tell her about you, and then about that guy, and she'll conflate it somehow. She'll blame you. And me, of couse, but she'll blame you more. She'll want me never to see you again. I **know** her; she'll do all she can to get you out of my life. And when she focuses in on something like that, she's relentless; she will not stop.

"You know, I think I understand for the first time that my life is **my** life. This horrible thing that happened somehow showed me that. Even if the attorney said I'm eighteen; I don't **have** to call my mother. Maybe . . . I mean, I might not tell her about this at all. That might be the best thing."

"I don't know," Ron says. "It just seems strange, is all. I mean, you're really close to your mom, aren't you?"

"Well, you're really close to me, right?"

"Yes." He smiles. "**Yes**, Sadie."

"But you keep certain things from me."

He looks away. "Yeah."

Sadie stares past him. She watches people going down the sidewalk: a middle-aged woman walking a dog wearing a pink dress with ruffles; a group of tourists, fanny packs on, smiling and pointing at this and that. Saturday morning, she leaned into a car window to give a strange man directions and he took her. What if he had killed her? She tries to imagine this, herself lying sprawled on the floor, her eyes wide open and lifeless, but it won't compute. Already the whole event is beginning to assume fantastical proportions, to fade like a bad dream, and she's glad about that.

If she tells her mother what happened, Irene will ask a million questions and Sadie will have to relive the experience. Then, because of her own fears, Irene might tell her not only that she has to stop seeing Ron, but that she has to live at home when she goes to college. And it's certain that Irene will tell Sadie's dad—"**I have to!**" she'll say—and it will hurt him, it will kill him, and this kills Sadie.

So no, she decides. She's not going to tell her mother. What good can it possibly do? Ron's the one who can console her; he's the one who saved her, he's the one she can talk to about what happened. He won't push her; he'll wait until she's ready to talk. Sadie will think of some excuse to offer her mother for why she was missing. She doesn't really feel bad about deceiving her. It's self-preservation. And besides, if there's anyone who can understand keeping things to herself, it's Irene Marsh.

A couple of weeks ago, Sadie read an article in the paper about kids living in college dorms who were allowed to have pets, and she asked her mother if they could go to the shelter and adopt a kitten for Sadie to keep in her room, so long as her roommate agreed. Irene thought it would be a good idea; look how much joy Shadow had brought to both of them.

They were in the kitchen when they were talking about this. It was late at night, and Irene had just finished an Indian-style marinade for the chicken she would be serving to Valerie and a couple other women friends the next night. Her mother was tired, and when Sadie saw the bags under Irene's eyes, the sagging of the flesh on her cheeks, she got that mixed feeling of tenderness and irritation that she felt toward her mother more and more often, lately. Irene was older, and it was starting to show. It seemed to bother Sadie even more than it did Irene, though Sadie was hard-pressed to say why. It wasn't because Irene's getting older suggested too blatantly that Sadie's own youth would inevitably fade. It wasn't that she was embarrassed by a woman who used to be undeniably good-looking who now looked washed out and weary. No. It was that Irene's aging had launched something inside Sadie that she didn't understand, and that she was ashamed of: a hard-edged impatience, a burgeoning anger; at times, a near revulsion.

But that night, Irene sat at the banquette in the kitchen and smiled up at Sadie. It was an invitation to join her, and although what Sadie really wanted to do was go and talk on the phone with Ron, she slid in opposite her mother. "What kind of kitten do you want?" Irene asked.

"Orange guy," Sadie said.

"That's what my first kitten was," Irene said. "An orange tabby, with blue eyes." And then she told Sadie the story:

Irene was twenty-two, and had just moved into her first apartment. And this was the first pet she'd ever had, chosen from a big litter that Irene had driven out to a faraway suburb to see. She'd always wanted a kitten, but her parents had disallowed it, so as a little girl, Irene used to cut pictures of cats from magazines, keep them in a shoe box, and rotate them out. Her paper kittens got laid on her pillow for sleep, got put beside her plate when she ate her meals. She taped them to her window so that they could watch for her to come home from school. She had names for every one of them.

She told Sadie that she was so excited to go and get the cat, she had to keep taking her foot off the accelerator to avoid speeding. When she got there, she had no difficulty at all in making a selection: the kitten she chose, chose her—it walked up to her, sat at her feet, looked up and meowed. Irene named the kitten Gracie, and she bought it a blue collar with a silver name tag, two toys, and the best food she could afford. She prepared a bed in a box, using one of her flannel nightgowns to line it, though the kitten preferred to sleep with her.

After only four days, it died. Irene had no idea why; she woke up one morning and the kitten lay unmoving at the foot of her bed. She wondered if the tenants before her had put down some sort of poison that the kitten had found. She wondered if the kitten had been born with a fatal anomaly. She didn't take it to a vet, for what could they do? Instead, she buried it in a nearby field, and decorated the little grave with the kitten's collar and a bouquet of wildflowers. "I never told anyone about this," she said, and then laughed at the tears she wiped away. "Good grief; I don't know why I'm crying, it was so long ago!"

"You didn't even tell Valerie?" Sadie asked.

Irene shook her head no.

"Why not?"

"Oh, she was out of town when I got it. And then, when she came back, there didn't seem to be any reason to tell her. The cat was gone."

"But it would have helped you to tell Valerie!" Sadie said, and Irene said, "No it wouldn't. She would have tried to make me feel better, but she wouldn't have been able to. And anyway, telling her about it would only make it bigger in my own mind. It would move it out into the world. I wanted to keep it as small as possible, so that it would go away sooner. I needed to keep it to myself."

So this need for a kind of secrecy, for autonomy, is something Sadie comes by honestly. And anyway, isn't sparing her parents the details of what happened to her a kindness? They'll only worry. Or blame themselves. She'll call home when she's feeling a little more stable. When she feels sure of the story she'll tell.

She looks over at Ron. "Can we go somewhere and just talk?"

Ron drives to Golden Gate Park, and they leave the car on the Fulton Street side. In a wooded area, they find a grassy place and lie down beside each other. When Ron very gently takes her into his arms, she begins sobbing.

Ron says nothing, just holds her.

"I thought he might kill me," Sadie says, finally. "And I was thinking how to be about that, I was trying to think of how to **be**. And I was going to try to be like my cat."

"Like your **cat**?"

She laughs, despite her tears. "I know it sounds stupid, but he was . . . When he died, he was **okay**. And I wanted to be okay. I wanted to be grateful. Even though I was dying. I know it doesn't make sense. But you can't imagine what it's like when you think you might die!"

"Yeah, I can, Sadie."

"No," she says. "It's just an abstraction until something like this happens. You have no idea, Ron."

"But I do know what it's like. That's part of what I was going to tell you today."

"What do you mean? You said it was good news, what you were going to say."

"Yeah, it is."

"So tell me."

He sits up, and she does, too, wipes her face and takes his hands. "**Tell** me!"

"Okay, so . . . When I was fourteen years old, I was diagnosed with cancer."

"What? What kind of cancer?"

"Colon," he says, then adds quickly, "But it's gone. That's the good news. Last week, I was at the five-year mark and I got all the usual tests. I went in yesterday for the results, and they told me everything was negative."

She stares at him, doesn't move.

"Negative meaning good," he says. "He told me I'm one hundred percent cured." He laughs. "It's **gone,** man."

Now she breathes out. She looks over at him: his hair, his ears, his soft mouth.

"I don't get it," she says. She means life.

"Me, either."

"But you . . . Why didn't you tell me this?"

"It wasn't time."

"Well, tell me now," she says.

"What do you want to know?"

"I want to know everything. I didn't even know kids got colon cancer."

"They don't, usually. One kid in one million is the statistic we were given. It was so weird, the day I was diagnosed. I had no idea anything big was wrong. I'd been having a little trouble with, you know, my bowels, and my mom took me in for a quick look-see, it was time for a regular checkup anyway. So he does this and he does that and then he says, 'Ron, did you know we have some new fish out in the waiting room?' He had this cool aquarium in his office, I used to love to watch the fish there. He said, 'How about you go and check out the fish? I want to talk to your mom for a bit.' I wasn't really worried. Nothing hurt. I was fine. The day before, I'd hit a grand-slam home run. I was **fourteen.**

"I went out to the waiting room and sat watching the fish, and after a while, the doctor called me back in and I could see my mom had been crying. I thought, **Oh, no, something's wrong with my mom,** but then I saw in her eyes that it was me. I remember I got really cold, and I wanted to run. I thought, **If I get out of here, I won't have to hear it, and it won't be true. It won't** be.

"I looked at the door, and the doctor must have sensed I was thinking about bolting, because he moved to stand in front of it. He said, 'Ron, your mom needs to tell you something.' So she stood up and came over to me and she took my face in her hands and she said, 'Ron, you're going to be fine, but you're going to have to have an operation and then some medication for a disease we've just discovered that you have.'

"'What disease?' I said, and she told me colon

cancer, and she just kept looking right in my eyes. And all I could think of was my dad, who died of that disease, how weak and thin he was at the end, just totally wasted. I said, 'Dad died from that.' And she said, 'You are not Dad. And we're going to get through this one day at a time. Today is the hardest day.'"

He looks over at Sadie and smiles. "It was a hard day, but it wasn't the hardest."

"Did you have to have chemotherapy?"

"Yeah."

"Did you get sick?"

"Oh, yeah."

"Did your hair fall out?"

"Some. But I learned this rubber band trick; I put a rubber band right at my hairline, and it helped keep the medicine from going to my scalp. I lost a lot of hair anyway, but not all of it. You couldn't really tell."

"Were you scared?"

He looks up into the sky. "Yeah. My mom told me I'd be fine, but I did some digging around and I saw that the chances of surviving were practically nil. That was the hardest day, when I read that. Kids don't fare well with colon cancer; it acts more aggressively in them, and it usually gets diagnosed later. By the time it's found, it has spread all over. So that got to me. I read all that and I felt really scared. I thought a lot about death, what it might really be, what it would feel like to die. And then, all of a sudden, I just knew I'd be fine."

"How did you know that?" Sadie asked.

"Well, I didn't **really** know it, of course. It was more . . . I guess I kind of insisted on it. My mom had lost my dad to cancer; and I just decided that was enough for her to take."

Sadie shakes her head.

"So anyway . . . Can I ask you something? Is this a big turnoff?" He laughs.

"No."

"It's not a turn-**on**, is it? Because that would be just as bad. That would be weird."

She rises up on one elbow and looks at him. "It makes me see you better. It makes me know you better, too. I want to know every part of you."

"Yeah, me, too. You, I mean."

She lies back down, picks up a blade of grass and considers it. "So did this just completely change your view of life?"

"Well, it was a pretty intense education, right? At first, I didn't know what to think. On the way home from the doctor's office, everything looked so vivid. Really beautiful. I saw everything like I was seeing it for the last time or something. But then I kind of got used to having cancer. People say you can get used to anything, and it's true. One thing that's lasted is that I always try to find . . . the **better** part of everything. Like when I went for chemotherapy,

I really liked this one nurse. So when I had to go for treatments, I didn't think about how sick I'd get; I thought about how I'd get to see Leslie; she was really pretty and she always made me laugh. I guess my general orientation toward life is something that cancer gave me. The idea that, no matter how long we live, we don't live long enough, so we'd better appreciate each other. And we'd better, you know, take risks, speak up. . . . I for sure learned that there aren't many situations where you don't have a choice about how you want to **be** about it. So when you said that about your cat . . . I get it."

"Yes," Sadie says.

"Anyway. That's why I didn't want to sleep with you. I didn't want to get too involved if . . ."

"But now we can get involved?"

He smiles. "Oh, I'd say we're involved all right. I'd say it's a little more than that."

Inside, she feels a wide ripple of pleasure. Of enormous relief. "I like you so much," she tells Ron. "I love you. Actually."

"**Love**'s a big word, Sadie."

"I know. I know it is. But I do."

"Okay, I need to tell you something. I had decided that, if I got bad news, I'd break up with you. I wouldn't want you to have to be in on whatever followed. But if it was good news, I promised I'd tell you something else.

"First, you have to know I was always a very

determined little kid. My mom told me about one time when I was three years old and was in trouble for climbing on some piece of playground equipment she'd expressly told me not to play on because I was too small for it. And I said to her, 'It's my life.' I'd not heard that expression; it just seemed so clear to me that the decisions I made were really up to me and me alone, even at that age."

"Ah!" Sadie said. "So we both came to the same conclusion. You just beat me by fifteen years."

"Right. Then, when I was twelve, I actually asked my mom if she could sign something for me so that I'd be able to get married."

"Who'd you want to marry?" Sadie asked.

"Cindy Hollinger. Class beauty. But, as it turned out, also class asshole."

"That's the trouble with beauties," Sadie says.

"You don't have that problem."

"Yeah, well, I'm not a beauty."

"I think you are."

She swallows, looks away from him.

"Sadie? Are you okay?"

Silence.

"Did you just now think about what happened to you?"

She nods, and then she turns toward him. He pulls her close, and they lie still for a while. There's a group of children playing nearby, and their sounds are so happy and bright.

Finally, "What else?" Sadie asks.

"What else?"

"There's something else you wanted to tell me."

"Oh. Right."

"Tell me," she says.

He looks over at her.

"Tell me! Just say it."

"Okay. This probably isn't the right time, but I'll tell you anyway. As soon as you're ready, I want to marry you."

She laughs.

"I mean it," Ron says.

"Okay," she says. "Well, let's go do it."

"You think I won't? I will."

"Aren't you afraid of marriage?"

"No. I've always known I wanted to get married. I guess I was inspired by my parents."

"Yeah, well," Sadie says. "For me it was the opposite. I had a front-row seat for watching a marriage fall apart."

"So you learned what not to do. I learned what to do. Between the two of us . . ." He looks over at her.

"I don't know what to say."

"I shouldn't have told you all this. Not today."

"It's okay. I'm glad you told me."

"You know, my dad died young, but because they were married so young, he got to be with my mom for a pretty long time. They got married when they'd known each other for just two weeks. Two weeks!"

"How old were they when they got married?" Sadie asks.

"My dad was eighteen; my mom was sixteen."

"What a recipe for disaster!"

Ron shrugs. "And yet." He puts his finger gently to a nearly transparent green bug that has landed on his arm, and it flies away, and Sadie thinks the bug was lucky to have been on Ron's arm.

He says, "I actually think getting married young might be the best thing to do. You grow up together, and you grow close, doing that. I look at people now, it's fucked up. They wait too long. They're too set in their ways and they can't compromise. And they have babies when they're, like, old, and that's just not right. Not fair to the babies and not fair to themselves."

"Plus the babies have more problems," Sadie says. She once heard a conversation about that very thing between two older women walking on the street ahead of her. Sadie figured they were mad because their children were dawdling over giving them grandchildren.

"Hey, Ron? Did the doctors ever tell your dad he was cured?"

"No. Nope, he never got to hear that."

"Oh. I'm sorry."

"Do you believe in God, Sadie?"

"I don't know."

He looks at her. "You don't know? So you're an agnostic, then?"

"I'm not even sure enough to be that."

"I believe in God," Ron says. "And sometimes I believe I feel my father's presence. I mean, I really do."

"That's nice," Sadie says, softly.

"I told him all about you," Ron says. "He approves of you."

"Good."

They lie quietly for a while, listening to the voices of people passing through the park, all the different languages: French, German, something Sadie identifies as Spanish but Ron says is Portuguese. When she asks how he knows, he tells her he speaks Portuguese—he learned it because someone told him it was difficult. He also speaks French and Spanish fluently, and now is learning Japanese.

Sadie is pleased with his knowledge, proud of it.

The sun drops lower in the sky, and it grows cooler. Ron asks, "Are you hungry?"

"What time is it?"

"That will let you know if you're hungry?" he says, laughing.

"I don't know. Yeah."

"It's six-thirty."

"Okay, yes, I'm hungry. Let's go and get some dinner."

"Where do you want to go?"

She thinks for a minute, and then she says,

"Someplace quick. We'll eat, then I'll tell you the rest of my plan."

He pulls her toward him and tilts her chin up. "Can I kiss you?"

She nods, and when he presses his mouth gently to hers, she thinks of how nice they must look, a couple under the trees, their arms wrapped around each other. They are a force against the world, young people who know how to love, who are brave enough to.

19

Late Monday night, John peers at his bedside clock and tells Amy, "It's after one, on a school night. We should go to sleep."

"First tell me just a little more," she says. "I love hearing about this, and besides, I'm not tired. Are you?"

He considers the question. "Actually, no. I feel like I just had a great workout. Which I did."

She sits up, leans against a pillow, anchors her hair behind her ears. She does not bother to cover her breasts, something Irene always did, and he isn't sure how he feels about it. There is a bit of the Puritan in him, he supposes; he embarrasses easily over things such as this. And it makes it hard for him to concentrate on what he's saying. He sits up beside her, kisses her forehead, then stares straight ahead.

"Do you mind my asking all these questions about you?" Amy says.

"Not if you'll answer my questions about you."
He looks quickly at her, then away.

She pulls the sheet up over her breasts. **Got it,** he
imagines her thinking. He regrets himself: she is
lovely, her breasts are beautiful; and now he has
made her self-conscious. But she only says, "So.
Erector sets and Tinkertoys. What else?"

"Blocks, before that," he says. "My mom says I
loved playing with blocks. I'd make towers as high
as I could, then knock them down and start over.
Apparently I did this for hours."

"In your little striped shirts and corduroy pants
and Buster Brown shoes?"

"And **suspenders,**" John says.

A marriage counselor once told him and Irene
that they needed to know about each other as children, that it would help bind them together in
important ways. But at that time, he already knew
a good deal about Irene as a child; she'd told him
things, and he'd asked her a lot of questions. He
knew that, all through fourth grade, she used to lie
in bed trying to figure out what the highest number in the world was, and she would nearly weep
in frustration because, no matter what she thought
of, all you had to do was add one and there, it was
higher. He knew that when she was twelve years
old she once snuck into a church and stared at the
crucifix, because a Catholic girlfriend had told her
if she watched carefully, she could see Jesus bleed.

She said she stared so long she thought she **did** see bleeding. He knew she made cookies to give away to strangers she met on the street; he knew that for years she longed for a sea horse she saw advertised in the back of a magazine; he knew that, in Brownies, she was too shy to sing the "Day Is Done" song at the ends of the meetings and so got booted out for being uncooperative. He knew that, when she went to the hospital to have her tonsils out, she thought her parents were going to leave her there because they didn't say they'd be back in the morning. He knew she used to go over to her best friend Sally's house every Saturday morning and that they would practice kissing on Sally's parents' bed. He knew that losing her virginity was anticlimactic, that she'd smoked dope for the first time when she was eighteen and hadn't liked it. He knew that she had never been given a birthday party, and, more astonishing, she saw nothing unusual about that. He knew that she once kept a dead bird in a shoe box under her bed for a week because she thought love could cure it. He knew that she had once shoplifted makeup—a tester lipstick in the color Creamy Toffee—and then felt too guilty to use it.

Irene was not as curious about him. She did not like to hear any stories involving his mother. After she heard a few, she asked him not to tell her any more. It seemed to hurt her, though she did not say that—rather, she said it made her angry. What he saw in her eyes when he told her those stories was not anger, though. It was a kind of vulnerability she was loathe to show anyone.

She did know his first job was teaching skiing to little kids, and that he was soon given the position of lead instructor. As such, he was approached by the other teachers to ask the boss for a raise. When he did, the guy fired him, so John started his own school. He ended up with one third of the school's clients and eight of the instructors, and he did very well. She knew that the next year he went to Europe and hitchhiked all around: Brussels, Luxembourg, Florence, Athens, Paris, Marseilles, Zurich, Munich, Dublin. He was galvanized by what he saw: old, old buildings that not only had been maintained but were being **used**. People were eating, drinking, and being entertained in urban spaces. He was a product of middle-class suburbia, but he had seen the light. **This,** he thought, was what was needed in America. This was what he'd do. Irene liked that story. She told it to their friends, in front of him, and he was proud when she did that. But that was pretty much all she knew.

When he tells these same stories to Amy, though, she seems to want to know even more; he's flattered by it, and it gives him hope that they really are forging a solid relationship. At first, when she began asking questions, a kind of weariness fell upon him. **Here we go,** he thought. **What's your favorite color, what's your favorite food?** It was like reading the same picture book over and over to Sadie, when she got fixated on one of them. But there was a kind of pleasure in reading it to her, too, a kind of anchor that, if John couldn't get in one place, he could at least get in another.

And so he will answer all of Amy's questions and she will soon know that he adores grapefruit and hates mango, that his blood sugar bears watching, that he once built a sailboat in his living room, carried it out sideways, and sold it immediately; he didn't want to sail it, he only wanted to build it. She'll know that his first professional project was a dilapidated nursing home that used to be a mansion, that he rented rooms out to college kids while he restored it, in order to fund it. She'll know that he can do carpentry and plumbing but not electrical, because the first time he tried to wire a light he was shocked so badly he was knocked off a chair and that was enough electrical for him. She'll know that for his second project he looked around for wrecks of buildings that had been abandoned and called the owner of one to ask if he'd sell. He met with the man, a very wealthy businessman who had inherited the building and really wanted nothing to do with it. The man liked John and ended up giving him the building. "But I have to tell you," he told John. "There's a pretty sad bunch of people living there who haven't paid rent in a long time: junkies, prostitutes, dealers. They're not going to be real happy at the prospect of things changing."

The day after the paperwork was done, John got in his car, a used Jaguar that was on its last legs, and drove over to look at the building. On the way, he turned up the radio and sang along. He couldn't help it; he was thrilled. But when he got to the building, there was a formidable-looking black man sitting on the front steps. He was dressed all in black and wore a choker made of silver dollars. He watched John get out of the car, watched him approach. John nodded and sat on the steps beside him, offered his hand, which the man refused. "I'm John Marsh," he said, "and I'm the new owner of this building."

"Yeah," the man said. "Well, I'm the manager of this building. You dig, motherfucker?"

"I'm here to have a conversation, not a confrontation," John said. "If we have a confrontation, you're going to win. But here's the deal: I'm going to rehabilitate this place. You don't have to pay rent; nobody does. I ask only one thing. I know the building hasn't been cared for, but don't wreck it any more. And let me know when you all are ready to go."

The man nodded. He looked over at John's car, then at him, and John was struck by how red the guy's eyelids were. The man said, "I know the yuppies on they way in."

John had a thought to defend himself, to say he'd bought the car for a song because it looked so beautiful, choosing style over substance as usual, and that he'd be lucky if it lasted a month. But he said nothing. He supposed he was a yuppie.

In six months, the guy called. "We out," he said, and hung up. And John began the work of his life, restoring old buildings to the beautiful structures they once were, reinvigorating them, which has sustained him in a way nothing else can.

He looks over at Amy. "I've told you a lot about myself. Tell me one thing about you."

"What do you want to know?"

"Oh . . . maybe something nobody else knows."

"I was runner-up to the prettiest girl in fourth grade."

"Something else. Something really personal."

"Okay. I hate to brush my teeth."

He laughs. "Why?"

"Because it's boring. So I take little walks while I brush my teeth. Sometimes I do things, like dust, or make the bed one-handed—I'm very good at making beds one-handed."

"So you hate brushing your teeth. Tell me something you love."

"Oh, striped shirts. Bacon on Sundays. The birds every morning. Reading the first paragraph of a book and knowing you're going to love it. And even though I can be a kind of impatient person who hates waiting for things, some things I don't mind waiting for. Some things are worth waiting for, and, in those instances, there's great pleasure in the anticipation." She looks away from him, saying this last, and he wonders if she's talking about them. He hopes she is.

He wants to tell her he admires her. He wants to tell her he thinks she's wonderful, and when he does, he'll pull the sheet back down from her breasts. But just then the phone rings, startling them both. "Excuse me," he says, leaning over her to pick up the receiver. "I don't know who **that** could be." And he doesn't. But he feels a shift in the air, a sense from Amy that he **does** know who it might be, that she is suddenly and uncomfortably reminded there is more to him than she knows.

As soon as he says hello, Irene starts talking.

"John, it's me, I'm so sorry to call so late, I'm really sorry, but I don't know what to do. Oh, this is probably so unnecessary, but I didn't know what to do."

Irene, he mouths to Amy, rolling his eyes.

And she smiles, but she has moved away from him, he can feel it. She'll say maybe she should go as soon as he hangs up, he can see it coming. He holds up one finger, and she nods. But then she does get up and pulls her dress over herself. She does not put on her underwear, he's happy to see, so maybe she's not leaving. She points to the other room. He understands. She wants to give him privacy. Irene is still offering her long-winded apology.

"What's **up,** Irene?" he says, and the irritation in his voice is more than he intended.

There is a moment of silence, and then she says, "It's Sadie."

He freezes, then manages, "What happened?"

"I don't know, probably nothing. But she went on this rock climb—"

"What happened? Did she fall?"

"I don't **know**. I don't know where she **is**. She hasn't called, she hasn't come home, and she doesn't answer her cellphone."

He gets up, starts pulling his trousers on. "Did you call the police?"

"Yes, I filed a missing person report. They seemed to think it was no big deal, but—"

"What else?"

" . . . What do you mean?"

"I mean what **else**?"

"Well, I . . . I keep calling her. I left a message on Meghan's phone."

"Did you call all the hospitals?"

"No."

"Well, call the hospitals, Irene! Did you call anyone she went climbing with?"

"No."

"Why not?"

"Because I don't know their numbers."

"You know their **names,** don't you?"

Silence.

"Irene?"

"She told me some names, but I forgot. I mean, she—"

"Get off the phone and call the hospitals. I'll be there as soon as I can."

"You don't have to come, John. Everybody but me thinks she's fine, that she's just . . . She's probably just . . . You don't have to come. I just wanted you to know. I thought you could maybe give me some ideas. Which you did. I'll let you know if—"

"I'm getting ready right now. I'll get the first flight out."

Amy comes into the room after he hangs up.

He looks up at her. "My daughter is missing. I have to go to San Francisco."

"She's **missing**?"

"Yeah."

"For how long?"

"For three days."

"Didn't you tell me she was going rock climbing?"

"Yes. And she hasn't come home yet. And she didn't call her mother at all, as she said she would."

"Well . . . I can see why you're worried, but this is not so uncommon at her age. I have a friend whose daughter went to the Boundary Waters and didn't come home until five days after she said she would. Sometimes kids just—"

"Look, I know my daughter. This isn't like her. She's in trouble."

He goes over to his closet, starts packing.

"Maybe . . . I should go home?" Amy says.

He turns around. "Yeah, I guess I'm . . . It might be a good idea. I'm sorry, I just really need to get out there and be with my wife."

"I understand."

He turns to the closet to pull out a couple of shirts, and when he turns around again, she is gone.

For a moment, he feels bad, and considers going after her. He ought to go after her. But he doesn't want to think about Amy. He feels that everything that just happened between them is a pretty illusion, a ride on a carousel. Here is his world: Sadie.

20

Late Tuesday morning, Irene carries an armload of linens into the living room. She's so relieved that John is coming. He's the only one who understands the kind of love she has for Sadie—not only understands it but shares it. He's the only one who seems to agree with Irene that this situation is serious. For the first time in a long time, she feels allied with John against what feel like outsiders. The last time this happened was many years ago, when a couple finally left their home after what might most kindly have been called an uninspiring evening, and Irene closed the door after them, then turned around and merely looked at John, who said, "I know. Can I rag on them first?"

He called her from the airport saying he'd gotten on the 6:55 A.M. He's due in at 11:39, fifteen minutes from now. She offered to pick him up, but he said she should stay there—he would take a cab in. She wants to prepare a bed for him—he's been up all night; he's one of those people who can never sleep on a plane, and anyway, his worry will have kept him awake. She doesn't want him to stay in a hotel, not under these circumstances. But she can't put him in Sadie's bed; that would seem to suggest that Sadie is not coming back. She can't put him in bed with her. The sofa bed is far too short for him and uncomfortable, besides; not for the first time, she regrets not paying more attention to how it felt as a bed. She supposes she could call and get some sort of rental bed delivered, but she doesn't want to add one more thing to her plate. She decides that she herself will sleep on the sofa bed.

As she puts clean sheets on her own bed, she remembers a time when she and John had first gotten together and went to stay for a long weekend in a lake house with another couple, friends of John's. One night, the couple went out for groceries and declined John and Irene's offer to come along and help. "Stay and enjoy yourselves," they said. John suggested he and Irene go skinny dipping, which they did, but the water was icy cold and they ended up lying in the couple's bed to get warm—their own beds were rudimentary cots that offered little warmth or comfort. They ended up making love, and Irene worried about leaving a stain. So they stayed connected after John's orgasm and, giggling, moved as one unit off the bed and onto the floor, then into the bathroom. There, they separated, laughed, cleaned up, and then made love again, on the bathroom floor. There was an ease between them at that time, there was such pleasure in being together.

She stands still, staring into space, remembering this. Odd to think that the embittered couple they became used to be that couple. Sad how the strongest thing between them came to be rigidity, wariness. Resentment, too, a feeling on both of their parts that they'd been wronged again and again, and no acknowledgment coming from either camp, to say nothing of an apology or a promise to try to do better. She wonders sometimes whether it would have helped if they'd stayed in therapy. But they both hated it. They both resisted it. And anyway, by the time they went, it was too late. They had lost some essential thing necessary for staying together. As Irene told Val, their pilot light had gone out. They had no patience, no sense of humor or perspective about themselves. What they did have was a great and abiding—and, for a long time, unifying—love of Sadie. Always, there was that.

Irene goes to the window and stares. Across the street, she sees a man at the bus stop reading the paper and imagines a headline: MISSING GIRL FOUND DEAD.

She doesn't understand why Valerie is so nonchalant about Sadie being gone; Henry, too. Maybe they're right in saying that Irene is overreacting to a situation that will simply turn out to be her daughter making a statement about not being a little girl anymore in the only way that Irene will pay attention to. In just a few weeks, Sadie will be in college, and then all bets are off. Irene has heard of parents who tell their college-bound children that they no longer have a curfew, feeling that they might as well try out unlimited freedom at home, where there is still a safety net. She supposes she should have done that. She supposes she should have done a lot of things differently.

She goes into Sadie's room and sits on the edge of her bed. She looks at the perfume bottles on her dresser, the things on her wall, her high black boots tossed into the corner. A few hours earlier, Irene made a futile search through Sadie's drawers and closet, looking for anything that might yield a clue as to her whereabouts. But she found nothing hidden other than a stuffed animal Sadie used to sleep with, a floppy-eared rabbit shoved into the corner of a high shelf in the closet. Irene held the rabbit against her chest, and smelled the perfume Sadie wears now. It came to her that there must have been times when her daughter went back to this bedraggled animal, looking for a kind of comfort her mother couldn't provide. Sadie kept the rabbit, Irene supposed, in the same way she kept the book about paper boats on her dresser, the book with the story of the boy sitting outside in the darkness after having launched his little fleet: **I hope that someone in some strange land will find them and know who I am.**

Irene lies on the bed and looks up at the ceiling,

wondering what Sadie thinks about when she lies here this same way. She herself feels a great weariness, but she imagines Sadie feels a kind of restlessness, an urgency running through her almost all the time, in the way that teenagers do. Irene remembers that feeling of needing to do **everything,** right now, even though she also believed that she would live forever, young.

But who can know their own children, really? After a certain age, their longings and deepest feelings are shared with someone else. Irene supposes it's possible Sadie is with some boy, now. Some young man who stands ready and able to see the young woman Sadie is, someone whom her mother has not yet recognized because she practices an ongoing kind of denial. Every time she folds Sadie's thong underwear, she sees instead the small cotton underpants printed with roses or princesses or kittens that her daughter used to wear. Oh, they've had the proverbial Talk, which mostly consisted of Irene starting to say things and Sadie interrupting her to say, "Mom. I **know.**" Irene has many times gratefully acknowledged the particular kind of wisdom Sadie has, her general good sense and trustworthiness. But mostly Irene sees Sadie as someone years younger than she actually is. Maybe it's because, when Sadie is gone, what will Irene have?

Oh, where is she? Once again, perhaps for the hundredth time, Irene dials Sadie's cellphone; once again, she gets no answer.

She concentrates on breathing, and on the thought that soon John will be here, and then there will be two of them sharing this burden. She feels she's been walking a tightrope not only for these last several hours but for many years. Ever since she left her marriage, actually. At first it was so exhilarating, the view so fine, the sense of danger not so much frightening as enlivening, engaging all her senses. But now her shoulders ache and her neck is stiff and she is tired of maintaining her balance. She hadn't counted on danger becoming monotonous; she had forgotten she'd grow old.

So many times, Irene has watched couples who are out together and has felt sorry for them because all they seemed to share was a familiarity with one another. A predictability. No heads bent forward together in urgent conversation. No sudden bursts of delighted laughter. No **sparks**. Instead, a quiet kind of calm, even a gentle—or not so gentle—bickering. But even in the bickering there was a sureness of each other that neither demanded nor required anything beyond the other's presence. How she longs for that now! That is the subtext behind every silly ad she writes: she wants not romance but the reliability and comfort of an old friendship. How do you get that when you've never met the person, when what you share is not a personal history but a tattered and revisionist version of what your life has been up to now? The subtext behind all **that**—all the stories Irene tells about herself, all the questions she answers—seems to be: **I guess you had to have been there.** A translation, a retelling, is not a shared experience, and in the sharing is everything. This she has finally learned, and, in the way a person too old to learn to drive learns anyway, she is clumsy with the knowledge, overly aware of it.

In Irene's kitchen is a piece of framed, off-white linen on which is embroidered: **A crust that's shared is finer food/Than banquets served in solitude.** She bought it for the beauty of the embroidery, feeling that the sentiment was not only tacky but not true for her: Irene always liked the idea of a banquet served in solitude. What could be better? All of the pleasure without any need for reciprocity. A selfish enjoyment like a massage is supposed to be, though Irene can never enjoy a massage because she always feels compelled to take care of the masseuse. The truth is, Irene can rarely really enjoy anything given by another person because of her concerns about what must be given back and, she supposes, because of her own warped sense of what she deserves—or, more to the point, does not deserve. But a banquet in solitude, a Beauty and the Beast kind of offering, all coming from behind the scenes, with no need—no **way**—to reciprocate: perfect!

That was then. That was years ago. She has changed, she has grown up at least this much, and she now understands fully—ruefully—the spirit of that epigram. Only last week she stood before it with a pile of towels in her arms and read it yet again, and she felt a dull ache settle in her chest. She imagined herself with a partner, sitting on wooden porch steps, sharing a crust. Raisin toast crust, the butter collected into little pockets, and the taste divine. Such a meager offering yielding such fine results. Then Sadie appeared, and Irene asked if she had any dirty towels in her room. If she did, Irene would wash them. Which was to say, **I can at least take care of you.**

Irene imagines John coming through the door, hastily packed suitcase in hand, his cowlick at attention because he will not have cared one whit about grooming himself. In his face will be the same anguish she is feeling. She thinks she will embrace him, which she has not done for so long. But she remembers what it was like. She remembers how it felt to put her arms around him and to feel his arms around her; he always rested his clasped hands just above her sacrum in a way that she liked very much, and his hold was neither too tight nor too loose. She remembers his smell; she remembers how his voice reverberated in her ear when he held her against him and spoke. His voice was deep, soothing; people used to tell him he should do late-night radio.

She lifts her shirt and lays her hand across the

bare skin of her belly, then closes her eyes and feels herself relaxing, despite everything. She should put on some decent clothes. She should fix her hair a little. She will, in a minute. He always liked her in green, she remembers that.

21

Bone weary and throat aching, John climbs into the cab at SFO and gives the driver the address. "First time to the city?" the driver asks, with a kind of gloating self-satisfaction that puts John over the edge.

"You know, this may come as a surprise to you, but not everyone thinks this place is fantastic," John says. "And **most** people have been here, I'd venture to say. It's not like it's the Galápagos Islands."

The guy starts to turn around in his seat but elects instead to give John a quick once-over in the rearview. Then he turns the radio on. He's a young man, a kid, really, a thin, bespectacled guy whose long hair is pulled back into a ponytail. He wears a denim shirt open at the neck, a blue jean jacket with a discreet tear at one shoulder. It feels to John that he's an artist of some sort, a musician maybe. John has a kind of talent at guessing people's occupations; on more than one occasion, someone has looked at him, astonished (or, in some cases, with a great deal of suspicion), and asked, "How do **you** know?"

"You a musician?" John asks.

"No." He turns the radio up louder.

Okay, John thinks. **I don't blame you.** He looks out the window at other drivers, many of whom are on their phones, and feels the usual irritation, the same kind of irritation that he supposes is often directed at him when he's driving and on the phone. He figures everyone more or less shares the same belief: No one should be on the phone when they're driving except oneself.

When they reach the avenues and John can see the ocean, he watches the waves roll in and a kind of calmness descends, a kind of chagrin, too. "Listen, I'm sorry I was so short," he tells the driver. Micah, his name is, if the information encased in plastic on the back of the seat is accurate.

"No problem. I guess I just always assume everyone's in the same mood I am. You know?"

John nods. "Yeah."

"You here for a funeral?" Micah asks. "If you don't mind my asking."

"No," John says, and the cold he suddenly feels runs all the way to the soles of his feet. He points ahead. "You're going to want to take a right in two blocks."

"Yeah, I know. I got you covered. Don't worry.

You can just sit back and relax, okay? I'll have you right to the door in about ten minutes."

John sits back. But he does anything but relax. **She could be home,** he keeps saying to himself, even though Irene has not called him to say so. He hadn't called her when he landed, either, because he didn't want to hear Sadie was still not there.

When they pull up to Irene's three-flat, John gets out of the cab and looks up at the second-floor window to see if Irene is watching for him. No. He pushes the buzzer to get let in the vestibule door but hears nothing. He pushes again. Damn it, the thing is broken. He goes to stand beneath the living room window. **"Irene!"** he yells. No response. He takes out his cellphone to call her—what the hell is she doing?

Maybe, he thinks, Sadie got home and Irene is in her bedroom with her, yelling at her, and doesn't want to be interrupted. He hopes Irene **is** yelling at her; he hopes Sadie's that safe. He does have keys, ones that were given him when Sadie and Irene first moved in, and he understood without being told that he was not to use them except in an emergency. Well, this qualifies.

He takes out his wallet and finds the keys stashed behind a picture of Sadie—she's standing before this very place, grinning. It's a recent photo, one she gave him when she last visited. Seeing her face unnerves him; his hands tremble as he puts the key in the lock. The hallway smells of something: rice? Behind one of the doors on the first floor he hears someone loudly talking on the phone: **I'm telling you, they're taking over the neighborhood; they're buying the place up with cash!** Somewhere in the back of his mind, he thinks what he always does when he comes to visit here: **How can Irene and Sadie live so close to other people? Don't they want their privacy?**

He bounds up to the second floor and breathlessly knocks at the door, then lets himself in. He sees no one.

"Irene?" he says. "Sadie?"

He walks down the hall and comes first to Sadie's bedroom door, which is cracked half open. He pushes it open all the way, hope in his throat, and there's Irene, sound asleep. Asleep!

"Irene!" He says it loudly, cruelly, as he meant to, but Irene looks so frightened when her eyes jerk open that he regrets it.

"What are you **do**ing?" he says.

"John." She sits up, swallows, pushes her hair out of her eyes. She's wearing a pair of yoga pants and a gray T-shirt; she's lost weight since he last saw her.

"What are you doing?" he says, again.

"Well, I've been up all night. And I just lay down here for a minute, and I . . . you know. How was your trip?" She's still half asleep; she must be, to ask such a ridiculous question.

"You might want to stay up, Irene. Our daughter is missing. You might want to be paying attention."

She crosses her arms, her hands gripping her elbows tightly. "Oh, John, please. Don't blame me. I didn't do anything except let her go rock climbing, which I only did because you talked me into it."

"Assuming that it was safe, Irene! Assuming that, since you're the one who's **here,** you would know if it was **safe.**"

She says nothing, stares at the floor, rocks nearly imperceptibly back and forth.

He drops his bag and goes to sit on the chair in the corner of the room. "Has anything else happened?"

She shakes her head.

"Anybody call about anything?"

"No."

"I was thinking on the plane . . . What about Sadie's computer, do you think there's anything on there that can help us?"

"It's not here."

"What do you mean it's not here?"

"It's not here, John! I can't find it! If you want to look for it, look for it! I've looked everywhere, and it's not here! I don't know; sometimes she takes it over to Meghan's; once, she forgot it there."

"Where does Meghan live?"

Irene doesn't answer.

"You don't know where Meghan lives?"

"They moved recently, and I . . ." She looks up

at him. "No. I don't know where Meghan lives. She and Sadie don't have playdates anymore."

"Well, did you call Meghan's parents?"

"They are unlisted."

"Why are they unlisted?"

She only looks at him.

He takes in a breath to calm himself down. "Okay. Okay. You did call the police. You did manage to do that."

"You know, John, I have been sitting here waiting and every second is like a day and I was so glad you were coming because I thought we could **help** each other, I thought we would **console** each other, but now—"

"**Console** each other? **Console?** Irene, I don't even know how to respond to that. We need to focus on Sadie, not on making you feel better!"

"I didn't **mean** that. I didn't mean **me**, I meant . . ." She sighs, shakes her head. "Why are you so angry at **me?** The police weren't even concerned when I filed the report, it was like they were just trying to humor me. **Oh, so what, an eighteen-year-old isn't calling her mommy to report in.** The guy at the desk didn't even sit **up** straight! She's not a minor; apparently she has the right to disappear. And everybody seems to think she'll come back today and that I'm just being hysterical!"

She stands, grabs Kleenex from the box on the nightstand, and John sees a huge pile of used tissues there. She looks away from him to say, "They'd say you're being hysterical, too, flying out here like this."

"Do you think we are? Overreacting?" His voice is normal now, his anger dissipated. Why **is** he so mad at Irene? She **didn't** do anything.

"No, I think we both know Sadie, and they don't. This is not like her. There's something wrong. I can feel it."

"Do you think she's hurt?"

Irene nods, miserably.

He does not want to ask this; he is afraid to, in part because he respects Irene's intuitive abilities, but mostly because it is a horrible and impossible question that should never, never be asked about anyone's daughter. But he hears himself say, "Do you think she's dead?"

"No. No. I don't think she's dead." She makes a gulping sound, swallowing. "Honestly, John, I really don't. But I do think she's in some sort of trouble, and I just wish so hard I could reach her. Or that I'd get some news of some kind that would at least let me know—"

The phone rings, and they both freeze. Irene looks at him, and he squares his shoulders, sets his jaw, and picks up the receiver. "Hello."

"**Dad?**" Sadie says.

"Oh, thank God," John says, and sits on the bed beside Irene. "Sadie! Where are you?"

"What are you doing in San Francisco?"

He has to laugh. He just has to. Irene snatches the phone from him. "Sadie," she says. "Are you all right? Tell me! Are you all right?"

She listens for a while, smiling, her face radiant, and then her expression changes. "Get home right now," she says. "Right this second."

"What?" John says. "What is it?"

Sadie speaks again and John tries to put his ear next to the receiver so he can hear, too, but Irene pulls away from him. She gestures angrily into the air, as though she is pushing something away. "I don't care. You get yourself home right now. And don't you dare bring him with you!"

"**What is it?**" John says. "What happened?"

"I said I don't **care**," Irene tells Sadie. "You come here alone. You show your father and me the respect we deserve and you get home right now and you come home alone. I cannot even . . . You come home right now. Please please please come home right now." A pause while she listens to Sadie, and then she says, "Absolutely not. If you want to talk to him, you can do it here." She hangs up and stares wild-eyed at John.

"What **happened**?" he says.

For a moment, Irene sits unmoving, her mouth slightly open. She looks like a boxer who's just taken a hard blow to the head.

Then, "It's bad," she says.

"What happened?"

"She got married."

"What?"

"I know. She got married. Oh, my God. She's eighteen years old and she got married, John."

"When?"

"Last night. In Reno. To some guy named Ron, whom I've never even met."

"Irene, what the fuck is going on around here?"

She looks over at him for a long moment, and, in spite of his anger, he admires the little star of brown in her otherwise green eyes; he'd forgotten about that. But Irene is angry now, too. She stands and points to the bedroom door. "Get out."

"Irene—"

"Get out!" Her voice cracks, yelling at him. "If all you can do is blame me, get the hell out of here!"

He throws his hands up. "Well, what would **you** do, Irene? What would you do if all this happened on **my** watch? Wouldn't you be angry at me? Wouldn't you blame me?"

"No. I would not. I would blame Sadie. And I would try to help you. I would expect that, as her parents, we would help each other."

She's right. He knows it. He hangs his head, stares at his feet. She's right. For all her faults, she was never someone quick to blame others. As he supposes he is. "I'm sorry," he says. "I guess we should talk about what we need to say to her."

"You know what, John? You know what?"

"**What,** Irene." He apologized! What else does she want?

But she says nothing. She leaves Sadie's bedroom, stomps down the hall to her own, and slams the door. He hears her sobbing.

From below comes the sound of someone banging on the ceiling, and a muffled "Keep it down! For Christ's sake!"

He goes into the living room and sits in a chair by the window to watch for his daughter to come home. After a few minutes, he hears Irene stop crying.

"Irene?" he calls.

No answer.

"Irene! I just have to ask you something!"

Again, no answer.

He goes to stand outside her door. "Did she say how far away she is?"

"She'll be here in about an hour."

"Listen, I'm sorry. I'm sorry I yelled at you. I'm sorry I blamed you. I was upset. I'm still upset. Jeez. She got married? Did you have a **clue?**"

Silence.

He rests his forehead against the door. "Irene, please come out." He waits a moment, then tries the doorknob, fully expecting that it will be locked. But it is not. He opens the door, then knocks anyway. She is lying on the bed, curled around a pillow, facing away from him. He walks slowly over to her. Her eyes are open, but she won't look at him.

Gingerly, he sits on the bed beside her. "You okay?"

"No." It comes out **Doe,** from her crying.

"You want me to . . . do anything?"

She sits up. "Make some sandwiches? I'm so hungry." **Bake some sadwiches.**

He starts to laugh, and then she does, too.

"Peanut butter and grape jelly?" he asks. Irene's favorite. He has never felt such a peculiar kind of joy. It almost hurts.

"I like black raspberry now."

"Should I make one for Sadie and her hubby?"

"Not funny."

He shrugs. "A little funny?"

"No."

"So, what do you think we should do? Ground her?"

"Go and make the sandwiches. I'll wash up. And . . . I put clean sheets on my bed so you can stay here. Do you want to stay here?"

"Uh . . ."

"Not with me! I'll sleep on the couch. But if you want to stay here, you can. This is kind of . . . It will be good to have you here for a while. This needs two."

"Yes," he says. "This most definitely needs two." He heads for the kitchen, then turns back to say, "Still heavy on the jam?"

"Yes." Her face softens, and she smiles. "Thank you for coming. I'm glad you're here."

"Me, too."

He goes into the kitchen and finds the peanut butter, the jelly, the bread, the plates, the knives. He makes four sandwiches. He knows Sadie better than Irene does. He always has.

22

Together, John and Irene stand at the window, watching Sadie come down the sidewalk. "She has him with her," Irene says. "He's coming with her!" She's furious that Sadie has disobeyed her explicit instructions.

"Well, let's just see what happens," John says. "I kind of admire the fact that he's willing to face the music."

"I don't want him to face the music!"

"Let's just see what happens," John says, again. He moves out into the hall; Irene goes to the door and opens it.

"You'll have to leave," she calls out to the young man, before she fully sees him. He and Sadie are rounding the stairs.

"I'm sorry," he calls back. "Sadie asked me to come with her."

Then he is before her and Irene crosses her arms and says, "Well, I'm asking you to leave. You go home, now."

"**Mom,**" Sadie says, and then, "You can come in, Ron. Never mind. Come in."

The young man steps just over the threshold, and Irene almost feels sorry for him. He's a nice-looking guy in jeans and a blue T-shirt, worry all over his face.

"This is my husband, Ron," Sadie tells Irene, pointedly. And then, "Hi, Dad."

John moves to embrace Sadie. "We were so worried about you!" he says. "I'm glad you're safe." He holds out his hand to the boy. "I'm John Marsh, Sadie's father."

"John," Irene says quietly. He has no idea how to handle this situation.

"I'm glad to meet you, sir." Ron turns to Irene. "I'm glad to meet you, as well. I won't stay. But I hope I'll see you again very soon."

Irene stands still, waiting. She fears speaking; she's afraid she'll yell, or cry.

"I'll call you," he tells Sadie, gently, and puts his hand on her shoulder, then turns to leave.

"Ron!" Sadie says. "You don't have to go!"

"It's okay," he says. "They need some time with you."

He holds his hand up, a wave of sorts, and locks eyes with Sadie in a way that excludes everything else.

Irene closes the door and turns to her daughter. "Are you out of your **mind**?" she says.

"Irene!" John says. "Jesus. Can we sit **down**? Can we **talk**?"

What fills Irene now is a wobbly kind of rage. She doesn't know who to be angrier at, John or Sadie. Easy for him to show up and be the even-tempered mediator! Easy for him to be the part-time parent who gets to say yes to everything because he never has to suffer the consequences of what he allows! She is the real parent, and she will handle this. She wishes he'd never come. He won't be of any use at all. He will make everything harder. "You keep out of this!" she tells John. "You don't even know what happened!"

"Neither do you, Mom!" Sadie says. "You don't know anything! You never do!" She goes to her room and slams the door.

John and Irene stand there. "Nice going," John says.

Irene goes into her bedroom and slams that door. There is silence, and then Irene hears John knocking at Sadie's door and saying, "Sadie? Can I come in?"

A muffled "Yes."

Irene sits on the edge of her bed, kneading her hands. What to do? Apologize? No. No. She is not the one who has done something wrong. That would be Sadie, who is now probably telling her father the whole story so that John can then absolve her of any responsibility whatsoever.

She goes into the hall and stands outside Sadie's closed door. Knocks.

"Not right now, Mom," Sadie says. "Please."

She opens the door anyway, stands there.

"Mom."

Sadie is lying on her bed, John sitting on the edge, his head down, his hands clasped between his knees. He won't interfere, then; she can say what she wants.

"I'm going out," she says. "I'm going for a walk. When I come back, I want you to tell me exactly what happened. I want you to tell me what's going **on.**"

Sadie nods.

Irene looks at John; he nods, too.

Irene goes for her jacket and her purse. She has no idea how these bricks have all just fallen on her head.

But Sadie is safe. And so she goes out the door and down the stairs.

She walks briskly around the neighborhood for half an hour, seeing nothing, really, but losing some of the tension that was making her feel she might fly apart into a million pieces. She goes up enough steep inclines that her legs are aching when she returns, and she climbs the stairs to the flat with some difficulty. She lets herself in and hears Sadie and John in the kitchen.

She finds them at the banquette, eating the peanut butter and jelly sandwiches John prepared earlier. Irene pours herself a glass of milk, grabs a sandwich, and goes to stand beside her daughter. "Scootch over," she says, and Sadie does.

Irene puts her sandwich and milk down, then puts her arms around Sadie, squeezes her.

"I just got jelly on your blouse," Sadie says, and Irene says, "I don't care."

"I sort of can't breathe," Sadie says, and Irene lets go.

"Tell me," she says. "Please."

Sadie sighs. She looks over at John, and he moves his hands in a small but expansive way that seems to say, "You have to tell her, too."

"I was waiting for Ron," Sadie says. "We were going to take a driving trip up the coast."

Irene has to clench her teeth to keep from saying, **"You told me you were going rock climbing!"** But then Sadie tells her about the car that pulled over, the man who took her, all he did, and Irene sits still, her head empty of anything but gratitude for the fact of her daughter, sitting here with her, alive. Three people; a family, peanut butter and jelly sandwiches, half-drunk glasses of milk.

23

John awakens and for one second tries to think where he is. Then he remembers: Sadie missing. Sadie home. The relief at seeing her safe, the horror at realizing the extent of the danger she was in. The way he and Irene peppered her with questions after Ron left, and how all that seemed to do was shut her down, turn her more and more in to herself.

"She's in shock," Irene said, after Sadie had gone to bed and the two of them were sitting and talking in the kitchen. "She can't talk about it now because she hasn't even realized what happened—or might have."

"I think she does realize that," John said. "But for some reason, she's not willing to talk to us about it."

"But why would that **be**?" Irene asked, and her eyes were full of confusion and sorrow.

"She's not ready," John said. "Maybe we just have to give her time." He did not add that he thought Irene's questions were too loaded with her own emotions to give Sadie room to respond. He felt that Sadie was balancing a precarious load, but she was balancing it; it was not up to her parents to shout instructions from the sidelines. Rather it was up to them to let her know that she was loved, and supported, and safe. They had to let her know that they were here when she needed them, and they had to deal with the fact that she might **not** need them, at least not in the ways they expected, or thought she should.

Just before Sadie went to bed, she told her parents that she had answered a million questions at the police station, that she didn't want to talk about it anymore, it was done, it was over, she just wanted to forget about it now, and go on with her life.

"A life that includes a sudden **marriage** after having been **kidnapped**," Irene said, and her voice held too much anger to get the response John thought she was hoping for.

Sadie turned to Irene and said, "I don't **belong** to you, Mom! I am my own **person**. My life belongs to me, including everything that just happened to me. It's mine to do with as I want or need to. Just back **off**!"

"Fine," Irene said, when it was anything but.

John sat in silence with Irene for a while, then told her about an experience he had had when it had been his fault that a child was injured. When he was nine, he'd talked a playmate into riding his bicycle along a retaining wall, something John did often, despite the fact that he'd been told numerous times not to. When his friend, Paul, had tried it, he'd fallen and fractured his leg, which had never healed properly. "You know how long it took me to apologize?" John asked Irene. "Twenty years. Twenty **years**!"

"But . . . why?" Irene asked.

"I was so guilty," John said. "The guy ended up with a million complications; he walked with a limp afterward, he couldn't play sports anymore, other kids made fun of him, it was awful. I just didn't know what to say. I didn't know how to start the conversation. I ran into the guy at O'Gara's one night. We were both drunk. **Then** I apologized."

"It's not the same," Irene said.

"It's the same in this way," John said. "I had to wait until I was ready to talk about something that was really hard to talk about. I think Sadie's . . . Maybe she is in shock. But I think she's a little embarrassed, too."

"Embarrassed about what?" Irene asked. "She didn't do anything!"

"She got into the car," John reminded her.

Irene nodded. "Yeah. Remind me to yell at her about that."

"You think she doesn't **know** it was stupid?"

Irene said nothing, just sat there, rubbing her knuckle with her thumb. Finally, she said, "I'm losing her more every single day." And then she went to bed.

He turns on the bedside lamp to check the time: 3:18; 5:18 in St. Paul. He closes his eyes again but then decides to get up. There's no use trying to go back to sleep; whenever he awakens like this, he never can. He sits on the edge of the bed, wondering if he'd wake Irene if he went into the kitchen. He's hungry. There's a sandwich left over, lying on the counter. He can grab it and the milk carton without turning on the light or making much noise. There are chocolate chip cookies in the tall glass cookie jar, too; Irene always has cookies in the cookie jar, one of the things he liked about her.

He goes into the hall and pads silently down the bare wooden floor. When he passes Sadie's bedroom, he hesitates, then quietly cracks her door. Her bedside light is on, but she is sound asleep, facing him, one pillow beneath her head, another held tightly against her. He looks at her bent knees, her tousled hair, the familiar, straight line of her eyebrows, her dark lashes below. He watches for the rise and fall of her chest just as he did when she first came home from the hospital. **Ah, Sadie.**

He starts to tiptoe in to turn out the light but then wonders if maybe she intentionally left it on. One of the things he asked her was if she still felt afraid, and she flatly denied it. Still.

He wishes she'd let him come to the trial; he'd like to see the man who caused his daughter such distress. Well, he'd like to murder the man who caused his daughter such distress, actually, and that's one reason Sadie told John not to come: she didn't want to have to worry about her father when she was trying to take care of herself. She wanted only Ron to come with her. John had seen Irene's face when Sadie said that, and the message in it was perfectly clear: **We'll see about that.** It was perfectly understandable that Irene would want to go with her daughter to the trial; in fact, John thinks she should, and hopes that Sadie changes her mind on this point. But if there is any lesson Irene and John are beginning to understand, it is this: Sadie is eighteen. She really can do what she wants, now.

In the living room, he is stealthily moving past the sofa bed when Irene sits up and gasps.

"It's me," he whispers, then adds, unnecessarily, "John."

Silence, and then he can hear a muffled laugh.

"John Marsh," he says. "Your ex?"

She turns on the light, blinks in the brightness. "What are you doing?"

"I'm hungry."

"Oh. Want some nachos?"

"Yeah! Do you have some?"

"I'll make some."

"I don't want to wake Sadie up. I'll just get the leftover sandwich."

"She never wakes up once she goes to sleep. And anyway, I threw that sandwich out."

"**Why?**" It used to make John crazy, the way Irene wasted perfectly good food. He'd put something in the fridge that he fully intended to eat later, and she'd throw it out. Over and over. He'd ask her where the sandwich or piece of pie or left-over pasta was; she'd say it was rotten and she threw it out. He'd say no, it wasn't rotten; she'd say yes, it was. Over and over and on and on. "I would have eaten that sandwich," he says.

"Well, in full disclosure, I only threw it out after I took a bite. From each half. Plus I sucked the jelly out." Irene sits up and reaches for the bathrobe at the foot of the bed, slips it on. "Anyway, nachos are better."

He follows her into the kitchen, watches as she wraps an elastic around her hair to make a ponytail. Next, he knows, she will don a bib apron, then wash her hands. Irene, cooking. A pleasant memory. One of the few.

"Do you still make them the same way?" he asks.

"Tons of cheese and jalapeños, yup."

"Good."

She opens the oven drawer and pulls out a cookie sheet, and as she is turning to place it on the counter, she drops it.

"Shit!" she says.

They both freeze, waiting to hear a sound from Sadie's room. Nothing.

"See what I mean?" Irene says. "Sorry for the swear."

"'Sorry for the **swear**'?"

She shrugs. "I'm trying to quit."

"Quit swearing?"

"Yeah."

"Oh," He slips into the banquette, picks up the salt shaker and inspects it. "You need more salt in here."

"Up there," Irene says, and gestures with her chin to a cupboard.

John gets the salt, and fills the shaker over the sink. Irene is close enough that he can smell her shampoo.

"How are you, Irene?" he says, not looking at her. "I mean, really. How are you?"

She laughs. "You mean because I said I'm trying to quit swearing?"

"No. I don't mind your swearing."

"Yes you do. You told me once it embarrassed you."

"Only because you used the f-word in front of my biggest client."

"I didn't know he was your client. It was a big party. A lot of drinking going on, too. I didn't know he was your client."

"Anyway," John says, "it wasn't that big a deal. The guy was a jerk. Now I'm glad you did swear in front of him, but then . . . it was a little embarrassing, yes."

She reaches into a cupboard and pulls out a grater. "Want to do the cheese and I'll do the jalapeños?"

"Sure."

She takes a package of cheese from the fridge and hands it and the grater to him.

"This isn't Monterey Jack," he says, looking at the label.

"No, I use queso fresco now. It's really good."

"I always liked Monterey Jack."

"Well, I use queso fresco now."

"Okay." He sits at the table and gets to work.

For a while, it is quiet but for the sounds of John grating and Irene chopping. It's nice. Irene used to always invite him to help her in the kitchen but he never really wanted to. Now he understands that it wasn't the help she was asking for; it was the companionship. She gave up early on asking him to help; she used to turn on NPR to keep her company.

He finishes grating the cheese and tastes it. "You really like this better than Monterey Jack?"

"Yeah."

"Come on, really?"

She turns around from slicing peppers to look at him. "You know, John?" She's peeved; her hand is on her hip, her brow furrowed.

"What? I'm just asking if you really like it better."

"As opposed to **pretending** to like it better?"

"Jesus Christ, Irene."

"**What?**"

"I only meant that maybe Harold influences you and—"

"Who's Harold?"

"That guy you work with. The food guy."

"Henry."

"Oh. Right. Henry. I just thought he might be influencing you or something. Not that . . . I mean, I know he's a nice guy and all. Sadie is nuts about him."

"I see," Irene says. "So according to you, I can't even make a decision about cheese that isn't suspect."

"I didn't say that."

"And since Sadie is nuts about Henry, he's a nice guy. Well, he's not such a nice guy, John. He's a temperamental ass a lot of the time. A **lot** of the time."

John puts down the cheese, leans back in the banquette.

"Irene, what are you so pissed off about? Can't you just . . . Why are we even talking about cheese? Do you realize what's happened here? Do you realize we could have lost our daughter? My God, Irene, she could have been **killed**!"

"And you're blaming me!"

"I'm not blaming you!"

"Yes you are. You **are**! You think I have a terrible relationship with her and that this never would have—"

"I don't think you have a terrible relationship with her!"

"Oh, yes you do, and don't you dare deny it! You're always putting on that long-suffering attitude, trying to pretend you're not telling me what to do with her when you **are** telling me what to do because **you know best,** right, John? You always know best! But you don't know! You're not the one here with her! You're not the one who sees her the most!"

"And whose fault is that, Irene? Huh?"

"Stop yelling." Her own voice is quiet, now.

He repeats the question, and she comes to sit opposite him. "It is not my fault that we got divorced, John."

"No?"

"No. There were two people in our marriage, in case you hadn't noticed."

"Well, there were three people affected by it, Irene. Okay? In case **you** hadn't noticed. And I don't think you did notice. Or care."

Irene twists her face up, starts to cry. "What the hell do you know about what I care about? Nothing!"

"Doing really well with the quitting swearing," John says. "All right, look. Let's just focus on Sadie. Okay? Let's just take care of her. I'm thinking . . . I might as well tell you, I'm thinking about taking her home."

"What are you talking about? She is home."

"No she's not. You took her away from home."

"She doesn't even like Minnesota."

"In fact, she does. But I wasn't talking about Minnesota."

"What were you talking about, then? What are you **talking** about?"

"I'm talking about me."

Irene stares at him.

"I'm her home," John says.

"And I'm not? Are you crazy?"

"Why don't you ask Sadie?" he says. He gets up from the bench. "Good night."

He walks back to the bedroom. That was a low blow. That was unfair. He doesn't care. He climbs into bed, pulls the covers up. "**Bitch**," he mutters.

From the kitchen comes the sound of the garbage disposal. She's probably throwing out the cheese because he grated it. He closes his eyes.

After a while, he hears a knock, and then the door opens. Irene comes over and sits at the bottom of the bed, stares into her lap. "Guess what, John. You're not Sadie's home. I'm not, either. That boy is."

She looks over at him, shrugs. "She named a successor. I guess I don't blame her. You know why I think she didn't tell either one of us about Ron Whatever-His-Last-Name-Is? Because she didn't want us to ruin it. That's her experience of what we do with relationships that are supposed to be loving. We ruin them."

"I don't think—"

"I'm going to bed. I just wanted to say that I'm sorry. I really am. From now on, we'll take care of our daughter. And that's all. Good night.

"Oh! By the way? Henry doesn't use queso fresco. He uses queso panela. But I use queso fresco, so . . . Good night, John."

"Good night."

"Are you warm enough?"

He sighs. "Yes."

She moves out of the room soundlessly. Like an apparition. Like the spirit of something dead and gone.

24

On Wednesday morning, Sadie hears a knock on her door. "Sadie? Can I come in?"

Her dad. She gets out of bed to let him in.

"I'm just off to the grocery store. Do you want anything?"

"A get-out-of-jail-free card?"

"Come on, you can understand why we need a little time with you. Is it really so bad being here with us?"

She shrugs.

"We just want to make sure you're okay."

"Right," she says. But she regrets the coldness in her tone. Her father looks like hell. She doubts he's slept much, but then who has? She imagines they've all been going over and over the events of the last several days.

"Granola," she says. "And raspberries."

"Okay," he says. "I'll be back in a bit."

"Hey, Dad?"

"Hey, Sadie."

She smiles. "It's not bad being with you."

"Okay."

After her father leaves her room, closing the door gently behind him, Sadie flops down on the bed. Last night, when the three of them had dinner, Irene spoke gently to Sadie, saying that she thought she understood why this happened, but Sadie would come to see that the idea of getting married, although perhaps a natural reaction, was a mistake.

"Why do you call it a natural reaction?" Sadie asked. "You think this is all a rescue fantasy? You think Ron is my white knight because he called the cops?" Privately, she wonders if there isn't some truth to that.

"I do kind of think that," Irene said. "But even if it isn't true, you are far too young to be married, Sadie. And I want you to know that Dad and I will help you out of this."

"Mom. I **love** Ron."

"I'm not disputing that."

"But do you believe me?"

Her mother sighed. "Look. Ron seems to be a very nice boy, and thank God he called the police. But you shouldn't have married him. You don't realize how much you'll miss by being married, Sadie! You're so young, you're entitled to live a young person's life. You need to explore, to try out things that marriage will prevent you from doing."

"Try things out," Sadie said. "Such as other men."

"Well, frankly, yes. But that's only a part of it. You need to be free, Sadie, to let yourself go in the direction you need to. Let us help you out of this, it will be pretty simple to do."

Sadie laid down her fork. "So you don't believe I love him. You can't **conceive** of me loving a man. You know why, Mom?"

"I didn't say that, Sadie!"

"But that's what you think."

"All right," her father said then. "Just . . . Let's everyone settle down."

"Wait a minute," Irene said. "Wait a minute! Let me talk." She looked at Sadie. "I believe you are fully capable of loving a man. Although to me, Ron is a boy. But let's just put that aside. Let's say he is a man. I believe you are capable of loving him. I believe you do love him. But what does that mean, Sadie? Does it mean you should be married at eighteen? What's the rush? Honestly, I'm just asking the question."

"You can't understand," Sadie said. It was true. "It's a waste of time for me to try to explain it to you guys." For one moment, Sadie thought about revealing Ron's illness to her parents. But she didn't want to. It didn't belong to them. They would distort it, use it as another reason for her not to be married. She could just see it, Irene saying, "His doctors could be wrong! He could relapse! Do you want to be a **widow**?"

"You never give me enough credit," Sadie said.

"You are a very responsible young woman," Irene said. "But you're too young to be married. It's not just me saying this. Your dad and I agree completely on this. Tell her, John."

"I think your mom is right," he said.

And then Sadie lost it. She yelled, "Well, look at you! Look at the two of you! Look what happens when you wait so long! You get too old and you can't be with **anyone**! The two of you are **pathetic**!"

That shut them up. She felt bad, saying it, but it was true. It would be one thing if her parents liked being alone, but they didn't, anyone could see that.

After that, her mother sat there, her eyes empty. Her father wouldn't look at her or her mother. Sadie spoke softly then, asking something she had always wanted to know. "Why **did** it take you so long to get married?"

"We're not talking about your father and me, Sadie."

"Well, maybe we should!"

But her mother got up and walked away. Then her father did, too. Sadie went back to her room and closed her door. She heard Irene on the phone, telling Henry that she would need more time off, at least a week. "Be**cause**," she said, and then lowered her voice so that Sadie could no longer hear her.

Later that night, Henry came over. Sadie heard him ask if he could talk with her, and Irene, still smarting, said, "Be my guest." She heard him walk down the hall, the floorboards creaking in the place they always did. She heard him hesitate outside her door, then knock gently. At first she didn't respond, but then, reasoning that he hadn't done anything wrong, that she'd always liked him (and also that he might have brought her something wonderful to eat), she opened the door.

He stood holding a basket of something that smelled buttery, chocolaty. Before he said a word, he lifted the napkin. Chocolate croissants. A mini-ramekin of butter, and one of raspberry jam. "Did you make the jam?" Sadie asked.

"Of course."

"Well . . . thank you."

"Eat one," Henry said.

"I will."

"No, now."

She laughed and took a bite. "**Staggeringly** good," she said.

"Yes?"

"Yes."

"So . . . may I come in?"

She stepped aside, conscious of the fact that, in her wrath, she had thrown things all over her room.

Henry went to the chair in the corner, removed a pile of clothes she'd flung there, and sat down. He sat at the edge of the chair, his legs crossed, his back straight. "I see we're sorting and organizing," he said.

She sat on the bed, took another bite of crois-
sant.

"So. Your mother tells me you got hitched."

"I got married, yes." Delicately, she removed a
crumb from one corner of her mouth.

"Have I ever met the guy?"

"No."

"Have I ever **seen** the guy?"

"No."

"Well, **that's** exciting."

"Look, Henry—"

"No, I **mean** it."

"Okay."

There was an overly long silence, and finally
Sadie said, "You'll like him."

"I'm sure. Why wouldn't I?"

"Well. Talk to my mom."

"I will talk to your mom. But first I want to talk
to you. I just want to see if you're okay. Are you
okay? Are you absolutely sure you did the right
thing?"

"I'm fine. And yes, I'm absolutely sure. It's nearly
impossible to explain, but—"

"Oh, you don't have to explain it to me. I fell in
love at sixteen with the person who was right for
me. But I let him go because I was sixteen. I've
regretted it every day since." He looked at her, his
head tilted. "Can you imagine? I mean this literally.
Every single day."

"I didn't know that."

"Nobody knows that."

"I'm so sorry, Henry."

"Thank you."

"But . . . didn't you ever try to contact him, in all these years?"

"That would require a séance, I'm afraid."

"He died?"

Henry nodded. "Two years after we broke up. Car accident. I read about it in the paper. I actually went to the funeral." He forced a smile. "**So.** But listen, as long as we're having our little pity party . . . Did your mom tell you that James left me?"

"No!"

"Well, he did. He called me a few hours after he left, and I didn't even pick up. I was sure he'd changed his mind and was coming back. But no. That's not why he was calling. He was calling to tell me the day he'd be back to pick up the rest of his things. He and his new friend, Bruce." He inspected his nails. "**Bruce.**" He looked over at her with an expression she had never seen on him before: unguarded. Soft. Weary.

"I'm just saying, Sadie. You know? I'm just here to congratulate you. You know I'm your friend. I hope I can cater for you, if you decide to have a wedding. Your mom will want you to have a wedding. A real one."

"My mom wants me to get an annulment."

"Oh, I know. But I'll talk to her and you'll talk to her and she'll talk to herself, and, when she's done processing all that, she'll want you to have a wedding. For the cake, I'm thinking deconstructed hazelnut butter cake with salty caramel filling and chocolate ganache for dipping. Won't that be fun?"

"Yeah. Sure."

"Okay, that was a test. Because that would be déclassé. You truly are your mother's daughter. I want total control of everything. Everything. I don't want so much as a **thought bubble** from you."

She laughed. "Fine."

He stood and adjusted his scarf, his shirt. "Your mother loves you so much, Sadie. She wants to make sure you haven't made a terrible mistake, something you might regret for the rest of your life. You have to admit this is rather . . . **rash**."

"Uh-huh. She loves me a lot. That's why she told me once that she didn't have to have me." It hurt again, saying it.

"She **didn't** have to have you."

"Well, that sucks. To hear that. She shouldn't have told me that."

"Oh, come on. She was angry when she said that. You were fighting, right?"

Sadie said nothing.

"So your mom was frustrated, she was hurt. She's a person—i.e., fuckup—and she said something stupid. She didn't say she wished she'd never had you, which, incidentally, my mother told me a million times." He rolled his eyes, crossed himself. "Your mother said she didn't have to have you, meaning that she went out of her way **to** have you. If you ask me, she was saying she loved you. That's what she was saying. Oh, listen, Sadie. You know who does it right? You know who does loving right?"

"Who?"

"Nobody. I mean, people can't even . . . If you get a cat because you just **loooove** cats, you're going to have plenty of days when you **hate** it because it's acting like a **cat**. Do you know what I'm saying?"

Sadie nodded.

"And another thing. When I was in high school, I had a poem taped over my bed. I read it every day. It was about a person asking another person, over and over, 'What is two plus two?' and getting all pissed off because the answer given was always four."

"See?" Sadie says. "This is why I don't like poetry. What does that even **mean**?"

"It means that some people are always going to think in a certain way. And they're never going to understand people who think so differently from the way they do. They **can't**. So it's best to stop asking for something someone simply can't deliver. Change the question, you know?"

"Which is precisely what I'm doing," Sadie said. "But I'm not asking. I'm telling."

"I know. But it's going to take some time for your parents to accept that. They can't see you clearly because of all the yous they see every time they look at you. I mean, seeing you off to **kindergarten** probably almost did them in, I'm sure. That's just the way parents who love their children **are,** they're just absolute **goosh** bags.

"Look, I know Irene pretty well, and I can tell you she's trying to understand. She really is trying. She may never agree with you, but she's trying to understand. It will make your life so much easier if you forgive her. Why don't you forgive her? I don't mean for saying something. I mean for being something."

"I already have," Sadie mumbled.

Henry was on his way out of her room, and he turned around. "What?"

"I already **have**."

"Fabulous. You might want to let her in on that."

Sadie opens the window to the warm day. She can see seagulls wheeling in the sky; she can hear their faint cries. She leans on her elbows and looks down at the street below. She really does feel like a prisoner. But she will honor the agreement she made to stay home and spend time with both her parents. For one thing, last night she had another nightmare, and when she awakened, she was so glad she was at home, in her own bed. She got her rabbit out and held him, though she made sure to hide him again as soon as she woke up.

It's been so long since her family has all been together. And, despite all the yelling and fighting and confusion, it's been kind of interesting. She watches her parents watching each other, and she wonders what they're thinking. Sometimes she sees things that make her understand how they got together: a shared perspective, a similar sense of humor. After all this time, they still finish each other's sentences. They still have inside jokes. "C'est Robespierre," Irene said last night at dinner, and her father burst out laughing, said, "M. Smokes!" and then they both laughed and said together, "There is no tax on Mr. Max!"

"What are you **talking** about?" Sadie asked, but neither of them answered. Finally, her father said, "Nothing," and her mother said, "It was a long time ago."

"**When?**" Sadie said.

"Hey," her father said. "Want to play poker?" So they played poker, and the clock ticked on the wall and the hours went by and it only came up once more that night, had she thought about annulling the marriage? No, she had not. Tick, tock.

After they all went to bed, Sadie called Ron and held the phone under the covers with her. His warm voice. Him. Mostly they talked about mundane things, what each of them had done that day, how his mother and her parents were thawing or not. But there was something new in their talking to each other, now. Sadie had once seen something on the dining room wall of some people she babysat for, a wedding gift they'd received. A piece of what looked like parchment paper on which were these words: **I am my beloved's/And my beloved is mine.** That was what was between them now.

She knows she will never tell her mother about the sweetness of Ron and her finally having sex on their wedding night, of all the quaint things. Everything bad that had happened became a distant, nearly unreal thing; Ron was all she saw. She wishes she could explain to Irene that, when she and Ron made love, she understood the idea of consummation in a way she never had before, the idea of commitment. She lay trembling under him when he entered her, and he kept asking, "Am I hurting you?" his own face full of pain at the thought that he might be. And she kept saying, "No, no, I'm okay," because even though he was hurting her, she wanted that hurt, and she was all right, she was more than all right, she was safe and she was **home**.

Afterward, he held her so tenderly, and she was full of calm. At one point a breeze came through the open window of the funny old hotel where they had stayed that night, it passed over them like a benediction, and it came to Sadie that the only ones who needed to understand how and why they had gotten married were they themselves. And this realization gave her an enormous rush of freedom. She had a thought to tell Ron that she needed to go outside, she needed to stand under the big black sky and the many stars because this room was too small for such a feeling, but she didn't. She rested her chin on top of Ron's head, and measured the rise and fall that corresponded to her breathing, and she let the little room they were in contain her happiness.

She would not tell Irene about that, nor would she ever tell anyone else, not even Meghan, because it belonged to the institution of Ron and her, as would many things to come; she felt she'd lain the first things down in the hope chest, long past hope.

25

At ten o'clock on Thursday morning, Irene is in the kitchen, ironing. She has out the wicker basket in which she keeps her large collection of vintage handkerchiefs, and she is methodically going through the pile. She draws comfort from the scent of warm cotton, the rhythmic creak of the ironing board, the ease of folding the hankies into perfect squares. She enjoys looking at the various designs: the cabbage roses and purple pansies and forget-me-nots; the four-leaf clovers and interlocking hearts and carved pumpkins and Christmas trees; the embroidered initials, the kittens dressed in overalls on the children's hankies. She likes carrying clean and pressed hankies in a sandwich bag in her purse; it has happened more than once that she has come upon someone crying with nary a Kleenex in sight, and it pleases her to offer a hankie on such occasions. Once, a woman in the security line at an airport stood quietly weeping, wiping away her tears with her hands; and she offered profuse thanks when Irene gave her a hankie. But then she began crying much harder. Irene wasn't sure if that was because she so appreciated the gift or because, now that she had a handkerchief, she was really going to let go.

John and Sadie have gone for a walk; Sadie wanted to show John some of her favorite parts of the city, and to have some time alone with him, too, Irene thought. She was glad for it. She knew it was good for the two of them to be together that way, and she relished the oasis of solitude she was granted. But soon after they left, she began feeling terrible. She called to make a lunch date with Valerie; then she dragged out the ironing board.

For years, now, she has ironed handkerchiefs when she is upset. She irons handkerchiefs or she lays the table. The first time Sadie came home from school to find their dining room table set for two—with the good floral china, and the silver, and the little individual salt and pepper shakers—she'd been in third grade. She asked, "Who's coming for dinner?" She and her mother never ate from those dishes; they were strictly for special occasions.

"No one," Irene said.

Sadie moved closer to look at the way Irene had positioned everything just so; she touched the white linen napkins pulled through their mono-grammed silver rings.

"Then why is the table all fancy?" she asked.

Irene leaned against the doorjamb that separated the dining area from the kitchen, wiping her hands on a dish towel. "I just think it looks pretty. Don't you think so?"

Sadie shrugged. "Yeah, I guess."

"Well, that's why," Irene said. "I just like to look at pretty things."

"But . . . you don't think someone is coming, right?" Sadie asked. She spoke slowly, carefully. She ran her finger along the gold edge of a plate, keeping her eyes down. Even then, she understood far too much about her mother's loneliness. Even then, she was taking on a burden she should not have had to bear.

"No, silly!" Irene said. "It's like when you used to have tea parties, remember? Remember how you used to like to set up all the little teacups and saucers?"

"But I was little," Sadie said.

Irene clapped her hands. "Guess what I made you for a snack? Come quick, and wash your hands."

Sadie ate her snack, her half apple decorated with raisins to look like eyes and grated carrots to look like hair, and then she went to her room. Later, she called for her mother to come to her room.

When Irene arrived, she saw that Sadie had found her old tea set and set it up on a quilt on her floor. "Welcome to my party," she said, and Irene took off her apron and sat down. Sadie had made construction paper flowers with pipe cleaner stems, and arranged them in a jelly jar vase. She had made name tags: MOMMY. SADIE. They had water and saltine crackers, which each of them pronounced delicious. And that night, Irene lay in bed weeping, trying hard not to make any noise.

She looks at her watch. Too early to leave for lunch, but she's going to leave anyway. She turns off the iron, unplugs it. She goes out into the hall for her jacket and purse, then back to the kitchen to see if she's turned off and unplugged the iron. She never used to have to do this, check things twice. She worried about her faculties until she confided in Valerie, who said, "Oh, I check things three times. At least! Sometimes I feel like I'm walking around in a circle, over and over, checking things. I feel like that little boy who turned to butter."

"What do you mean?" Irene asked.

"You know," Valerie said. "That boy? With the tigers? Who went around and around in circles under the tree until he turned to butter?"

"Oh!" Irene said. "Yes! But didn't the **tigers** turn to butter?"

Valerie looked at her blankly, and Irene felt immensely better about her own abilities.

Driving to the Huntington Hotel, where Valerie has offered to treat her to lunch, Irene thinks about having left the basket of hankies on the ironing board. She should have put them away. If Sadie and John come back, Sadie might tell her father about the last time her mother hauled those hankies out. Sadie had come into the room when Irene was ironing the Minnesota handkerchief. "She looked so sad," she imagines Sadie saying. "I think she misses Minnesota."

"Does she?" she imagines John saying.

Irene has seventeen state handkerchiefs thus far, all decorated with little motifs representing what the state is famous for: last Christmas, Sadie gave her Iowa and Texas. Irene especially liked the Texas one, the bowlegged cowboys whirling their lassos, the bluebonnets, the oil wells. But most of all she loves the Minnesota one, with its lakes and leaping walleye and North Star.

"Do you ever miss Minnesota?" Irene asked, when Sadie came in that day to grab an apple from the fruit bowl. She fixed her gaze on the iron, moving it slowly back and forth over a handkerchief that was already wrinkle-free.

"I go there twice a year," Sadie said, biting into the apple.

"I know, but do you ever wish you lived there?"

"Do you?" Sadie said. "Is that why you asked me?"

Irene said nothing.

"Mom? Do you miss Minnesota?"

"Not really," she said.

By the time Irene parks the car, she has twenty minutes to kill before she meets Valerie. She sits in the park across from the hotel watching a small group of older Japanese women practicing qigong. It's lovely, a slow-motion kind of ballet, and the faces of the participants are both focused and peaceful. She wonders if she should start classes. Valerie and Ben go, and they keep telling her she should come with them. But Irene is not a joiner. Never has been. Her favorite teacher in elementary school was the one who said Irene could stay in at recess because she didn't like group sports.

Irene closes her eyes and lifts her face to the sun. She tries to imagine herself alongside Valerie and Ben, doing qigong. She thinks it's wonderful that they do the classes together. She envies Valerie everything about her relationship with her husband. They are the model for what she wishes she could have. Valerie and Ben have never stopped having fun, have never lost interest in one another. But their loyalty to each other builds a wall around them. If Irene and Valerie are on the phone when Ben comes home, Valerie gets off. "My man is home; I've got to go," she always says, and there's not nearly enough irony in it to suit Irene. "You don't have to get off the phone just because he comes home!" she said, once. "This isn't 1950!" And Valerie said, "I know I don't have to. I want to."

A shadow blocks the sun, and Irene opens her eyes to see if clouds are rolling in; rain was forecast.

But it's not a cloud, it's Jeffrey Stanton, the man she met on the day she quit work.

"Jeffrey!"

"Irene Marsh! What are you doing here?"

"Meeting a friend for lunch. At the Huntington." She looks at her watch. "In about ten minutes."

He sits on the bench beside her. "Well, we've got a little time. What's new?"

"I'll give you the Cliffs Notes," she says, and fills him in on Sadie's marriage. She has no idea why she's told a man who is little more than a stranger such an intimate thing. It just burst out of her.

He's perfectly calm about it, though. "I guess your work's cut out for you," he says, smiling. And then, "Would you like my opinion?"

"Why not?"

"I think you should have the boy and his parents over. Invite them for dinner or something."

Irene nods. Fat chance. "Ron's father died. He only has a mother."

"Well, invite her," Jeffrey says. "You may not want to, but you know how it goes; if a parent denies something, a kid only wants it more. In the end, maybe you'll just have to accept this."

"I don't **want** to accept this."

Jeffrey says nothing, and, after a moment, she shakes her head and sighs. "I know."

"It's not the **worst** of all possible things," he says.

"I suppose not."

"Hey, you know what? I was going to call you tonight."

She looks at him, shielding her eyes from the sun. "Were you?"

"Yup. I've got tickets to a Giants game next week, right behind home plate. Would you like to go? Dinner will be provided either at the game or afterward, your choice."

"Oh, Jeffrey, I don't know."

"No big deal. I just thought you'd like it."

"I haven't been to a ball game since I was a little girl and I went with my grandpa. I asked him what the priests were doing on the field."

"The priests? . . . Oh! The **umpires**! Well, they do forgive sins."

Next week, Sadie will be gone. John will be gone. It might be fun to go to a ball game.

Jeffrey leans forward. "Throw this into the mix: If we don't eat at the game, I was going to take you to a joint with the **best** meat loaf. You're a retro kind of girl, right? They put relish trays on the table. Celery sticks with cream cheese."

"Sounds great." She imagines sitting there with him, enduring again the stares of younger women wondering why he's with **her.**

He looks at his watch and grimaces. "Uh-oh, gotta go. I'll call you." He kisses her cheek and starts walking away.

"Jeffrey? How about if I call you?"

He turns around. "Aw, Irene. You're not going to go with me, are you?"

She doesn't know what to say.

"I get it," he says. "No worries."

She watches him walk away.

When Irene goes into the restaurant, Valerie is already seated. Irene sits across from her.

"Guess who I just ran into in the park."

"That younger guy who took you out to lunch?"

"How do you know?"

Valerie points to the window they're seated next to.

"Oh."

"What did he say?"

"He kind of asked me out again."

"**That's** nice."

"I'm not going."

"Why not?"

"He's in his early forties!"

"So?"

"So to him, I'm . . . you know."

"No, I don't know. What are you to him?"

"Just . . . I'm not going, okay?" It comes out louder than she meant; the men at the table next to them all turn toward her, then resume eating.

Valerie speaks quietly. "Some men like older women."

"I know. He was married to a much older woman. But . . ."

"But what?"

"It's just not comfortable for me. That's all. I'm not going."

Valerie sighs. "You know I love you, right?"

"Uh-oh."

"Just listen."

Irene folds her hands in her lap.

"You know I love you, but you are one of the most exasperating people I have ever met.

"Honestly. When **are** you comfortable, Irene? You know, when we were in college and we'd get together with a bunch of people, you were always the first one to leave. And you did it so unceremoniously! You'd just all of a sudden leap up and say, 'Well, I have to go,' and **poof!** You'd be gone. We used to talk about that, how you could never just . . . stay."

"You talked about me after I left?"

"Yeah. It was weird how you always did that."

"Well, I **did** have to go."

"Why?"

"Because I had stuff to do."

"Wrong answer."

"I think I know my own answer."

Val looks at her, says nothing.

"I had to leave because I had stuff to **do**, Val."

"Such as . . . ?" Valerie butters a piece of bread, takes a bite. Chews, her eyebrows raised expectantly.

"How should I know? Stuff! I can't remember what all I did. But I had things to do!"

Valerie lays down her bread. "You know what, Irene? I don't think you had so much to do. I think you left because **you just can never stay.**"

"Uh-huh. Well, we've been friends for ten thousand years. I'd call that staying, wouldn't you?"

"Yes. That's a kind of staying. With me, your one really good friend. But do you remember that fight we had when we went to New York together when we were in our thirties? I don't even know what it was about. But we had a fight and then you told me we were done, our friendship was over. I was sitting on the bed in the hotel room crying and you were totally unmoved, you just walked right out the door."

"I came back," Irene says.

"Yes. Because I came out in the hall and literally dragged you back and **made** you stay."

For a long time, Irene says nothing. The women sit there, looking anywhere but at each other.

And then Irene says, "I don't stay because . . . because I don't want to screw things up. I feel if I stay too long, I'll screw things up. Okay?"

"But Irene, don't you know this? When you leave, **that** screws things up. I wish you would . . . I don't know, I wish you would put down your armor and let things in. Let things happen!

"I just got a letter from a man I knew a long

time ago, asking me to do a favor for him, to put him in touch with a mutual friend. I first met this guy when he was fifty. Now he's almost eighty. When I saw his name on the return address I thought, **Wow, it's Ellis Coates, I haven't heard from him for years, for over twenty years!** I opened the letter thinking about how I always kind of liked him, he was handsome in that rugged sort of way, and he could be really funny, too. But he was always wrecking his relationships, one after the other, and he was overly intellectual. Depressed a lot, too. I read his letter with real interest, wondering what all happened to old Ellis, how he might have changed over the years. And he . . . Well, I have it. Listen to this."

Val pulls the letter from her purse and reads aloud: "**I am sitting here in abject misery, wondering whether I should stick my head in the oven or, given my preference for Woolf over Plath, go rock shopping instead. And then who pops into my head but you, someone ever able to lend a sympathetic ear. I have just ended a yearlong relationship with a woman whose neediness finally . . .** Well, there's a bunch of stuff about how this woman just didn't measure up, a bunch of stuff. And here's what he says at the end: **I wish I had better news to share, but you may recall that I have always found it tedious to pretend. I do dare to eat the peach.**"

Val puts the letter back in her purse and sighs. "So. What has changed for Ellis Coates? Nothing. And it was just stunning to me, how he has not changed one bit and I guess he won't, he's **eighty** now. I mean . . . We do get old, Irene. Time passes. And then we're done.

"You know, I used to have this Little Match Girl fantasy that, at the time of our death, we would be carried out of here in the arms of an angel. This really buff angel. And we would be looking back over his shoulder and seeing our whole lives. And I so wanted to be able to say, **What a great ride that was!** And if we do get carried out in the arms of an angel, I **will** be able to say that; I **feel** that. But you . . ."

Valerie reaches up to press her fingers into the corners of her eyes. "Damn it. I don't want to cry. I just want to tell you that I want **you** to feel that way, too, because you're my best friend, you neurotic old crank, and I love you and I can't yank you back into the **room** all the time, you have to yank **yourself** before it's too **late!**"

A waiter glides to their table and refills their water glasses, then glides away.

Irene blinks back her own tears. "Can we not talk about this now? I want to talk about it. Just not now. Let's talk about something else."

"Okay. Okay. Things are better with Sadie, huh?"

"What makes you say that?"

"Because the first thing you said was not about her."

Irene opens the menu.

"It was about that man," Valerie says. "That **quite handsome** man."

"Yeah, let me just decide what I want, here."

"Oh, I already ordered for you."

"How do you know what I want?" She studies the entrées. "I want the pear and blue cheese salad."

"Done," Valerie says.

"Am I that predictable?"

"Sorry." Valerie takes a drink from her frosted glass.

"I do not want Diet Coke, however," Irene says, picking up her glass and looking into it.

"What do you want?"

"Raspberry iced tea."

"Taste it," Valerie says.

Irene takes a drink; it's raspberry iced tea. "You know what my mother used to tell me all the time?"

"What?"

"**You think you're so smart!**"

"So how are things?" Valerie asks. "What's it like living with John again?"

"It's . . . I don't know. I don't know how it is." She looks at Valerie, shrugs.

"Oh, hon," Valerie says.

"What?"

"It's hard, huh?"

"Sometimes it is. But then, at other times, it's kind of wonderful. It was always that way between us, so . . . complicated. So much withheld. It must be nice having a marriage like yours. Open. Even. Safe. You have a perfect marriage."

"Nobody has a perfect marriage."

"You do," Irene says, and leans back in the chair as her and Valerie's salads are set before them.

"Anything else?" the waiter asks.

"Dessert, after," Irene says. "As long as she's paying. Your most expensive chocolate dessert."

They are quiet for a while, eating, each of them lost in thought, and then Valerie says, "I'm going to tell you something, but you must promise me never to tell anyone else."

"What is it?"

Valerie looks around the restaurant, then leans in closer to Irene. "I fell in love with my qigong instructor."

Irene waves her fork. "Everybody does that."

"Everybody does what?"

"Everybody falls in love with their spiritual adviser. Or therapist, or whatever. As a child, I myself fell in love with St. Francis of Assisi. It was the animal attraction. So to speak."

"Yeah, but you didn't sleep with him."

"Well, setting aside the fact that he was dead, what are you saying, Val?"

"I think you know what I'm saying."

"**You slept with your qigong teacher?**"

"Shhhhh!" She looks around again. "Keep it down; someone I know could be here!"

"You slept with your qigong teacher?" Irene whispers.

"Yes!" Valerie whispers back.

"Are you **crazy?**"

"No. I fell in love with him. And I told Ben that. That I'd fallen in love with him, I mean."

"But not that you slept with him?"

She pokes around in her salad. "No. Not yet."

"But you're going to?"

"Well, that's what I have to decide."

"**When?**"

"When do I have to decide, or when did this happen?"

"When did this happen?"

"It started a couple of months ago. I went without Ben to a class, and the instructor, his name is YeeYee, and I—"

"His name is **what?**"

"It's YeeYee, and don't make fun of it! It's just a name, no different than your name, really."

"Oh yes it **is**, uh-**huh**."

"Do you want to know what happened or not?"

"Yes. Tell me every single detail."

"I'm not going to tell you all the details."

"What are you going to tell me?"

"The skeletal outline, I would say."

"Why not the details?"

"Because they're not any of your business."

"I am your best friend, Val."

"Still not any of your business."

Valerie's phone rings. She pulls it from her purse and holds a finger up, answers it. "Hi, Benny. What's up?"

She listens, then says, "Great. I've always wanted to go there. But listen, Irene and I are just finishing lunch. Can I call you back?"

She hangs up. "Ben and I are going to the new fusion place on Green Street tonight."

Irene says nothing.

"Irene?"

Still, she keeps silent.

"What, you're mad at me because I had an affair?"

"I'm mad that you didn't tell me," Irene says. "How come you get to ravage all the clothes in my emotional closet and I don't even get to open your door?"

"That," Valerie says, "is the weirdest and worst metaphor I have ever heard in my entire life, and that includes Fred Peterson's dumb poems about his grandmother's pies that he used to make us listen to."

"Yeah, well, if you'd gotten up and left like me, you wouldn't have had to hear so many of them. Remember this? **Cinnamon me. Sugar me. Make me bake into myself.**"

"Oh, God, I'd forgotten that. Oh, poor Fred."

There is a protracted silence between the two women, and finally Valerie says, "Oh, all right! Here's what happened. I stayed after class to ask a question about a pose. He showed me something which involved his putting his hand near my crotch. And I just . . . I just spun around and kissed him. And he kissed me back. And we . . . Right on the floor."

"On the floor of the studio?"

Valerie nods.

"Wow. The floor. Didn't it hurt?"

"Yes, it did. In lots of ways. I went home afterward and cried so hard I was howling. But I went to his apartment the next day and we did it again. It was . . . Well, don't get mad, but it was the same day you called me over because Don had dumped you. When we drank those martinis. When I left, I took a cab to his place. And that time it was in his bed. He undressed me, and when he saw the lace on my cami, he said, 'Is this lace from Belgium? Are your earrings Tahitian pearls? Because that's what you deserve.' And he touched me with such . . . reverence. And he looked so deeply into my eyes and he . . . just . . . **saw** me."

"Oh, please. You don't think Ben sees you?"

"Ben and I were having trouble at the time. We were in this thing where we were just really having trouble. He was basically ignoring me. And I him. And so the prospect of having such a gentle and romantic and attentive lover was something that was so appealing. Maybe it was a little midlife crisis. I thought, **I just want to try this. I'll probably never have the opportunity to try this again. And it won't hurt anyone.**"

Irene says nothing.

"I know," Valerie says. "I know it hurts everyone. Especially when YeeYee started telling me to leave my marriage."

"That's when you broke it off, right?"

"Nope."

"You're still seeing him?"

"Nope."

"Then . . ."

"He broke it off," Valerie says, the color rising in her cheeks.

"Wow. You got dumped by your qigong instructor?" Irene can't help it; she starts to laugh. "Did you say, **Oh, YeeYee, please don't leave leave me?**"

"Yeah, it's not really so funny, Irene."

"I know it's not. I'm sorry."

The waiter comes over to their table. "Everything delicious here?"

"I'd say so," Irene says.

"Anyway," Valerie says. "This was just to clue you in on the idea of 'perfect marriages.' The truth is, if he hadn't called it off, I would have. Honestly. I was coming to my senses."

"But . . . Why didn't you tell me you and Ben were having such bad trouble?"

"Because you would have told me to leave. And I

would have. You know, sometimes marriage is iron. Sometimes it's tissue paper. And I think the times it's tissue paper are when you need to keep things to yourself. Or you can end up making a mistake that you'll regret forever. Do you know what I mean?"

Irene nods. Yes, she does. Now.

26

Outside, the rain is coming down so hard, John feels as though it might come all the way through the roof and the flat above to soak him. He talks louder into the phone. "You wouldn't believe how hard it's raining here," he tells Amy.

"Is it? It's raining here, too."

"Good for your garden."

"Bad for walking dogs, though."

" . . . You got him?"

"I got him." John can hear the smile in her voice. He's a little miffed; he'd thought she would wait for him to get the dog she'd shown him. But apparently she hadn't understood that he might have liked that. Or hadn't cared. Well, maybe he doesn't even want a dog, even part of one. He's been thinking that there are some advantages to not having pets. You can travel far more easily, that's for sure, and maybe he would like to travel more often, after all. Now that he's getting older. Weren't you supposed to travel more when you got older? Maybe

Irene was onto something when she complained about staying home all the time, all those years ago.

"So . . . did you name him?"

"I did." Another thing John might have wanted to participate in.

"And?"

"His name is Dickens. And I think he's going to be great. Right now, he's . . . Well, he's a puppy."

John hears a key turning in the lock and tells Amy, "I think Sadie just came home."

"Oh, okay, we'll talk later," Amy says, and hangs up before he can say goodbye.

John lies still for a moment, phone in hand, trying to gauge this: Was she angry at him for wanting to talk to the daughter he would be leaving again soon? Was she simply trying to accommodate his need to get off the phone?

"Sadie?" he hears Irene say.

Because it's not Sadie who just came in. As he had known it would not be; Sadie is in her room, learning to use the apps on the new iPhone he bought her. But he hadn't wanted to tell Amy he wanted off the phone because his ex-wife had come home.

He comes out into the hall and sees Irene standing there, dripping wet. Her hair is flattened to her cheeks, her clothes soaked, her purse dripping steadily.

"Hi," he says.

"It's raining," she says, breathlessly.

"Oh? I hadn't noticed."

She laughs and takes off her sodden jacket, hangs it on the coat tree. For a moment she stands there in the little puddle she has made, as if wondering what to do next.

"Want a towel?" John asks.

She nods gratefully.

He goes to the linen closet, searches for the biggest one he can find, and brings it to her. "You know, I've heard that an umbrella comes in handy in situations like this."

"Overrated," Irene says. "It's kind of fun getting this wet."

Her eyes are sparkling. She's happy. It's the first time he's seen her this way since he arrived. She towels off her hair, starts in on her neck, her arms. "You're going to need another towel," he says, and goes to get one.

He starts to hand it to her but instead bends down and begins drying her legs himself.

"John," she says quietly, taking the towel from him.

He steps back, leans against the wall, crosses his arms.

"Where's Sadie?" Irene asks.

"In her room, in apps heaven, I imagine. I got her an iPhone."

"We need to talk."

"I was going to get her one anyway. For when she starts school. Now I don't have to mail it. Is that all **right** with you?"

She looks sharply at him. "What's wrong with you?" She keeps her voice low, so Sadie can't hear, gestures toward the kitchen, and he follows her there.

"What are you so pissed off about?" she asks after they've gone through the swinging door.

He doesn't know. Because she looks so pretty all wet. Because he has to leave his daughter again. Because Amy bought a dog without him. "I thought you were mad at me for buying her a phone."

"She **needed** one. I'm **glad** you got her one. I think it's **nice**."

"So . . . what do we need to talk about, then?"

She points to the banquette. "Want to sit down?"

"Nah, it's okay."

She sits, and looks up at him. "I've decided to ask Ron and his mom to dinner tomorrow night. I wanted to know if you thought it was a good idea."

"Yeah, I think it is a good idea. Is that all?"

"Will you sit **down**?"

He shrugs. "What? It's a good idea. What do you want me to say?"

"Fine. We won't talk about it."

"Irene. You asked me about something; I said it was a good idea; why do we now have to talk about it? What's there to talk about? I mean, **after** the dinner, I'm sure there'll be something to talk about. Unless you want to consult with me on the menu. Which would certainly be a first."

"Okay, John. I am now going to tell you something you've heard from me a million times. I cannot **talk** to you. Why **is** that?"

"Because you have to make everything so complicated, Irene!"

"Well, **forgive** me, but I think our eighteen-year-old daughter having gotten **married** after a **traumatic experience** does have its complicated aspects. And perhaps may be a subject that's worth devoting some **discussion** to, whether we focus on the fact that she refuses **therapy,** or that the boy she married will soon be sitting at our table with his **mother** and we haven't a clue what we might **say** as a show of—"

"I'm going for a walk," he says.

He grabs an umbrella from the stand and heads out into the street. He'll take the bus downtown and back. He'll ride around, look at some buildings.

After he reaches the corner, a bus comes almost immediately. John settles into an empty seat at the back and looks out the window. He thinks about last night, when he couldn't sleep and went into the kitchen for a glass of water. He was as quiet as he could be, hoping he wouldn't wake Irene. Tiptoeing past on his way back to the bedroom, he heard her whisper his name.

"Did I wake you?" he said. "I'm sorry."

"I was awake. I never sleep anymore."

"Yeah you do."

"I know, but not like before."

He moved over to the sofa, sat on the floor with his back to it. He could feel Irene watching him, and, after a moment's consideration, he moved his hand back toward her and she took hold of it.

"I feel so bad," she whispered.

"Just remember," he said. "It could have been so much worse. What if that lunatic had—"

"I know, don't say it. Don't even say it. But she got **married**. And it's just not right. It won't work, I know it won't. And then she'll have to get divorced."

"To say nothing of the possibility that she'll get pregnant," John said.

"I keep thinking she **is** pregnant. I asked her, and she got all huffy and said no."

"I asked her, too. Same reaction. Only she added, 'Some people marry for love. You should try it sometime.'"

"She said that?"

"Yeah." He started to turn around and look at her, then didn't. This was nice, the way they were talking to each other. Better not rock the boat.

"They don't even know each other," Irene said.

"I told her that, too."

"I mean, we at least knew each other very well."

Now he does turn around. "Do you think so, Irene?"

"Yes! Don't you? We knew each other. We still do know each other."

"What's my favorite color?" John asked.

She laughed.

"No, what is it?"

"It's . . . Is it blue?"

"It's green."

"Well, okay. Sorry. But what does that prove? I mean, what's my favorite color?"

"Your favorite color? You say it's red. But it's actually turquoise."

"No, John, it's **red**."

"So how come you never buy red clothes or red things or wear red lipstick or even eat red food?"

"I eat beets. I love beets."

"Look at all the dishes you bought that were turquoise: all the bowls and plates and platters. Look at your jewelry. Look at your artwork, your clothes. Your favorite color seems to be turquoise, Irene."

She lay flat again. "This is stupid. Let's talk about something else."

"Hey, I have an idea! Let's talk about Sadie."

"Yeah, let's do."

Silence, and then, "John? I have to ask you something. Do you think this is my fault?"

"What, her getting married?"

"Yes."

"Well, if that's true, it's both of our faults."

"I'm the one who raised her," Irene said.

"I had her, too, for the first eight years of her life," John said. "And I'm involved with her now. I don't see her every day, but we talk a lot."

"I know. She likes you better. She always did. I shouldn't have taken her from you. I should have let you raise her."

"You know what, Irene? I look at Sadie, and I think you should take a bow. I mean it." He kissed her hand, intending for it to be the only affectionate physical gesture he might offer, intending it to be friendly and not intimate, but it moved deep inside him, the touch of her skin against his mouth. He stood. "I'm going to sleep."

For a long time, in a silence sparked by possibility, she said nothing. And then she murmured something that sounded like **okay**, and turned away from him. He went to the bedroom and lay on top of the covers, wide awake. He looked at the outline of perfume bottles on her dresser, at her hairbrush lying there, next to an ornately engraved silver mirror her grandmother had given her for her tenth birthday, which her mother wanted to take away from her, saying it was inappropriate for a child so young. But her grandmother insisted that Irene would appreciate it, which she did, and apparently still does. He went to the dresser and picked up the brush. It was heavy in his hand, cool to the touch. He wondered what Irene thought about when she brushed her hair; it was still thick and really quite beautiful. Still a deep auburn, though apparently she had some help in that regard. He had noticed more and more silver showing up in his own hair. But you didn't see him trying to hide it.

He put down the brush, looked at himself in the mirror. He straightened his pajama top, hiked up his bottoms. Then he came back out into the living room. She was sleeping, now. He sat in a chair and watched her. He looked at the curve of her hip and the spread of her hair across the pillow, and he thought of other times he had done this, stood watching the rise and fall of her chest, trying sometimes to interpret the movements in her face caused by fleeting thoughts or dreams. He thought of the night he brought her home from the hospital after Sadie was born, how deeply she slept then; he couldn't rouse her to eat, but her eyes would fly open at the faintest whimper from her child. He thought of a time they'd had a pretty spectacular night of sex, and she'd fallen asleep in her getup as she called it, a red, lacy nightgown he'd seen on a mannequin and brought home to her on Valentine's Day. She didn't like to fall asleep with it on; she feared Sadie seeing her in it. Most often, she would change back into her usual sleepwear: one of his T-shirts and a pair of her flannel pajama bottoms. The other day, he'd seen one of those T-shirts in the laundry basket and he'd been glad for it.

He thought about going to watch Sadie sleep, but there was only so much a man could take in. Or bear.

"End of the line!" the bus driver says.

Indeed.

John sits still for a moment, lost in regret, and then sees that the driver is checking him out in the rearview, trying to see if he's okay.

John stands quickly and holds up a hand. "Thanks!" he says, and goes onto the street. The sun is out now, the city brilliant in the light, and his heart lifts in spite of himself. Give the city its due: it actually is a dazzling place. He'll walk around, see what's for sale. Just for fun. Just for the relief of putting business in his brain.

27

For some time, Irene sits at the kitchen table, thinking. Oil and water, she and John seem to be, even now. She doesn't know why.

She makes a cup of tea and nurses the idle hope that Sadie will hear the noise and come into the kitchen, seeking out her company. She doesn't, of course. She stays in her room. And why not, when the pattern has been that all Irene does is try to talk her out of something she's fiercely committed to? Irene was convinced that Sadie had been—possibly was still—in shock, that she had (again, **understandably**) rushed to the illusion of safety that her boyfriend and marriage represented. But now she was home! She was safe! She could take in a breath, reassess the situation. Surely she could see that she had made a mistake.

But now Irene wonders if the person in shock isn't herself, if her own ability to reason and perceive isn't hampered by a maelstrom of feelings, by her sense that she's not quite in her own body, not able to employ any kind of rational thought. In the end, her daughter, her healthy and intelligent and strong daughter, is eighteen, and she's gotten married. Is that the end of the world?

She finishes her tea, washes out her cup, and on the way to Sadie's room decides to offer her daughter the gift of truly listening. Sadie knows how Irene has felt about this marriage; she seems to understand the reasons for all her mother's objections. But maybe Irene doesn't really understand how Sadie feels.

On the way home, Irene thought that, of all the terrible fates that can befall one's child, getting married too young didn't even register. John has helped her to see that. Never mind that the two of them can't seem to find a place of lasting comfort; he does help her gain perspective when it comes to their daughter. He has always done that. Damn it; she **likes** him, why can't they get along?

She knocks on Sadie's door.

"Yes."

"It's me. Can I come in?"

"Yeah!"

Okay, Irene thinks. **She's in a good mood. Don't blow it.**

When she opens the door, Sadie is sitting cross-legged on her bed, making a list. "What are you doing?" Irene asks.

Sadie puts the list aside, covers it with a magazine. "Just trying to think of things we'll need."

"Can I see?"

Sadie hesitates, then hands her mother the list. **Dishware,** Irene reads. **Cheap vacuum. Dresser (use crates?). Mattress. Two lamps.**

Irene's eyes fill, and she puts down the list and reaches for her daughter. Sadie is stiff at first, and then she is not. She hugs her mother back, then pulls away to sit expectantly before her.

"When we first got married," Irene tells Sadie, "we got so many presents. A lot of fancy stuff that I had no use for, really: Silver trays, fancy cutlery. Cheese boards and fondue pots. Ice tongs, for Pete's sake! But you know what I did like? I liked the little juice glasses with oranges on them. They were the kind of thing you could get at the dime store for next to nothing, and I just loved them. I used to set the table at night for breakfast the next morning. Two coffee cups, two plates, two forks, knives, and spoons. I'd fold the paper napkins into triangles, and stick them in the tines of the forks, very fancy, you know."

Sadie smiles.

"Someone gave us an electric coffeepot, and I would set that up, too, put in the grounds and the water the night before, and then leave it on the table ready to be plugged in, so convenient for when you wanted another cup! I thought we'd sit there every morning like Ward and June Cleaver."

Sadie's smile fades. "Didn't you?"

Irene shrugs. "Not so much. We hardly ever had breakfast together until you came along."

"Why not?"

"Well, mostly because your father didn't like to eat breakfast."

"He does now."

"Well, he didn't then." Her voice has gotten thin, edgy.

"I believe you, Mom."

"I'm sorry. I just . . .

"Okay. Let me see if I can say this. I think what's bothering me most about your being married is that I'm scared for you, Sadie. That's all. I want you to be happy in a marriage, and marriage is just so hard."

Sadie studies her mother's face. "Why? Why do you think it's so hard?"

Irene looks across the room and out the window, where the sky has cleared and a redemptive ray of sunlight brings out subtle pastel colors in glass that is normally clear. She can smell the scent of after-rain, that hopeful mix of concrete and water and leaves and fresher air. She wishes, suddenly, that she were sitting on a bench outside alone, nothing on her mind but a jostling mass of birds at her feet, going after the crumbs she throws. Because Sadie's question is too big, it's too difficult to answer.

Finally, she says, "Here's an example. Your dad and I had been married about two weeks when I came home from work late—I used to do that now and then, stay late and catch up on paperwork. And after I left the hospital, I'd gone to get these smoked sausages that I liked. I was really hungry, and I wanted to cook up some of those sausages when I got home. Your dad was sleeping and I tried to be really quiet, but he came into the kitchen and said, 'What are you **doing**, Irene?' I still remember exactly how he said it. He was so pissed off, standing there squinting in the light. And I told him I was making sausages, I was hungry. He said, 'It's ten-thirty!' and I said, 'Oh, okay. I'll just tell my hunger that you said that.' And he went back to bed, and I just stood there thinking, **I can't cook sausages late at night anymore.** And indeed, I never did again."

"Mom," Sadie says. "Can I speak honestly?"

"Yes. Please."

"So what?"

"Okay," Irene says. "I know that's kind of a stupid story, but I only mean that once you get married, you—"

"First of all, you could have told Dad to go to hell. In a nice way. You could have said, 'You know, once in a while I'm going to need to eat late, so get used to it.'"

With some difficulty, Irene holds her tongue.

"Or you could have decided that, since he had to get up early, you'd eat out when you wanted to eat late at night."

"But I wanted to come home and eat," Irene says.

"And Dad wanted to sleep. Jesus, Mom."

"Please don't talk that way to me."

Sadie looks at Irene, shaking her head. "We are not at all alike," she says, finally.

Irene says nothing. It hurts to hear her daughter say this, with such superiority, with such evident relief.

"So . . . Did you want something?" Sadie asks. "I mean, when you first came in here?"

"Yes. I wanted to ask you to invite Ron and his mother to dinner tomorrow night."

"Really?"

"Yes."

"Really."

"Yes!" Though now she is not so sure anymore.

"What time?" Sadie asks.

"Seven."

"Okay," Sadie says, happily. "I'll ask."

Irene looks around the room. Sadie has made a pile of things to be thrown away. In it is a Barbie doll, lying so her legs are splayed at a ridiculous angle. "Throwing away your dolls?"

"Well, I thought I'd donate them somewhere. Although they might not want that one on top. I gave her a haircut. Didn't turn out too well."

Irene smiles. "I did that once. I cut my Ginny doll's hair, and it looked awful. I tried to glue it back, and then it looked even worse. I was going to throw her away, but I thought it was unfair. So I buried her. I gave a funeral, and all the neighborhood kids came. We had cookies and cherry Kool-

Aid afterward." She smiles at Sadie. "Huh. My first catering experience."

She goes over to pick up the doll, straightens her legs. Then she holds it up to face Sadie and speaks for it in a high voice. "Hey, Sadie!"

Nothing.

Irene puts the doll back in the pile. Nothing works anymore. Nothing.

She stands. "Sadie? I can help you with household things. I have a lot I can give you."

"Thanks."

"And also, I want to say that . . . Well, I'm almost there."

"Okay."

"But if you could just tell me one thing," Irene says, coming to sit on the bed beside her daughter. "Right before you took your vows, right before you said 'I do,' was there any hesitation? Did you feel any ambivalence at all?"

"No, that was you," Sadie says, looking directly into her mother's eyes.

So it was.

"All right. I'm going tell you something," Irene says.

Sadie waits, wary.

"I had a friend in high school who got married when she was seventeen, the day after graduation. Lisa Weltner. I still hear from her every now and then. I think she has the happiest marriage I've ever seen. So I just want to say, I know you can get married young and have it be successful. There. There's your first wedding gift from me."

"Thanks, Mom. Seriously."

"Although I must also tell you the guy she married was five years **older.** Five years makes such a difference at this time in your life." She looks at Sadie. "I mean, you'll grant me that, right?"

Sadie leans back so violently she bumps her head hard against the bed frame.

"Are you all right?" Irene asks, automatically.

"How come you can't give with both hands, Mom? How come you have to give with one and take away with the other?"

"I'm only trying to suggest that you haven't acknowledged that so much of this is . . . Sadie, I believe you care for Ron. I believe you love him. But what you're undertaking is so much harder than you know. Not because you're so young. **Nobody** knows how hard it's going to be until they're in the middle of it, no matter what age they are when they get married! But by entering into this so young, you're just handicapping yourself further. Couldn't you have waited a couple of years to get married? Couldn't you have trusted that everything would last that long? What are you so afraid of that you had to get married so soon?"

"What were you and Dad so afraid of that you had to wait so long?"

Irene sighs.

"I need to be alone, now," Sadie says. "Please."

Before Irene goes out the door, Sadie says, "So . . . is dinner still on?"

"Yes," Irene says, but she thinks her daughter probably knows something about what she is feeling. Which is that she wishes she could rescind the invitation. She's not ready after all. Even if she wants to be, she's not.

"Can Meghan come?"

Irene turns around. "Sadie. Sadie. One of the reasons I'm struggling with this is that you seem to think this is . . . This isn't fun. This isn't a **lark**. This is serious. My inviting these people to dinner because—"

"**These people** are my husband and my mother-in-law. And the only reason I'm not living with them right now is because Ron wants me to try to get things right with you before we find our own place."

Irene ignores this, which is a little like ignoring a knife in your side. She speaks calmly. "Inviting Ron and his mother to dinner is not so much a social event as it is—"

"An inquisition?"

Irene looks at the thin band of gold Sadie is wearing on her left hand. Sadie told her she and Ron picked it out at a pawnshop. She thinks of a friend of hers, whose daughter recently got a two-carat diamond and was planning a wedding that would cost over one hundred and fifty thousand dollars. Irene thought it was gross. She remembers thinking, **I hope when Sadie gets married, she keeps it simple.**

"I'm trying to meet you in the middle, Sadie. I really am."

Sadie nods. "Yeah. When's Dad coming back?"

"I have no idea."

Irene closes her daughter's door, goes into her bedroom, which at the moment is not even her bedroom, and closes that door, too. She sits at the edge of her bed, stares into her lap.

Fine. Let her go. Good riddance. She sees John's sneakers by the bed, and she picks up one and flings it at the closet door. **When's Dad coming back?** She picks up the other shoe and throws that one, too.

From Sadie's room come the muffled sounds of her talking. Telling someone about her nutty mother, no doubt. Good riddance.

28

"Okay, so we'll be there at seven tomorrow night," Ron says. "My mom wants to know what we should bring."

"Peace," Sadie says.

She hangs up the phone, leans back against her headboard, and listens to see if there are any more sounds coming from her mother's bedroom. No. It's quiet now. Sadie looks at her watch: seven-thirty. When **is** her dad coming home?

Irene just can't settle down. Sadie can't have practical conversations with her mother the way she can with her dad; she can hardly talk to her at all. For instance, she'd told her father that she and Ron had decided he would pay the first few months' rent on whatever apartment they found; she would buy the necessities from the money she'd been saving for dorm extras. After that, they'd split everything. They'd both be in school starting in September, but they'd each have a part-time job. In fact, Sadie had already secured hers; as soon as she got into Berkeley, she went to student employment and got a job for the fall in a research lab, where she'd be cleaning out the cages used for white mice. Ron will find something half-time at night, he's said. And Ron's mother has agreed to help them with groceries if they need it. They'll get by. "You might need a little help with cash," her father had said. "When you need it, let me know." She could see the struggle in his face, the way he wanted to tell her that this life was not what he wanted for her, but he made way for what **she** wanted; he respected her.

But her mother. At first, hoping for the best, Sadie had tried to explain to Irene what it was that made Ron so special to her, right from the beginning. She did not say that she hadn't introduced him to her because she was afraid Irene would ruin everything; she said she hadn't introduced him because she wanted to be sure that her own feelings were real. And then, more quickly and certainly in a far different way than she'd ever imagined, she'd seen that they were. She actually took her mother's hand and moved closer to her when she said this, when she tried to explain that the horrible thing that had happened to her was not the reason she wanted to get married but that it had served as a kind of catalyst for something that seemed destined to happen anyway. The moment hung in the air, Sadie's chest ached with longing for her mother to understand, but then Irene pulled her hand away. "Uh-**huh**," she said.

Sadie heard the disbelief, the condescension in her mother's voice. As she later told Meghan, a deaf person would have heard it. She thought, **That's the last time I'll confide in you.**

But then what had she expected from a woman whose "wedding album" served only to parody the institution? Once, a few years after her parents' divorce, Irene was cleaning out a bedroom closet when Sadie came into the room. It was a hot summer day; Sadie had been outside playing with friends and wanted to come in for the relief of some air-conditioning. On the floor of her mother's bedroom, on top of a pile of dresses and skirts, was a thin white leather album, silver script across the front saying, **Wedding Memories.** With Irene buried in the closet, continuing to toss out clothes and shoes, Sadie flipped through the pages. On the first page, written in pencil, was the name of "The Bride," **Irene Alexandra Dunsmore**, and "The Groom," **John Robert Marsh.** Next came a copy of **Our Wedding Invitation**, which was quite pretty, a ring of flowers encircling elegant gold typeface. The next page held the signatures (in ink, Sadie noticed) of guests who had attended the wedding. After that, there were pages that were meant to hold photos. But in the one labeled **Our Wedding Cake**, there was a picture of a Hostess cupcake. On the page for **Our Bridesmaids**, there was a picture of three ancient women sitting on a park bench, all with canes, all with stern faces. Later,

Sadie would come to know that the picture had been torn out of a magazine. But then, at eleven years old, she was simply confused. **My Gown** featured another page from a magazine, a redheaded, sultry woman wearing gold lamé pants and a polka-dot halter top. At the point when Sadie reached that page, Irene backed out of the closet. "Whew!" she said, smiling over at her daughter. But when she saw the wedding album in Sadie's hands, she snatched it away.

"What **is** that?" Sadie asked.

Irene said, "Nothing. It was just a joke."

"Where is your real album?" Sadie asked. She had seen other wedding albums, big fat ones; some of her friends' parents had them within easy reach, or displayed them with pride on their coffee tables.

"We didn't have one," Irene said.

"Why not?"

"Because they're just silly," Irene said, and Sadie heard some anger in her mother's tone. So she got a drink of water and went back outside. She never saw the album again; she assumes her mother threw it out that day.

Sadie lies down on her bed, rests her pillow over her stomach. She used to love her mother so much. Maybe it was too much. Maybe she should have allowed herself some righteous anger at Irene for taking her away from a father she adored, for being moved somewhere so far off, meaning she rarely got to see him. Maybe she should have had some screaming knockdowns with Irene about how she never got a vote and she was plenty pissed about it. All the things her father had missed! The school plays and concerts, the athletic events in which Sadie had performed so well, the teacher conferences, the countless nights he was not there to lie on her floor and philosophize with her. But she had never confronted her mother about all she had missed with her father. It lived hidden within Sadie, that anger; it did not announce itself even to her except as a vague ache that came and went, came and went. It behaved itself. It did not give in to itself. Until now. Now something is uncoiling.

Sadie thinks that she kept so many things from her mother because she saw herself as the stronger of the two, and so she put up with Irene's neediness. Her oddness. For example, the way she came in on her mother standing nude before Valerie that day. What does someone do in the face of behavior like that? What does someone do with a mother so removed from self-knowledge that she won't even admit to her own loneliness? Irene acts as though she wants to have a long-lasting relationship, but then all she does is sabotage herself, one way or another.

Her mother would be the first to deny this, of course. "**What?**" Sadie imagines Irene saying, if ever Sadie offered this observation. "I'm trying! Are you kidding me? Can't you see that I'm trying?" But to Sadie's way of thinking, she's not trying at all. The space and time that Irene is saying Sadie needs? That's what her mother needs for herself. She needs to stop plugging the hole and find out what's causing the leak in the first place. Instead, she goes from one stupid relationship to the next, never really investing herself and then saying it was the man's fault she didn't. Sadie has borne witness to this all her life. Ron was right when he suggested that her mother has taught her well what a good marriage partner must be—not like Irene.

Sadie looks around at her room. She remembers various incarnations of it; how once she had a bright yellow table and chair beneath her window where she sat to teach school to her stuffed-animal pupils. She used to have flowery curtains that Irene made for her, and for which she herself had selected the ribbon for tiebacks. She remembers how Irene redecorated her room for her thirteenth birthday while she was in school, giving her the bright red beanbag chair she wanted, as well as a much bigger dresser, a computer desk, and a framed poster of Michael Jackson.

Oh, and she remembers Irene sleeping on the floor beside her bed when a flu virus that Sadie caught took a worrisome turn. She remembers feeling bad about her first junior high breakup, telling her mother, "David doesn't like me anymore. I didn't do anything. He just doesn't like me anymore." Irene, seemingly more distraught than she, all but wrung her hands, saying, "I'm so sorry, I know this hurts, but believe me, there will be another boyfriend." And when Sadie said, "When?" Irene went out on a limb and said, "Three weeks," and she was right, in part because Sadie, having heard what she interpreted as a directive, made it happen. That was when her attitude was that one boy was pretty much the same as another. That was before she met Ron and, through him, a new self.

When she called Ron, he was with his mother, looking at an apartment in Berkeley that a friend of hers was renting out. "I think it will be perfect for us," he said. "If you like it, we'll take it. She'll give us a really good deal, four hundred dollars a month, and it's on Hillegass Avenue, really pretty. We'll be able to walk to classes."

"Go ahead and rent it," Sadie said

"But you haven't even seen it!"

"I know. Surprise me. Again."

"Ma!" she heard him say. "Sadie's parents would like us to come for dinner tomorrow night at seven. Okay with you?"

Sadie could hear his mother's response: "Of course! Naturally!" She sounded like such a happy person, grounded and at home in her own skin. Ron has told Sadie that his mother is someone who is able to navigate a life lived alone; she doesn't seek out the company of men. She goes out occasionally, but mostly she is content being by herself.

Recalling that, Sadie feels a sudden rush of protectiveness toward her own mother, and this both surprises and gladdens her. She puts her hand up on the wall that separates them and spreads her fingers wide. "Mom," she says, so quietly she's not sure she's really spoken.

29

On Friday evening, Irene adds a thin stream of olive oil to the salad dressing she's making, whisking it in perhaps a little too vigorously. Dinner is half an hour away, and she's nervous. And she's still hurt, still angry, still confused. She feels like a marble on a moving floor; she just can't get positioned and **stay** there. So she's taking it out on extra-virgin olive oil and fig-flavored vinegar. "**Never** buy flavored vinegars," Henry told her, not long ago. "Buy a good **plain** vinegar and then **add** the flavor using **fresh ingredients**." That day after work, she'd stopped and bought three flavored vinegars including this one, which she thinks tastes just fine. Also three flavored oils, which she found less tasty.

While Irene finishes meal preparation, John sits at the banquette, drinking wine. He'd poured a glass for each of them, but Irene's wine is as yet untouched. She's not sure she should drink anything. She fears the volatility of her emotions. She could cry or yell or otherwise embarrass herself. She's never been much of a drinker, and tonight is not the night to experiment.

"He's not even that good-looking," Irene says and whacks a clove of garlic with the side of her knife. She whispers this, though Sadie is in the shower and wouldn't hear her if she spoke normally.

John shrugs. "I don't know." He's barefoot, fresh from the shower himself. He looks good; he went out today to buy a few clothes. He hadn't packed much, hadn't cared to even think about what he might want to wear at the time he left. But now he sits in a nice blue-and-white-striped shirt Irene ironed for him, and she thinks he looks handsome, though she supposes now is not the time to tell him. She'd just finished ironing the napkins she'll use tonight when John came home, and so she offered to iron a shirt for him—the board was set up, the iron still hot. "Give it here," she said, holding out her hand. There was the briefest hesitation before he accepted, as though this would be too intimate an act for her to perform for him. And there is a kind of intimacy in ironing a man's shirt, smoothing your hands across the collar, along the sleeves, over the back. Handy as John is, he has never learned to properly iron a shirt. So he gave her the blue and white one.

"Did you buy any others?" she asked.

"I did, but I don't think I'll be needing them. I'll

be going home on Sunday; I'll get them ironed there. You know."

"Oh," Irene said. "Okay." She bent her head to navigating the small spaces between the buttons.

"Think I'll go and talk to Sadie," he said, and left the kitchen.

Good, Irene thought. For suddenly she was cavernously miserable, very close to tears, and she didn't want John to see.

Now she adds the garlic to the dressing, whisks again.

"Do **you** think Ron's good-looking?" she asks John.

"I suppose."

"Well, I don't."

"I don't think it matters, Irene. I mean, do you, really?"

She puts down the knife, grabs her glass of wine, and comes to sit opposite him. "No. It doesn't matter how he looks. I'm just . . . I know it doesn't matter how he looks. It matters how he is. If he were her boyfriend, I'd really like him. As her husband, I just want to kill him."

"Well. You want him to go away."

"I want them not to be married."

"Yet they are. And apparently they're going to stay married."

Irene shakes her head. "I wish we could get her to see a therapist, just once. She'd believe a therapist who told her that all this is just a way to distract herself from what happened to her."

"Maybe," John says. "But what accounts for the guy wanting to get married so young?"

"Exactly," Irene says. "See? I've wondered about the same thing. He needs to see a therapist, too. There's something really wrong with him. Why would he want to get married? Why wouldn't he want to date a million girls?"

"Maybe he doesn't care about all that."

"He's eighteen! Why wouldn't he care about all that? When you're eighteen, **all that** is all there is!"

"Not for everyone," John says. "Not for me. When I was eighteen, I really wanted to be married, too."

Irene snorts. "You did not."

"In fact, Irene, I did."

She feels her mouth drop open, her eyes open wide: a sitcom reflex. "You were thirty-six years old when you got married! For the first time!"

"Because I was **scared**, Irene. I was **scared**. It **mattered** too much to me!"

"But you . . . You never told me that!"

"Look," he says. "Maybe we should just . . . I don't know, step back. See what unfolds. Let's meet his mother. Let's see what we think of him after we spend some time with him."

"Yeah, well, he could be a prince and I still wouldn't think she should be **married** to him."

"I know."

The timer goes off, and Irene pushes herself out of the banquette and dons her oven gloves. "So, fine. We're agreed then." She slides the pan of eggplant lasagna out, checks her watch. "This has to sit for a good fifteen minutes."

"Irene?"

"Yeah?"

"What are we agreed to?"

"What?"

"You said, 'We're agreed then.' What are we agreed to?"

She stares at him. "To get her unmarried."

"Ah," John says, and then, "We can't do that. She has to do that."

"But I don't think she will!"

"Then she won't."

"John, she's eighteen years old!"

He shrugs. "Exactly."

His phone rings, and he pulls it out of his pocket to check caller ID. He says to Irene, "Sorry; I'll be really quick, but I've got to take this."

He tells the caller, "Can you hold on a second? I'll be right there." He listens to something while he's sliding out of the banquette, then laughs. "Are you kidding? Of course!" His voice is warm, affectionate, flirtatious.

A woman, then, Irene thinks.

He goes down the hall, into Irene's bedroom, and closes the door. Irene rips lettuce and flings it into a bowl. After that she wipes her hands on her apron and stares out the window to the street below. Not one soul.

She centers a red pepper on the cutting board, and when the doorbell rings, she jumps so hard she nearly slices a finger off. But she doesn't. She lays down the knife, takes a deep breath, and goes to the door to let them in.

30

John sits in one of the living room chairs by the window and rubs his neck, arches his back. He's tired, but he's invigorated, too; for the first time since he got the call from Irene saying Sadie was missing, he thinks things are going to be just fine.

He'd liked Ron when they first met in spite of himself; he likes him even more now. He's an old soul, as is Sadie. John trusts him. He trusts Sadie, too. And Ron's mother is an absolute delight: direct, positive, clear, wise. She's French, named Huguette, and she still carries a trace of an accent. She uses phrases both charming and amusing: "yesterday night" for "last night," for example. "Easy as cake." About a certain restaurant that came up, "About that one I am luck warm."

Her carriage is that of a dancer: shoulders back, spine straight, and every movement full of grace. She wore a simple white blouse with a stand-up collar, a long black skirt, and a blood red shawl, and she looked like a million bucks. Her hair is long, still dark, and she wore it in a style his mother used to favor: a French twist, or at least that's what it was called then. She wore a single wide gold bracelet, gold knot earrings.

Irene said almost nothing to her at first, with the exception of thanking her relatively sincerely for a lovely bouquet and a very nice bottle of red wine, but eventually she warmed up. She appeared to be moved by Huguette's story of how she and her husband had themselves gotten married so young. John believed Huguette when she said that sometimes age really is just a number, not only for older people but for the young. "They know what they're doing," she said, looking over at Sadie and Ron. "They will be happy together, these two." John felt a lifting inside, a pride; he looked over at his beautiful daughter and for the first time thought, **It's okay, everything will work out.** It felt good to know that another adult, one whose investment in the situation was identical to his and Irene's, was so confident and approving. And Sadie saw his relief; she beamed at him from across the table, and he beamed right back.

He sits in the chair full of contentment, of relief.

Irene, however, is lying on the pulled-out sofa bed with one arm across her eyes, mute. After their dinner guests left, Sadie went with them. They were going to take Ron's mother home, then spend a little time alone. Sadie promised to come home soon afterward; she seems suddenly to have traded in anger and frustration over her self-described imprisonment for a kind of bemused affection. On Sunday, she and Ron will move into their apartment.

"Well, that's just it, then," Irene says, finally. She sits up at the side of the bed and looks over at John.

"I think it is," he says.

She sighs, fiddles with something on the waistband of her skirt, then untucks her blouse. Her still-long hair falls over her face while she does this, and she looks lovely to him: a barefoot, middle-aged woman, bathed in yellow lamplight, her hair free, her blouse loose around her hips. It reminds him of an earlier version of Irene, an earthy woman who displayed a kind of forthrightness that at first delighted him. Later, he grew weary of it, but that was when he'd grown weary of a lot of things about Irene, and he supposed he lumped all her characteristics together, both positive and negative.

He feels sorry for her; she's the one remaining holdout in all of this now, the only one who can't make the leap of faith everyone else has agreed to do.

"John?" she says.

"Yeah?"

"Do you think there's a group for parents with children who marry too young?"

"Probably. There's a group for everything else. And those groups really help people."

"How do you know? You've never gone to any of those groups."

"Oh, but I have," he says, laughing, and then immediately regrets it, because here comes the next question, which he is not sure he's ready to answer.

"What group?" Irene says.

"Huh?"

"What group?"

And so he tells her about the group he went to and then, because he feels he has to, about Amy. How they met there, how they've been seeing each other a little bit. A lot, actually. Quite a lot.

"Ah," she says, nodding, when he's finished telling the story. "So she's the one who's been calling."

"She's one of the people. I mean, I've been talking to a lot of people about the project I'm doing next. Kind of a cool idea. I want to turn this building on Wabasha into a residential hotel. It'll have—"

"She's the woman who called when I was making dinner."

"Oh. Yeah. This evening? Right, that was Amy, yup. She reminds me of you, actually. Little bit."

Irene nods. "Well, I guess I'll go to bed, so . . ."

So get the hell out.

"Irene."

She looks at him, overly wide-eyed. "What?"

"I'm sorry. I didn't mean to do that."

"What, tell me you're seeing someone? Why shouldn't you tell me you're seeing someone? I'd expect that you were. I see people. I'm seeing someone, too."

"Are you?"

"Yes."

"Nice guy?"

She reaches over to straighten a pile of books on the table next to the sofa. "Yes, he's nice. **Very** nice." She smiles at this last, a private thing between her and herself, and John is a bit unnerved. "He's way too young for me, though. In his early forties."

"Yeah, that's . . . That is too young for you."

"Well, I'm not going to marry him! He's just fun to . . . have fun with. You know?"

John tries to imagine who this guy might be: what he looks like, what he does. But he won't lower himself to ask. It's none of his business, anyway. But early forties!

"Has Sadie met this guy?"

"No, not yet. Soon, though."

It occurs to John to say, "So why hasn't he been calling you?" But he won't say that. For one thing, it's possible that she'll say, "Oh, we **text.**"

"Are you and Amy getting married?" Irene asks.

John's hand flies to his chest. "Me?"

"Yeah."

"Am I getting **married**?"

"Oh, my God," Irene says. "You are. Well, congratulations."

"I didn't say I'm getting married!"

"No, but you're thinking about it. Aren't you?"

Damn it. He supposes he is. A little. "I think about it sometimes. But I don't think I'll do it."

"Go ahead," she says. "At least you're old enough."

They laugh, then, both of them, and then Irene puts her hands over her face. "Oh, God, I'm such a mess. I don't understand anything. I really don't."

"Irene?"

She doesn't move, won't take her hands down. "You should go to bed. I'm fine." Her voice is muffled, strained; but she infuses it with a desperate perkiness to say, "Good night!"

"Yeah, it's nine-twelve, Irene."

Her hands fall to her lap. "I know, but it's been a hard night. And nobody's been sleeping very well around here."

He moves to the sofa bed and crouches beside her, and now she does start to cry. She wipes under her nose, looks dolefully over at him. "Hi."

"Hi, Irene."

"I don't know why I'm crying."

"It's lots of things, I'd guess."

"Do you want to . . . ?" She pats the bed. "You can lie down here. If you want to."

He moves slowly to the other side of the sofa bed and lies down. A chaste, overly deliberate distance separates them. The space feels alive, like a third person.

"You're right," she says. "It is a lot of things." She rubs at her forehead, and the gesture is so deeply familiar to him. She always did this when she was puzzled or upset about something, wrinkled her brow and then rubbed it. She looks over at him and smiles, and he sees that the green in her eyes is aquamarine in this light. He sees, too, that her eyebrows are laced with gray, and it breaks his heart.

"You know what I found the other day?" she says.

"What?" He starts to take her hand, stops; then takes it anyway, and she lets him. He feels like when a butterfly lands on him; he scarcely breathes.

"I found our wedding album," she says.

"Really? It wasn't much of a wedding album, as I recall."

"No, we were just making fun of everything."

"Right." A sadness comes into him, and he is wary of it. He thinks about moving back to the chair.

"There was a picture in there, torn from a magazine," Irene says.

"The old ladies." And now it is not sadness that he feels but a great sense of shame. That this is the way they treated their marriage. Especially contrasted to the joy and pride and lack of ambivalence he has witnessed in his daughter.

"No, not the old ladies," Irene says. "This was a picture that wasn't glued in; it just fell out. Do you want to see it? It's in my bedroom closet. I'll go and get it."

"Just tell me." He doesn't want to see that album ever again, he realizes.

"Well, it was of a house, buried in snowdrifts.

Nothing else around it. Just these great big banks of snow, and a black sky, and a small wooden house, a kind of log cabin, I guess. And there was one window with a little light in it. But it made for a big presence, against all that snow."

"Huh," John says. He's not quite sure what she's getting at.

"Then I found another picture, also not glued in. It was of a black sedan, like a getaway car, driving away from sawhorses put up as do-not-cross lines."

She falls silent, and John turns to her. "So . . . what do you make of that?"

"What do you?"

"I don't know."

"Well," she says, "for me, it was a kind of metaphor, you know? That's what we were, in a way, that little house in all that snow. One little light. And the getaway car—"

"That was you," John says.

She looks over at him. "That was you, too."

"You think so?"

"I know so. In fact, wasn't it you who put that picture in there?"

"No!"

"Well, it wasn't I."

"I don't even **remember** it, Irene."

"Neither do I!"

Awkwardly, he takes his hand from hers. He doesn't belong on the bed now. But to get up and move at this moment would be an overobvious statement he's not sure he wants to make.

"I know what," he says.

"What?"

"Let's go out. Let's go out and have a drink at some fancy place."

"I don't want to. Thanks anyway."

"Aw, come on."

She laughs out loud. "This is ridiculous."

"Isn't it?"

"Really, John. I don't understand a single thing!"

"I know. Life. So, Irene? Let's go out."

She smiles. "Okay. Okay, we will." She stands and tucks her blouse back into her skirt. She reaches down for her shoes. One has slid beneath the sofa bed and she gets on her hands and knees to retrieve it. He always liked her ass, and it's still a nice ass. He wonders if that schoolboy has touched her ass. He looks away, and then when he hears her say "Ready?" he jumps to his feet and offers his arm, which she takes.

"Wait!" she says suddenly. "What about Sadie?"

"What about her?"

"What if she comes home and we're not here?"

"What, your married daughter can't stay in a house alone?"

"We'll leave her a note," Irene says, and it seems to be with some excitement that she says it. It's as though she's getting away with something. Maybe she is.

They go into the kitchen, and John stands watching her write the note. This, too, is so deeply familiar to him, the way her script is half print. The way she will sign the note "Mom" and then underline it, as though emphasizing her role.

Irene anchors the note under the sugar bowl on the kitchen table. "Ready?" she asks.

He thinks he is.

31

"Hello?" Sadie calls out. She stands in the middle of the living room, waiting. The sofa bed is pulled out but empty; the door to her mother's bedroom is closed. Are they **sleeping** together? The possibility makes for a rush of both excitement and disgust in her. What are they doing **sleeping** together?

She pads down the hall, stands outside her mother's bedroom. She listens: nothing. She knocks softly, then turns the knob. Empty.

For a moment, she panics, thinking something has happened to them. Ironic, when she thinks of how frightened they must have been when they didn't hear from her for so many long hours. And now, alone for the first time since she was taken, she feels a sudden, bone-chilling panic. She swallows past a huge lump in her throat and pushes open the door to the bathroom, pulls aside the shower curtain. She looks under the bed and in the closets in her bedroom and her mother's; she looks under the sofa bed. All that's left is the kitchen, and she moves slowly toward it. She snaps on the light and sees the note on the table, reads it, and nearly weeps with relief. She sits in the banquette and waits for her heart to stop racing, for her breathing to move fully in and out.

Maybe she should talk to someone about what happened; even though she now knows her parents are all right, she can feel fear of another kind pressing down on her shoulders, into her chest. She reads the note again: they have gone, will be back later, call if she needs anything.

Gone out where? Why?

She goes to the refrigerator and gets a carton of yogurt and takes it to her bedroom to eat it. She doesn't want to be in the kitchen. It's too big. Too many corners, too many shadows. Knives.

She eats the yogurt and then calls Ron. "Guess who went out on a date?" she says.

"Your parents?" he says. "No way."

"Way." She is surprised at how she sounds, saying this. Sad.

"What's wrong, Sadie?"

She clears her throat, laughs. "It's weird."

"Yeah, I'm sure it is."

"No, I don't mean them going out is weird. Although it is. What I meant is, it's weird that I don't know how I feel about it. Whether I'm glad. Or sad. Or mad!"

"Maybe all those things," Ron says.

"Maybe."

"Want me to come over?"

"No. It's okay. They'll be back soon."

"And?"

"And," she says.

"My mom really likes your parents, especially your dad."

"Too late, he's taken."

Ron is silent, and she says, "I'm sorry. I don't know why I said that. I know you didn't mean she liked him that way."

"No, she didn't like him that way."

"I'm **sorry.**"

He shifts his tone to say, "Hey. We're moving in together on Sunday."

"I know."

"Our own place!"

"Right."

"Sadie, are you sure you're okay?"

"Yeah! I just . . . I'm in my room. You know? I'm just sitting here in my bedroom."

"But you're okay. With everything."

"I mean, I'd be leaving anyway, right? I'd be moving to the dorm anyway."

"It's a different thing, to move to a dorm. Very much different from getting married. Sadie, I just want to tell you . . . I just want to say I love you and I don't regret what we did. If you do—"

"I don't!"

"Just listen. If you do, it's okay. We can undo this

and wait until later to get married. I'm not going anywhere."

"I don't want to undo this!" She tests out how it feels, saying this for herself alone and not in a defensive way to someone else.

"I mean, what would we wait for?" she says.

"For you to be really sure."

"Well, are **you**?"

"Am I sure? Yeah! I mean, I know we're young. We're really young."

"Oh, my God," Sadie says.

"What?"

"You aren't okay with everything! You're just trying to get me to say it for you. Do you just . . . Do you want out of the whole thing?"

"Sadie, I'm just trying to read you. Okay? You seem like . . . I'm just trying to read you. I told you how I feel and I meant it. I know we're young, but I feel ready. I just want you to feel that, too. It seems like you're all of a sudden questioning some things."

"I'm not!"

"Okay," he says.

"I'm really not."

"**Okay.**"

Sadie pulls her quilt up to her chin. "I think it's just . . . When I came home and nobody was here? I got scared. I got really scared."

"That makes sense. I think that things like that are going to come up now and then. A lot **happened** to you, Sadie."

"Yeah."

"It will take a long time to even realize all that happened, don't you think?"

"Yes. My mom thinks I should see someone about it."

"My mom does, too."

Sadie lets out a little laugh of astonishment, and Ron adds quickly, "In a good way. She likes you. She wants you to be okay."

"I am okay! Why won't anybody believe I'm okay? And now you!"

"Whoa," he says. "Back up. I don't quite understand what's happening here."

"I have to go," she says. "My parents are home. I'll talk to you tomorrow." She hangs up the phone. Her parents aren't home. She's alone. She walks around the house, back and forth, from end to end. Below her, she hears the sound of the neighbor's television set. She's not alone. There are people all around her. She could call Meghan, but it's not the same between her and Meghan, now. Meghan is distant, guarded, with her. She says she's glad for Sadie, but she's gone, somehow. She supposes Meghan would say the same thing about her.

Sadie goes to the living room window and presses her forehead against the glass, looks down on the street. She sees her parents coming up the block toward the house, their arms around each other. She flees to her bedroom and closes the door, turns out the light.

32

On Saturday morning, Irene arrives at the bookstore early. She's going to look at magazines for brides. She never looked at such things before she got married. Now, standing in front of the magazine rack, she is astounded at the great variety available. She selects several with an odd kind of embarrassment; she might be picking out porn magazines.

She carries a heavy load into the café, finds a window to sit by, and begins flipping through. The variety—in rings, in gowns, in cakes, in venues—is astonishing. She wants to try to enjoy the experience, but all she can feel is a kind of revulsion at what she sees as blatant exploitation.

She looks out the window at the people passing by, and starts when she sees Jeffrey. He's across the street with an older woman, one about her age, very pretty. She gives Jeffrey a smile, a kiss on the cheek, waves goodbye, and they walk off in different directions. Jeffrey is coming toward Irene. She turns her attention to the glossy pages of the magazines, but mostly she wonders if he'll see her sitting there.

She hears a knock on the window, and there he is. She smiles, he smiles back. He pulls his cell-phone out and points to her, and her phone rings. "Hello?" she says, laughing.

"That woman is a client of mine," he says.

"Oh. Very nice-looking."

"Guess what. I've decided to give you one more chance."

"You have?"

"Yes."

"Well . . ." She looks around at the near-empty café. "Why don't you come in and we'll talk in person?"

"Can't. On my way to a meeting. Why don't you say yes to the ball game, and we'll talk then?"

"Do I still get meat loaf?"

"Only if you act now. Limited-time offer here."

"Yes," she says.

"I'll call you next week."

"Yes, okay."

He closes his cellphone, mouths **I'll call you**, and walks briskly down the sidewalk. She watches him, thinking about what it will be like to see him again. It makes her feel good to think a man like him is actually interested in her, but in the end . . . In the end, **what**?

She thinks about being in the hotel bar with John last night. Despite their intentions to go somewhere fancy, they'd elected instead for what they came to first: a nondescript bar in a nondescript hotel. A dim room, five or six black vinyl swivel chairs lined up in front of a bar stocked with off brands; a blaring television set, a few round wooden tables, the surfaces sour with the scent of the cleaning rag. But they didn't care. They had arrived at a place of equanimity they had not enjoyed in years; Irene figured that John, too, wanted less to partake of any particular kind of atmosphere than simply to enjoy each other's company.

After they sat down at the corner table, John said, "I don't know about you, but I always think the safest thing in these places is to have a beer."

"I'm getting a Rob Roy," Irene said, and when John asked what that was, she said she had no idea.

"In that case, I'm getting one, too." John said.

After they were delivered watered-down drinks, the contents of which they could not identify (dishwater mixed with men's cologne? John suggested), they sat in silence for a while, watching the people at the bar. There was a line of three men sitting there, all dressed in suit pants and shirts with the sleeves rolled up, all hunched over their drinks and chatting in a dispirited kind of way whenever commercials interrupted the ball game. A solitary, overly made-up woman sat at the end of the bar, eyeing them and chewing on a swizzle stick. She was older, maybe sixty-five or so, with a frizzed-out blond perm and what must have been at one time a pretty spectacular body now stuffed into a blue silk dress, a glittery pin at the shoulder. The men, Irene and John decided, were in town for business; and what with the economy in the shape it was, this was the hotel they were assigned to stay in. The woman? They weren't so sure. "I don't think she's a prostitute," Irene said, whispering.

"Maybe it's my mom," John said.

Irene looked quickly over at him. What an odd thing to say, she was thinking, and what a sad thing, too. "If your mom were alive, she'd be in her eighties," she finally offered.

"Yeah," he said, looking down into his drink.

Then he looked up, smiling, and said, "Remember when Sadie was four and she helped me wash the car for the first time?"

"I do remember that." Sadie had helped wash, then dry the car; and when John had told her, "Okay, time to wax it," she'd flung down her rag, lay in the grass, and said, "Oh, God, take me now!"

"That was you in her," John said, but it was with a kind of affection that Irene had never before felt from him, about her tendency to overdramatize. A kind of acceptance.

She nodded. She didn't want to look at him; she didn't want to tip the balance away from this perfect middle. She stared into her drink to ask, "Remember when she was learning to ice-skate and she fell and broke her wrist?"

John grimaced. "How could I forget? I felt so

bad when I realized what had happened. She was hurt really badly, but she just kept on skating."

"That was you in her," Irene said, looking up.

He shrugged.

"You're so . . . not a complainer."

"I guess."

"John. I want to tell you . . . I just really want to say I'm sorry."

A long moment, and then he said, "I am, too."

"And also . . . I did love you."

"Yeah, once upon a time. Me, too."

She leaned back in her chair and regarded him, her head tilted. "Are you different now, John?"

He sighed. "That's a hard question. But I think I am. Are you?"

She stared soberly at him, felt tears starting to well up, and John quickly stood and offered her his arm. "Let's get the hell out of here," he said.

They walked up and down the hilly streets in the fog. They didn't talk much, but just before they rounded the corner to go home, John turned Irene toward him. "I have to tell you something," he said.

"What?"

"When Sadie was missing, I had this thought that, if she never came back, you and I would stay together. Because we would be all that we had left of her."

Irene nodded. "I had the same thought."

"And it brought me some comfort."

"Yes."

"But I also felt really guilty, thinking that."

"Of course. I did, too." She smiled. "You know what's kind of wonderful? No one will ever feel about Sadie the way that we do. Nothing will ever take away that bond between us."

He stood there, staring into her face. Then he hugged her tightly. "We did Sadie right," he said.

"Yes," Irene said, her voice muffled from being smashed into John's shoulder. Stepping back and looking up into his face, so close to hers, now, she asked, "What else did we do right?"

He looked at her, something came into his eyes, and she knew he was thinking about kissing her. She knew it because she remembers this about him, the way he so often looked at parts of her face before he kissed her: the line of hair at the top of her brow, her ear, her chin, and then, finally, her mouth, he looked at it right before he kissed it, as though he'd been waiting politely for it to be delivered, and was now so very glad for its arrival. "Hat-in-hand kissing," Irene had called it, when she'd first started dating John and had described the way he kissed to Valerie. "He starts out tentatively," she'd said, "but that's not how he finishes. He makes your **toes** curl, you know? That man can **kiss**." She's still never found anyone who can kiss like John.

She held still, waiting to see in what direction he'd go, because what he did next would dictate everything else that would follow. "What else did we do right . . ." he said, frowning. And then, "Well, I'm sorry, Irene. I can't think of anything."

A moment, and then she started to laugh and said, "Me, neither." And John laughed, too. They stood on the corner laughing and laughing. Finally, John made his face overly stern and shook his finger at her, then at himself, and said, "Not funny!"

"No," Irene said.

He threw his arm around her and began marching forward. He said, "Come on. I'm taking you home." He kept his arm firmly around her all the way back, and it took her a few steps to realize she had put her arm around him, too; it had happened that easily, that naturally.

Irene is startled by someone tapping her on the shoulder. She turns around to see Huguette. "Oh," Irene says. "Hello."

"I see you are sit alone," Huguette says. She gestures to the chair. "May I?"

"Of course," Irene says. "I'm just waiting for a friend."

"You are looking in the bride magazines?"

"Well. Yes. But the truth is, I'm having a hard time with all of this. I feel my daughter has made a terrible mistake."

"Oh, yes?"

"Not because of your son," Irene rushes to add. "It's just that they're too young."

"Too young to . . . ?"

"Well, to be married! Much too young to be

married! I mean, I know you married very young, and you think age is just a number, but that's not really true."

Huguette leans forward. "Perhaps this can be seen from two ways. In my life, I am right. In yours, you are. But we are right now talking about Sadie and Ron. What do you think they are too young to do?"

"They are too young to make a commitment such as this! Marriage is a very big commitment! Or should be." She adds this last more quietly.

"What else?"

"They are too young to have children."

"Ah yes! On this, I agree with you."

"And they are too young to give up the life of freedom they should be living now."

"This life of freedom. For what is it?"

"It's to have fun before they're settled down. To think about how they want to live their lives without the influence of another. Okay?"

"Okay. But . . . what if they can have fun being married? What if they can decide together how to live their lives?"

Now Irene grows angry. She looks at her watch. "I'm sorry to be rude, but I've got to go."

"Has your friend arrive?" Huguette turns around in her chair.

"No," Irene says. "I just . . . Look, I don't think this is very productive, the two of us talking. We have very different points of view. What I wanted was for my daughter to be really sure she wanted to be married, before she took that step. I don't feel she's mature enough to have made that decision. I mean, come on, do you really think your son is?"

"My son, yes. Your daughter, I don't know very well, but already I—"

"In addition to that, my daughter is dealing with something that happened to her that was very traumatic."

"Yes. Ron told me."

"Well, I think you can see, then, that this is not the time for her to be making rash decisions."

"Only she has. Here we have the fact before us. And now, the question: Can she stay with this decision? Is it good for her? For her, Irene. Not you." She stands, picks up her purse. "Sometimes we make choices in our lives. Sometimes our lives make choices for us. I wish for you some harmony in spirit."

Irene doesn't have any idea what to say. Huguette nods, and walks away.

A young woman comes in with an older woman who Irene thinks must be her mother, and they begin looking at a magazine together. "This is the dress I was telling you about," the young woman says, and her mother looks closely at it.

Then she looks at her daughter and says, "I think it's perfect."

"Really?" the young woman says. "Be honest, Mom."

Her mother smiles. "I am being totally honest. Now let's find shoes and a cake."

For one moment, Irene has the odd idea that Huguette sent them over. But of course she didn't; Irene has often seen young women poring over bridal magazines in this café.

Irene turns to her own stack of magazines. She has to admit there are some lovely ideas here. They truly are lovely.

By the time Valerie arrives, Irene has selected a few things to show her. About one cake, Valerie says, "**That** is Sadie!" Irene agrees. She'll buy this magazine, and when she gets home, she'll ask her daughter what she thinks about a celebration in October in honor of her marriage. Also, she'll ask her to forgive her. Then maybe Sadie will help her prepare dinner. She wants to make something wonderful, to send John off. Something he'll remember.

33

Sadie is sitting on the floor, wrapping fragile things in newspaper to put into boxes. At first, when she hears the knock at her door, she doesn't answer. But then she says "Yes?" in a way that she hopes will suggest she's far too busy to have another heart-to-heart. She's sick of heart-to-hearts.

This morning, when her mother was out, her father came in with some song and dance about how she shouldn't judge Irene for her wariness not only toward Sadie's marriage but toward the institution in general. He told her about one time when Irene was a little girl and was lying on the floor of the living room, coloring. Her parents were there, too, her father reading the newspaper, her mother mending. "William?" Irene heard her mother say. Her father did not respond. "William?" she said again; and again, her father did not respond. After the third time this happened, Irene's mother flung the mending basket down and went into the kitchen. Irene found her there, sitting at the table, her arms crossed, her eyes flat. "What's the matter?" Irene asked. "Go to bed," her mother said. "You should have talked louder," Irene said, and then her mother did look at her. "You stupid girl," she said. "The things you think will help."

"Your mother witnessed a lot of bitterness in both of her parents," John told Sadie. "She had no choice but to be scared of marriage, growing up that way."

"And what about you, Dad?"

"Huh?" he said, which was what he always did when he was stalling. Lots of males do that, she's noticed.

"Did you have the same kind of wariness?" she asked.

"No," he said. "Mine was different."

Then Ron had called, and her dad had backed gratefully out of her room. Ron was a little sad, believing that Sadie wanted out of the marriage they'd so hastily entered into. But he'd thought about it, he told her, and he'd decided he'd rather lose her than make her feel like she'd lost herself. He reiterated the fact that he wasn't going anywhere.

She wished she were with him. She missed him. "What are your **bad** parts?" she asked.

"Oh, I can get very moody," he said. "Also, I don't really care if my socks match."

In the end, she said she'd talk to him later that night, she was busy packing now. Which seemed to make him feel better, though of course she has to pack if she's moving to the dorm, too. She still hasn't canceled her room there. She could move right in, be a freshman student rooming with someone named Laura Erickson, a girl from North Dakota whom she'd written a couple of emails to, talked to on the phone once, too. She seemed like a nice enough person. She'd told Sadie she loved old Led Zeppelin, strictly vinyl. Sadie likes that, too. She asked if Sadie liked blue, because she wanted to bring some blue curtains, a simple style, no ruffles. Sadie loves blue and hates ruffles.

After that phone call, Sadie had thought about what it would be like, living in a big building full of kids her own age, and how much she had looked forward to the all-night chats she'd heard so much about. She'd thought about studying at the desk in the room, books and papers all around her, her gooseneck lamp shining light down. Maybe an empty pizza box on the floor.

But now here is her mother before her, an open magazine in her hand. "Look what I found," she says, and she shows Sadie a wedding cake made up of cupcakes.

Sadie looks at it, then into her mother's face. And bursts into tears.

Irene lets the magazine fall and goes to sit on the floor beside her daughter. She puts her arms around Sadie, rocks her gently side to side, saying, "I know."

Sadie pulls away. "No you don't! You don't know what I'm crying about!"

"Maybe not," Irene says. "But can I tell you what I think you might be crying about?"

Sadie shrugs.

Irene sits back on her heels. "I think you're crying because you're really confused, and you're angry about being confused. You think you've gotten yourself into something that could be dead wrong for you, but that to get out now might cause too much pain to too many people, yourself included. One second, you think this was the best decision you ever made; the next, you're horrified that you made it. You look at the marriage your parents had, and you can't trust that yours won't end, too. But more than anything, there's this: You really love Ron."

Now Sadie begins to cry harder.

Her mother moves closer, puts her hand on her daughter's knee. "Sadie. All I saw in my parents' marriage was loneliness and anger. They couldn't reach each other. So what I took away from that is—"

"I know!" Sadie says. "Dad told me."

"Okay. Well, did he also tell you about his parents' marriage?"

"I know his mom took off when he was real little. And that what he had left of her was in that cigar box."

"What cigar box?"

"The one he kept some of her stuff in. It was . . . I don't know, an empty lipstick casing. A scarf. The postcards she sent him. He kept it until the day before he left for college, and then he took it in the alley and burned it."

"He told you that?"

"Yeah. You didn't know that?"

"No."

"How could you not have known that, Mom?" Irene shakes her head.

"He knows way more about you than you do about him."

"Yes. I was selfish that way." She looks over at her daughter. "You're not like that, Sadie."

"I don't know what I'm like."

"Well, then I'll tell you," Irene says. "You are intelligent, loyal to a fault, inquisitive, honest. Caring of people and of animals and of the world at large. Full of joy, and easy to be with. Wiser than your years. Confident in your ability to make decisions and stand by them."

"Until now," Sadie says.

"Let's not say we're at the end of something," Irene says. "Let's say we're in the middle." She stands, awkwardly. "My knees hurt. I have to go sit on something. Come sit on the bed with me."

"I can hear you from here." Sadie doesn't want to sit on the bed with her mother. She wants to call Meghan and go out with her. She wants that fateful day never to have happened. She wants Ron to be sitting beside her, holding her hand. She wants her mother's knees not to hurt, for her not to be getting so **old** when she's so **alone**.

Irene says, "I just got back from the bookstore. And all the way home, this one thought kept repeating in my brain: **That was then; this is now.**"

"What do you mean?" Sadie asks. "Why were you thinking that?"

"Oh . . . For lots of reasons. Because I have a lot of regrets about how I lived my life in the past, and I think I let that get in the way of how I live now. And because I keep focusing on how I want you not be married, when you already are. In the bookstore café, I sat next to a mother and daughter who were really united in their happiness about the daughter getting married. And I felt so ashamed of how I've been behaving. Now, it's true that girl was older than you. But that doesn't mean that your love isn't as true, or that your chances aren't as good."

"Plus maybe the groom is only eighteen," Sadie says, smiling.

Irene laughs. "True. It's true! But anyway, when I was walking home, I thought, maybe that mother wanted her daughter to marry someone different than the man—or woman—she chose. Maybe she had a lot of things to object to. But here's what she was doing: standing with her daughter and saying, **This is your choice and I'm with you in it.** And that's what I want to say to you.

"I also want to tell you I'm glad for you, that you didn't let fear stop you from doing the thing your heart was telling you to do. It takes a lot of courage to get married, and a lot of work to stay married when the hard times come. And the hard times always come."

"**Why?**"

"Oh, because it's the nature of our species, that why. We're complicated and contrary beings. Who knows if we're really supposed to try to live in the way that marriage requires? Yet something in us seems to insist upon it."

"Mom?"

"Yes?"

Sadie waits. If she waits long enough, if she gets out of her own way, the right words will come, she knows that. She sits staring at the hole in the knee of her jeans, and finally she says, "Do you know the best thing you taught me?"

"No."

"See? I know you don't. But I'm about to show you. And can I tell you one more thing?"

"Of course."

"A **cupcake cake**? Henry would die."

34

All the way back on the plane, John scarcely moves. He looks out the window and thinks of Sadie, of Irene, and then, finally, of Amy. He feared at first that this trip away from her had made for a permanent rift in their relationship, that he had gone to a place he could not come back from, both literally and figuratively; and he wasn't sure that what he felt most about that was relief. But the few hours on the plane have told him otherwise. As the miles between him and California increased, his feelings for Amy and Irene grew clearer to him. Does he want to get married again? He thinks he does. Is Irene the one, again? No. He had a thought when he was staying with her, though, that maybe she was. When she sat up in bed and untucked her blouse, when her red hair fell across her face, it launched a thousand feelings in him, including one that said, **We could try again.** It was exhilarating, thinking that. For one thing, he would be where Sadie was, every day. And he might finally fashion with Irene the kind of safe haven he had always longed to have with her, **the palace of we,** as he used to imagine it.

He thought that surely Irene must have entertained the notion herself when he was there; he thought he felt a kind of longing to stay together coming from her, too, every now and then. When she handed him a breakfast plate with eggs scrambled wet, as he liked them. When she sat with him in worry about Sadie, and they were able to offer each other meager comfort—but comfort nonetheless—in the face of what might be a devastating loss. But he did not ask her. He watched her face during the last dinner they had together, to see if there was some kind of invitation, some kind of regret; he allowed space for her to say something before he walked out the door and downstairs to get the cab, but he did not ask her. At first he thought it was because he was afraid to. Then he realized he didn't want to. What he wanted was to go back to Amy. Because she offered him something Irene never could, or would: A sense of unwavering stability. A contagious joy. And he can give her something back that he never could—or would—give Irene: an unprotected love. Oh, he has come back to a love for Irene, but it is one not of passion but of compassion. Which is to say, she is his friend; and he is hers. Perhaps that's all they ever should have attempted.

When he lands in St. Paul, it is late to call Amy, but he does anyway.

Four rings before she answers. "Amy," he says. "I'm sorry to wake you. It's me."

"Oh. John. How are you? Is everything okay?"

"I'm back. Everything's fine. I wondered . . . Can I come and see you?"

"Well . . . It's kind of late."

"I know it is, but . . . You don't have to get up early tomorrow, do you?"

"No."

"So . . ."

"Uh. Maybe tomorrow?"

"I kind of need to see you, Amy."

"If you have something to tell me, you can just do it on the phone. I understand."

"What do you understand?"

"Well, John, I understand you're still in love with Irene. I knew it when you called her 'wife' and not 'ex-wife' when you were packing to go to San Francisco."

John stops walking, and the person behind him bangs into him with his bag. "Sorry!" the man says, and John waves his hand, **It's okay.** He moves to the side of the terminal, next to the Rocky Mountain Chocolate Factory, to continue talking.

"I said that? I called her 'my wife'?"

"Yes, uh-huh, you did, you called her 'my wife.' So I kind of knew then. I tried to tell myself that, when you came back, we would pick up where we left off, but—"

"That's what I want to do. Amy. That's what I want to do. I'm not still in love with Irene. I love her, it's true, but as a friend. Honestly."

Silence.

"Honestly!"

"Where are you?" she says.

"I'm standing in the airport next to the Rocky Mountain Chocolate Factory."

"Well, okay. Come over. And bring me a caramel apple."

"They're closed. But if you want, I can break the glass."

She laughs, and he thinks, if she can laugh, she isn't going to tell him anything bad.

When he pulls up in front of her place, she comes out to the curb and then walks up to the porch with him. "Do you mind if we sit out here?" she asks.

Uh-oh, he thinks.

He sits on the rattan sofa; she sits on a chair opposite, and again, he thinks, **Uh-oh.**

She smiles at him, her hands clasped together on her knees. "So I'll just tell you what I need to say, and then I'll listen to whatever you want to say. Okay?"

From inside her house, he hears her phone ringing. She looks toward the sound, then back at him.

"I have no idea who could be calling me so late," she says.

Here we go.

"Amy," he says.

She holds up her hand. "I get to go first, remember?"

"Right. Okay. Go ahead."

"Well, when you were in San Francisco, almost right away I could hear a change in your voice. And not just your voice, but your feelings. I could feel you moving away from me. And I kept trying to deny it, but I noticed it more and more every time we spoke."

She clears her throat, repositions herself. "I thought about how you were there with Irene, bound together in the way that crisis makes you be, and I knew that it would make you close. And then . . . Well, then you would rediscover feelings about each other, and that would lead to your wanting to be together again. Which is completely natural. I understand that. If I could be back with my husband, I would be, too."

John has been leaning forward, listening to her intently. With this last, though, he pulls back, stares at his hands. "I know you would be with your husband if you could, Amy. I think you had a great marriage."

"We did." Her voice is full of such simple sorrow.

"But love at this age is bound to be complicated. Don't you think? What I want with you is all we can make it be. I know you still love your husband. I know you always will. But you have the rest of your life to live."

Her phone rings again, and this time she stands to go in. "I'm sorry. I'd better see who this is."

She goes to the phone, has a brief conversation, and comes back smiling. He waits for her to tell him what it was about, but she doesn't, and he understands that he has no right to ask, really. Apparently, she's moved on.

Well, fine. He's tired. He'll spare her having to tell him.

He walks over to kiss her forehead.

"Are you leaving?" she asks.

"Yeah, it's late."

"But—"

"It's okay," he says. "Maybe I'll see you around."

She looks sad now; she pulls her sweater more tightly about her; the night air is cool.

He starts down the steps.

"John?" she says.

He pretends not to hear her, and heads for his car. He hears her door closing. He gets into the car, drives a block, then turns around and comes back to Amy's house, goes up to the door and knocks loudly.

When she opens it, she says, "Oh, good. Get in here."

He doesn't move. "Are we done?"

"I hope not."

"That wasn't some other guy calling?"

"No!"

"Why did you get that dog without me?"

"Because I thought I was losing you and I might as well at least have him."

"Well, I wish you hadn't named him already."

"We can change it. He doesn't come to it, anyway. I don't think he likes it. We can call him whatever we want, John. Come **in**. Please?"

He comes in and kisses her for so long it makes him dizzy. Then he goes to sit at her kitchen table and drink a glass of wine with her and listen to her talk. There is one story she tells in a long stretch of her usual meandering monologue that he intends to hold in his memory forever:

I was in my car yesterday at a red light, and I was singing along to Johnny Mathis, they were playing "Chances Are" on the radio and, oh, I just love that song, and as for Johnny Mathis, well. He was on the Phil Donahue show once—remember the Phil Donahue show? It was the first time women were given that kind of respect. I remember the first time I watched it, I thought, Oh, my God, he's giving a normal woman a microphone and just letting her talk! I mean, I thought it was a mistake, I just couldn't believe that he would give such respect to ordinary women! Who are so worthy of respect, but he was the very first one to

show that on television. Oh, I loved Phil Donahue, I got my favorite piecrust recipe from the
Phil Donahue show. But anyway, Johnny Mathis
was on Phil's show and this one woman raised her
hand and Phil went running over, that man used
to get such a workout every time he did a show,
he'd go running around to all the women who
wanted to say something and his suit jacket
would be flapping in the breeze. But this one
woman in the audience said to Johnny Mathis, "I
don't know if this is much of a compliment to
you, Johnny, but you sure make cleaning the toi-
lets easier." And everybody laughed, but everybody knew exactly what she meant, and you know
what, that remark has stayed with me all these
years. But wait, the point is, I was in my car at the
red light singing along with Johnny Mathis and I
all of a sudden felt someone watching me, and I
looked over and there was my neighbor Jenny, in
her car, and she was just grinning like the cat that
ate the canary. I rolled down my window and
said, "I'm singing along with the radio." "I
know," she said. "It's Johnny Mathis," I said, and
she said, "Oh, God, Johnny **Mathis**!" "'Chances
Are,'" I told her and she put her hand over her
heart. And then the light changed and she said,
"I'm going to call you!" And it was such a joyful
moment. It was just one of those accidental
moments of joy, singing in the car, someone you
like seeing you do such a silly thing and knowing

exactly why and sharing it with you. And I just think that we need to collect these joy berries wherever we find them and put them in our big yellow buckets. And you know who that was calling when you were here? That was Jenny, I'd left her a message after you called me and were coming over and I wasn't sure what to do. She called back to say that I'd better open up and admit my feelings to you and not let you go. So, you know. Stay."

35

On the Sunday after Thanksgiving, Irene answers the phone on the first ring. "Henry?" she says. She's expecting his call. After Henry and James's first counseling session aimed at reconciliation, James told Henry it was a "nonnegotiable need" that Henry stop working so much, so that they could have more time together. So Henry told Irene he was going to sell his business and he'd like to work for her. They're due to open tomorrow.

"Now, you know what kind of food I'm going to have," Irene had warned, before she agreed to hire Henry. "I'm talking green bean bake here."

And he sighed and said, "What can I say? It will require **nothing** of me."

But it is not Henry on the phone. It's John.

"Hi!" Irene says, so pleased to hear his voice. "How are you?"

"Are you sitting down?"

"Actually, I'm lying down."

"Even better."

Oh, she thinks.

She takes in a breath, then says, brightly, "You're getting married. Are you getting married?"

"I am. I guess it's **kind** of sudden, but I'm not getting any younger. And anyway, it runs in the family these days, right?"

"Well. Congratulations." Very quietly, she clears her throat.

"Are you okay?" he asks.

"You mean about your getting married? Of course I am. I'm happy for you."

She thinks she knows exactly what he looks like, right now. Like a little kid wondering if he's in trouble. His eyebrows furrowed, his cowlick standing at attention.

"Really, I am," she says.

"Things good with you and Jeffrey?"

"Uh-huh." No. After a month with him, she's back to being a computer jockey. But no need to spoil this moment for John. She hesitates, then says, "I had a dream about you last night."

"Tell me, but don't expect me to interpret it."

"It was really strange. I was moving all over the country, and everywhere I went, I kept seeing you. Once I was driving down a road somewhere in the mountains; they were very high mountains and a truck passed me on the other side of the road. It was a flatbed, really long, carrying lumber, and you were sitting at the end of the flatbed, next to a red caution flag. Although you weren't being very cautious, sitting there that way, your legs dangling down. And you were so young, you were young again, you had black hair and that mustache you used to have. And I was struck by how young you were and I looked in the mirror to see if I was young, too, but I wasn't. I was even older than I am now. I had all these wrinkles, like a really old lady."

John is quiet, and then he says, "You're not so old, yet. And it's **time** to throw caution to the wind."

"You're interpreting after all."

"Yeah, I guess I am."

"Did you tell Sadie, yet, about getting married?"

"No, I wanted to tell you first. She'll be a little sad, I think. You know how kids always kind of fantasize that their parents will get back together."

"Yes. They do."

"**I'm** a little sad, too."

Irene laughs. "I know. But mostly you're happy. And mostly I am, too. And Sadie will be."

"She'll need a little time."

"Probably so."

"But you'll be there to help her."

"You will be, too, John. As you always have been."

"Is she as happy as she sounds?"

"She seems to be. She really does. She loves college, she loves being married. I had them over for dinner last night, Huguette, too. We tested a bunch of new recipes: Tater Tot meat loaf got an A, all around. An A-**plus** from Ron, actually."

"Irene? I want to ask you something. Amy and I are getting married in three weeks. I want Sadie to come."

"Of course!"

"Okay. Well, I guess . . ." He falls silent, and she tightens her grip on the phone, holding back the feeling she knows is imminent for her, too.

"I'm going to hang up, now," he says.

"I know." Here it comes. Her throat begins to ache.

"You knew I was going to hang up?"

"I know it's hard for you to tell me this. But I really am happy for you, John."

"Thank you . . . Irene."

His voice is so soft now, overly familiar in a way that tears at her. She hangs up and sits still for a moment, then goes to her closet and takes down her wedding album. She looks through it again, and then she wraps it up tighter in the little blanket she used for Sadie when she was a newborn, and puts it back on the high shelf.

She turns the computer on, waits for it to boot up. On her desk, she has framed a picture of a cowgirl that Valerie affixed to a birthday present she gave her many years ago, knowing that Irene loved cowgirls, that she used to want to be one. The woman is rosy-cheeked, clear-eyed, and curly-haired, whirling a lasso over her head in order to catch whatever it is she's after. Irene studies the way the woman stands up in her stirrups, leaning into the wind. Then she gently takes the frame apart, careful not to tear the thin paper of the picture. She lays it on her bed, goes to the closet, gets down her wedding album, and brings it to the bed. Stuck between the last two pages is the picture of the little wooden house she'd told John about, isolated, buried in snowdrifts. She meant to ball that picture up and throw it away. But now she finds she cannot do it. There is a truth in it, a history of her and John that she regrets but wants nonetheless to honor. So she puts the picture of the little house back in the album, beneath a sheet of plastic, so it won't fall out again. But she also positions the picture of the cowgirl next to the house as though she's riding purposefully away from it.

She stares at the image, the cowgirl in her brown boots and blue skirt, her red blouse with the sleeves rolled up, her black hat tipped back far on her head, her intention fierce in her eyes.

Irene shuts her computer off. She moves to the chair in the corner of her bedroom. She puts her hands on her knees and closes her eyes and tries to empty her mind. Valerie told her recently that she does this every day: sits in silence, her mind empty, waiting for the spirit to come. "Sometimes it happens; sometimes it doesn't," she told Irene. "But it's always good for me to think of nothing, that way."

Irene waits. She does not think of nothing. She

thinks of how her catering company will have the best mashed potatoes on earth. She thinks of how she needs coffee. She thinks of the blouses she needs to pick up at the cleaners, the bills she needs to pay. She thinks of how she will fly Ron out to Minnesota to John's wedding, if he'd like to go. It might be nice for him to see the place where Sadie was born. And then she remembers a conversation she and Valerie had after one of Irene's many breakups. Valerie had said that maybe Irene should take a little breather from trying to find someone, maybe she needed to do something else. "Like what?" Irene had said. "Love is the answer. Didn't you pay attention in hippie school?"

"Love **is** the answer," Valerie had said. "But sometimes love isn't what you think it is. Sometimes, it's . . . I don't know, for you? For you, I think love is a sheep in wolf's clothing. I mean that it doesn't have to be so **hard,** Irene. Look closer.

"Remember how I always used to have that E. M. Forster quote taped to my computer? For so many years, I looked at those words every day: **Only connect.** But then I thought, **No.** Only connect **presumes something on someone else's part. It creates an expectation, a need to get something back from someone else. And what does that set you up for?** I also used to think the idea of nonattachment was bullshit. Was **wrong.** But now I see the wisdom of it. You put something out for your own sake, instead of having everything rest on what you get in exchange. So I changed **Only connect** to **Only love.**"

"Yeah, I don't do so well with love," Irene had said.

"You don't do so well with marriage," Valerie had said. "I don't think you've even begun to realize all there is for you to love. And I know you better than anyone, and here's what I know about you: You have so much love to give! But I feel like you're all the time digging in the tomato bin, saying, 'Where are the **apples?**'"

Irene sits longer. She closes her eyes tighter, breathes in more deeply.

The spirit does not come. Joy does not come. Illumination does not. But something does. Irene goes to the window and looks out onto the street, down at the people walking below. Some walk purposefully, sure of where they are going. Some walk aimlessly, in no hurry to get anywhere. Others are frankly lost. She goes for her keys, then heads out the door to join them.

Acknowledgments

My thanks, as always, to my editor, Kate Medina, to whom this book is dedicated. Her encouragement and support began in 1992 and has never wavered. I also want to thank others who do such good work on my behalf at Random House: Lindsey Schwoeri, Beth Pearson, Ashley Gratz-Collier, and Barbara Fillon.

At William Morris Endeavor, I am indebted to Suzanne Gluck and her assistants Caroline Donofrio and Mina Shaghaghi. Thanks also to Alicia Gordon in movieland; Cathryn Summerhayes in the U.K.; Laura Bonner, who handles foreign rights; and Claudia Ballard, who takes care of me and the magazines.

Many friends lent a hand in writing this book: Ross Mitchell talked to me about the complex feelings of children diagnosed with cancer, Jeff Appleman explained certain legalities involved with kidnapping, and John Rupp, my friend since we were eighteen years old, served as a model for John

Marsh's love of architecture, restoration, and the beautiful city of St. Paul, Minnesota. Elizabeth Cox convinced me of the value of sitting in silence. My writing group provided valuable support and insight, as always: champagne cocktails for Veronica Chapa, Arlene Manlinowski, Pam Todd, and Michele Weldon. Also, they were an appreciative audience to my chicken show, soon to be reprised, though in a safer venue. Finally, a huge thank-you to Phyllis Florin, who reads things for me practically every day of the week and never, ever lies.

About the Author

ELIZABETH BERG is the author of many bestselling novels, including **The Last Time I Saw You, Home Safe, The Year of Pleasures,** and **Dream When You're Feeling Blue,** as well as two collections of short stories and two works of nonfiction. **Open House** was an Oprah's Book Club selection, **Durable Goods** and **Joy School** were selected as ALA Best Books of the Year, **Talk Before Sleep** was short-listed for an ABBY Award. Berg adapted **The Pull of the Moon** into a play. She has been honored by both the Boston Public Library and the Chicago Public Library and is a popular speaker at venues around the country. Her work has been translated into twenty-seven languages. She lives near Chicago.

LIKE WHAT YOU'VE READ?

If you enjoyed this large print edition of
ONCE UPON A TIME, THERE WAS YOU,
here are a few of Elizabeth Berg's latest
bestsellers also available in large print.